The Parisian Dancer | Doron Darmon

Producer & International Distributor
eBookPro Publishing
www.ebook-pro.com

The Parisian Dancer
Doron Darmon

Translation: Esther Frumkin

Contact: admin@darmons.com
ISBN: 9789655752922

THE
PARISIAN
DANCER

DORON DARMON

"Create the reality that you desire out of the hard, frightening truth; even if it seems that everything is lost, find the strength to start over again."

PART 1

1

The fragrances of a summer morning in Paris of 1938, in the center of the Latin Quarter, were deceptive. The scent of strong boulangerie coffee with an endless array of butter and chocolate pastries, the market stalls, the flower sellers and the stair cleaners— people that only Paris could dream up. Marek winded his way up the stairs, suit jacket slung over his shoulders, stubble adorning his chin, and a Gitanes cigarette dangling from the corner of his mouth. In one hand he held a paper bag full of pastries, and in the other a poster for the Folies Bergère, the most distinguished nightclub of Europe, its cabaret-dancing and showgirls drawing the who'swho of Paris, along with tourists visiting the City of Lights.

He climbed the staircase of the building on Passage Brady until he reached the modest apartment where he lived with his wife Annette and their one year old son, Olivier. They had arrived in Paris in the mid-1930s. In a daring move, they emigrated from Poland, leaving their families and close friends behind at the mercy of groups of Polish extremists (if they had any mercy at all). Shortly after they left, their families were attacked in the pogroms of the mid-1930s.

Marek and Annette, alone without friends or family managed to find a place for themselves in a tiny corner of Paris' bohemian quarter. They were sure that now their dream of living a free life was coming true and what they had gone through in Poland would never happen here, in their new home.

The same year they left, Annette lost her parents and sister, who were murdered in one of the pogroms by an extremist group that burned down their house. Annette had not been herself ever since, becoming anxious about everyone close to her. Marek, who had witnessed the change in her, promised that he wouldn't let her suffer any more, that he would always be there to lead her to safe shores and protect what was dearest to her: the family.

Although the French had no love of strangers— an attitude that they developed during and following the First World War— in their immediate surroundings, the couple was welcomed with great warmth, made to feel part of the bohemian neighborhood they lived in. The Jewish Oppenheimer family was good to everyone they met and to those around them. Marek's philosophy of life was simple: wherever we give, we get; always be ready to give and help out, and it will all come back to you in the end. That's how the universe works.

Despite the difficulties the immigrant family faced in late-1930s Paris, they were happy with their lot. They were together, and their loving and giving were a source of life. Little Olivier was a product of that love: a wonderful child, mature for his age, with expressive eyes and *joie de vivre*. His name, *Olivier*— a French name— signaled their fresh start in a new land.

Within a few years of their arrival in Paris, Annette's hair was already beginning to gray, and she looked old beyond her years. Marek, though shorter than average, had a muscular build, a result of the athletic activity and physical work that he had kept up over the years. As a couple, they appeared to complement each other, though Annette looked a bit older than Marek.

Marek Oppenheimer worked at a printing press; a job that he landed after a long period of trying to "find his feet" in the French capital. After a strenuous night shift at the press, he would come home to his apartment on the top floor, where Annette and Olivier would wait for him for the family's ceremonial greeting of the day. The cool breeze blowing through the open window, the pastries that Marek would bring on his way home, Olivier playing with the newest daily poster— this was their quality time. Marek with his last spurt of energy following a long night's work, and Annette and Olivier who had just woken up. The time they spent together gave Marek love and renewed strength for the rest of the day.

Marek entered the apartment. Olivier came running towards him with tiny steps and hugged his leg. He looked up at his father, grinning from ear to ear, and mumbled in a contented voice: "Papa..." Marek responded with two words: "*mon bébé*" (my baby), accompanied by a joyful smile. Despite the difficulty in getting out the French words, the couple had decided to speak French as a first rule in their new life. Olivier climbed on to Marek and pulled the poster from his hands, letting it unfurl in all its glory.

Annette was surprised to see the poster. "What kind of education are you giving your son? Is that what he's going to learn? That women dance in see-through bodysuits with their breasts bouncing every which way? Don't you have any posters with children's drawings, with letters and words?"

Marek quickly responded, "This doesn't look natural to you? I personally think she's perfect," he said with a teasing smile, pointing to the lead dancer.

"Marek, my love," Annette responded with a serious face, "the door is always open. I'm not keeping you here by force," and turned her back on him.

He went over to her, hugged her from behind, and held her swelling abdomen with both hands. "Do you really think I would leave this round tummy?" He kissed the back of her neck and she lifted her arms, reaching behind to hold his head. *Don't move*, she thought to herself, *just keep kissing me...*

Olivier looked over at his parents, emitted a noise as if to say, "I'm here," and then turned his attention back to the poster. He struggled with it until he managed to spread it open before him, rejoicing at the beautiful sight of the woman in her colorful clothing. He touched the woman's breast and said: "Nana." Annette laughed. "Your son doesn't miss a thing..."

A small notice rolled out of the big poster, and Marek quickly took it from Olivier. Annette reached over and grabbed the notice from Marek's hand, screwing up her face at the sight of a drawing showing Hitler and the French prime minister under the title: "Is War Inevitable?" It was an advertisement for a conference of business people and leading thinkers.

"Dear, I don't know why I brought this home, but from what I hear, the situation is really uncertain… I don't know what this means. I don't know how real this is, but something bad is happening."

Annette asked: "That's it? Is it final? Do you really think there will be a war? I don't want to live in such an evil world… Where can we go…? How far away do we have to go to escape it? We've already left everyone once …"

"I can't tell you what's going to happen. It's hard to predict things that don't depend on us. I only know that if it comes closer to us, we'll have no choice; if we've decided not to stay in a place where we and our Olivier are in danger, we will have to pack everything up and keep moving on. Apartment walls don't bind us to the ground, life is more important." Annette looked at him without uttering a word.

"The pact that France signed with Poland does not bode well," Marek went on, "it leaves France with no choice. They'll have to fight. Otherwise, why would they have signed it? It's kind of funny that, as French people, we are now supposed to defend the Poles who tormented us. What I know is that at the moment, with the winds of war blowing, people are changing. Annette, we need to be ready for anything. We'll continue to hope for the best, but we already know that we cannot influence everything with the power of thought alone. We can only influence our own affairs."

They sat in silence opposite each other at the little kitchen table, Olivier perched on Marek's lap. The sounds of Paris waking up entered their apartment through the open window, bringing them back to the "here and now." How they loved their little island of sanity.

Their apartment building was located in the heart of the Latin Quarter, whose population consisted mainly of artists, painters, jazz musicians, dancers, philosophers; people who lent the quarter its special character. A place full of people who loved people.

Marek went off to sleep to recoup his strength after an exhausting night's work.

2

Marek was awakened by a tiny hand pulling at his nose. Having barely opened his eyes, he felt Olivier climbing on top of him. This was the sign for him to get up and get ready for their afternoon walk. The three of them left the apartment, Marek still half asleep.

Marek held Olivier's hand as they began descending the stairs. When they reached the first floor, they met Helena, their neighbor from the second floor, who was on her way up. She smiled a wide, welcoming smile. "Where is my love?" she asked playfully as she bent down to kiss Olivier on the cheek. Olivier smiled at her, pleased, and said, "Nana." Helena was the woman on the poster, the object of Olivier's love.

"How he has grown!" she exclaimed, rising back up. "I would actually prefer that he stays little and cute like this, so that I can always kiss him," she laughed.

"I'm sorry, but you know that nature will have its way," said Annette, feeling slightly uncomfortable.

***

Helena was originally from Italy. She was in her late thirties, athletic and statuesque, with a striking figure. In Italy, she had dreamed of becoming a stage actress, but just like Annette and Marek, she had been forced to give up her dream. Similar circumstances to theirs, but in a different country had compelled her to leave her family and friends behind and escape secretly to

France, hoping that the "capital of culture" would give her the opportunity to realize her dream.

She sought work upon arriving in France a few years earlier. Her first interview landed her a cleaning job in the home of a rich family in the Sixth Arrondissement. She did not despair, but continued her efforts to find a theater, even a small one, where she could fulfill her dream of becoming an actress. Her talents as a dancer eventually led her to a job interview at the Folies Bergère nightclub. Without knowing the character of the place, and perhaps also out of blindness or naiveté, she went to the interview.

The "interview" turned out to be bizarre and humiliating. "Let's go!" the producer prompted the candidates right from the outset. "Put on your dance outfits, let's see you as feminine as possible, like women should be!"

While they were waiting in the dressing room, the assistant producer came in and asked them for their measurements. When Helena's turn came, she wittily replied: "the narrowest and the tallest," and laughed.

"I can see," he said, smiling.

The assistant producer took a suitably sized outfit and tossed it at Helena. As she began to undress, he stared at her. She turned her back to him, feeling humiliated, as if she was some kind of object. As she was getting ready to put on the outfit, she realized that it was nothing more than the bottom half of a leotard with lots of feathers attached, while the rest of her body remained nude. She turned to the assistant producer, whose name was André, and asked angrily in a heavy Italian accent, "and what dances exactly am I supposed to perform in this outfit?!" The girls around her immediately began to chuckle.

"My child," André answered her in a slightly patronizing tone, "just the dances that you thought. Folies Bergère is one of the most valued cultural institutions in Paris. The city is famous for these dances. People come to Paris from all over Europe, and one of the sites they are certain to visit is our cabaret!"

A pretty girl named Michelle, who was already an experienced dancer at the cabaret, approached Helena and said, "don't be scared. Even though you will dance in the nude, it is still a highly respected institution. If you know how to make yourself a place here, you will also be very well compensated. And believe me. it will be much more than you expect."

Still uncomfortable, Helena stripped down put on the feathery outfit. Michelle gazed at her, thrilled by Helena's body— firm breasts, narrow waist, long legs. "My child, you will need to watch yourself here," she burst out. "Even though this is a respectable place, the men are still men. Sometimes, in their eyes we are nothing more than a toy that can be sold to the highest bidder," she said and glanced over at André, who hadn't taken his eyes off Helena the whole time.

After that, Georges, the choreographer of the cabaret show, told the girls to come up on stage. He arranged them in a straight line, and asked Michelle to demonstrate the dance moves that he wanted them to perform for the audition. Before they started to dance, he told them, "dear girls, you have the privilege to audition for the leading cabaret in Europe! Whoever gets accepted will merit a life that she never dreamed of! But know this, my dears: I will make you cry before you get on stage. When you stand on this stage, you must be ready to do anything! There are no questions here. I offer our clientele only the best! If any of you is not comfortable with this, it's better if you leave now, before we start."

Helena stood paralyzed, tears in her eyes. She felt hurt and wanted nothing more than to run away as fast as she could, but she remained in her place. Unlike the girls who had come seeking a more comfortable life, she still harbored a hope that she would someday become an actress. This place was only a waystation on the road to her dream, she told herself. With this thought in mind, she stood up straight, erect and proud. *I'll survive*, she thought to herself, *and not just survive: people will respect me. I will be the best.*

Standing in a line, the candidates began the dance routine. Helena seemed to float across the stage, her feet making no sound as they landed. The other girls looked clumsy in comparison.

Suddenly, Georges screamed, "stop! What are you? Women or she-bears? Dancing so heavily! Numbers five, seven, twelve, twenty-four – out! Have a great life! The rest— do it again. And this time, I want to see harmony in your movements."

The girls who had been asked to leave ran outside in tears, all except for one who, despite the embarrassing circumstances, remained standing on the stage, smiling. Georges shouted at her in rage, "I told you to get off the stage! You belong somewhere else!" Finally, he succeeded in making her cry too. Michelle went over and hugged her. "Georges, you're taking it too far!" she scolded him. She was the only one who could make him chuckle.

Helena went on dancing. After they performed the dance three more times, twelve candidates remained of the initial thirty-seven. They stood exhausted on the stage as Georges came up and joined them.

"My dear girls, today you are going to transition from young girls to women in every part of your body. On the stage and off it, you will carry the name of the Folies Bergère. You can be proud. Your lives are going to change entirely. But it will only happen on the condition that you do exactly as I tell you! Anyone who dares to rebel against my word— and that means putting on as much as one gram of fat without my permission— will find herself begging on the street."

"Georges, stop scaring them," Michelle interrupted him.

"My dear Michelle, I'm not scaring them. And if you don't want to hear what I have to say. the door is open." There was constant tension between the lead dancer and the crazy choreographer. Georges craved control, but he also loved Michelle and allowed her to speak her mind.

***

Pregnant Annette felt uncomfortable standing next to Helena in the stairwell. She was jealous, as her two men were Helena's captives. *Marek gazed at Helena in admiration*, Annette thought to herself, *in the way that a man looks at a woman who will never be his*. Olivier was drawn to her kind face and to her pictures on the poster that Marek had brought home.

Despite her discomfort, Annette thought Helena was more real than any of the other women in the quarter. Helena always respected her and knew to withdraw when she felt Annette was recoiling.

Annette turned to Helena, who was about to continue on her way up the stairs, and asked, "do you have any news from the family? What do they say?"

"Not much, just that the situation couldn't be much worse," Helena chuckled cynically. "The Italians, my dear, when they do anything, it is always accompanied by a great deal of noise. So, they've just gone crazy, and life has gotten very, very hard. My mother says that if I had stayed, they would have conscripted me to the militia! I am praying that they will hang on and stay healthy, that that they won't get hurt..."

Annette kissed her goodbye and they parted ways, but not before Helena gave Oliver a big, loving ug, the kind that mothers give their children...

Marek could not take his eyes off of Helena's legs as she climbed up the stairs. From where he stood, if he had continued looking, he would have seen the rest of her body as well.

"I'm here, in case you didn't notice!" Annette scolded him.

"I didn't forget for a moment! But sometimes, it's permitted to look at works of art... You know that it is permitted to look at the Chanukah candles, but it's forbidden to touch them," he grinned. He hugged Annette's waist, holding onto Olivier with his other hand, and the three went out for their walk.

By the time they got back, Olivier was very tired, as if he were the one carrying his two parents in his arms, and not the other way around. As they were climbing up the stairs, just when they reached the second floor, he cried: "Nana!"

Annette laughed. "She's not here, my little naughty boy." She pulled him close and sang to him. "Maman and Papa are always here at your side, and you are my little baby, close your eyes and dream. Maman and Papa will always be with you, and you are my baby, close your eyes and sleep. For we will always be here..." Olivier fell asleep in Annette's arms.

3

Marek worked overtime, until the early morning hours, in the printing house where he had been working since he first came to Paris. He had rapidly advanced to become the manager of all the operations there. The owners of the printing house, the Crémieux brothers, were grateful for Marek's work, and made sure to compensate him occasionally for his dedication. They called him "the dynamo." The native Frenchmen working at the printing house did not particularly appreciate Marek's enthusiasm. Despite all the support and help he gave them, they sometime called him "the immigrant" behind his back. He was generous and would often complete ten tasks himself before turning to help others complete theirs, modestly, never asking for any recognition or compensation. But the fact of his being an immigrant did not endear him to this sector of French society, which had become very patriotic since the The Great War.

The Crémieux brothers' printing house was like a museum of European history: the posters hanging on display along the walls told the story of Europe.

At times when Marek was tired from working, he would sneak a short break, mainly at night when the Crémieux brothers were not at the printing house. In demonstration of their faith in him, they left him a key to the main office, where he would relax in a chair, enjoying a Gitanes cigarette, and gaze at the posters which told, in a way, his own story as well.

It was a night like any other night. Marek sat in the owners' office, relaxing in an armchair that faced a poster from World War I. Gazing at it, he suddenly realized that it was identical to a new poster that had just been hung on the wall. *It's exactly the same thing*, he thought to himself, *the story repeats itself. How much evil and stupidity there is in this world... I hope they'll be smart enough not to start again. One rotten apple can spoil the whole crate. Someone has to be rational in this world and stop this..."* His mind raced with such thoughts.

The early morning light coming in through the window brought him back to reality. He went back to finish the last series of prints, and then wearily dragged himself back home.

When he came in, Annette had just woken up , and came to greet him in the nightgown that he loved so much. Marek forgot about the thoughts that had troubled him at work. Olivier was still sleeping, and Annette sat down on his lap.

"My love, the little thing in your tummy has gained weight," he laughed.

"Hold on a minute, are you hinting that I've gotten fat?"

"Not at all. You haven't, but your tummy has."

"You're wicked!" They embraced. He loved seeing her in her last month of pregnancy, more womanly than ever.

"You know, tonight I had some bad thoughts. Everyone at work is talking about how even though we're French and we've proven to the Germans what we're worth, this time something really bad is going to happen... When I was in the office, I looked at the war poster and I saw that nothing has changed. What was is what will be. The same words, the same explanations, as though everything has been written and is known ahead of time."

Annette sat up straight. "You're scaring me. So, maybe we shouldn't wait any longer? Let's just get up and leave! We did it once under pressure, I don't want to have to go through that again. I don't know if I'll have the strength to do it. I'm not alone anymore, Olivier is a part of me now... I'm very worried about the world he is going to grow up in. And soon, I will be a mother of two... It's not that I think that people here are evil like those we ran away from, but I don't know how things will develop. I'm not scared of them, but I'm scared of those who are likely to come here if what they are talking about really comes to pass."

"Do you really think it will come to such a situation? That Paris will experience what we went through in Poland? This is the city of culture, of lights... I agree that not everyone here thinks like that, but it's still a far cry from the savageness and evil that we experienced there. It shouldn't happen here."

"Marek, I'm just saying that you and Olivier are everything to me. I know that it weighs on you to hear that, but if something happens to one of you, I will never forgive myself. The time we have is short. You're the one who brought the poster home, aren't you? You said that if we would ever feel threatened, we wouldn't be tied to the walls of a home. That we wouldn't take any possessions, but just get up and leave. Life is more important than anything, isn't it? You told me that we have each other and that it doesn't matter where we are, as long as we are together."

"My love, we will still have enough time to take this step should it come to that. You're right, but there are still rational people who don't want anything to happen. Everyone knows the repercussions of war, and no one wants to live in a world like that. People naturally prefer comfort, goodness, calm... They would rather see a rosy future."

"I have always been the optimist of the two of us... That is what's kept us moving forward in every situation. Promise me that you will pinch me any time I sink into this despair."

"My love, I won't pinch you, but I'll kiss you every time it happens," he smiled at her.

"If so, maybe I should sink into despair more often..." she said with a loving smile through her tears.

Marek gave her a long kiss and the two cuddled up together until Olivier's voice announced that a new day had arrived.

4

Upon arriving in Paris, Marek and Annette had decided that she would not work at first. A little over a year after they had settled in the Latin Quarter, she started getting back to her profession as a seamstress. At first, she did repairs and dress fittings, and over time began to sew evening gowns for both bourgeois and bohemian women in the quarter. As a seamstress, Annette immediately became a clearinghouse for gossip among the women of the quarter. All of the gossip in the quarter flowed to her. Annette didn't fully understand their culture and the strange stories these women told her: who was going out with whom, who was separated from whom, and the worst of all in her eyes— women sharing stories of when it fell to their lot to share the same man…

The variegated colors of the Latin Quarter were on display in her house in all their vividness: starting with little betrayals while her clients' husbands were at work, stories of dancers and singers who lived in the quarter, the painters and philosophers, evenings of jazz, and what happened at the end of the show… Alongside the embarrassment she felt, Annette also enjoyed her unexpected immersion in Parisian society. She felt that the barrier had finally been breached between her and the society of her adopted country.

One of her customers was also their second-floor neighbor, Helena. Almost from the first time that Helena came for a fitting of a luxurious dress, she began to open up to Annette, no doubt thanks to little Olivier, who would half crawl, half walk about Annette's workroom while his mother was taking measurements of garments.

Olivier was delighted to see the many women who came to his mother. Each of them gave him a hug and a kiss, and sometimes a caress, with a motherly smile. He would return a smile of his own and raise his arms to be picked up, stirring their maternal instinct. His overtures were a simple request for love, and at the same time a desire to give love to those surrounding him, like that of any small child before he grows up and is exposed to the hard facts of life.

"You know," Helena began, "I really love children."

"I could not help but notice," Annette answered with a smile. "Every time you pass Olivier, you swallow him up with your eyes. But just be careful, he'll take advantage of that."

"I know," Helena smiled. "I'd be happy to watch him sometimes, and free you up for other pursuits," she winked at Annette.

Annette was a bit taken aback. After all, Helena was a dancer, and t just anywhere, but in a strip club, even if it was the most elegant in Europe… Gossip in the quarter had not passed her over; many women talked about her life of dissipation, about cars parked on the street containing men in tailored suits coming to visit her after the show, late at night… But she was able to see Helena as a person and not just a barroom stripper.

"I'd like that very much," Annette answered. "I see how happy Olivier is every time he sees you. Thank you, it's very nice of you to offer such a thing."

"Really, the pleasure is all mine. I know what it's like to be an immigrant from a foreign country, to be the object of gossip in this quarter… I know what it's like to be alone," Helena said, suppressing a lump in her throat.

Annette realized that all the stories she had heard about the woman standing before her did not convey any sense of the loneliness that Helena was enduring, the great sacrifice that she had made to realize her dream, and, at the same time, to escape the insanity, just as Annette had done.

"You're welcome to come visit us whenever you'd like," Annette said.. She felt that they shared a common destiny in a crazy world with an uncertain future.

Helena felt a warmth from Annette that she had not felt for a long time, an affection merited by who she really was, not by her body or a man's desire to have her for himself after watching her dance topless, her breasts exposed in the glare of the spotlights. Her only dream was to be an actress, but reality had served her a slap in the face; she had gotten sucked into a world that she had not known before, a world that she admired less and less as time passed, but which also gave her the strength to continue planning the fulfilment of her dream.

"You know, I left Italy for a few reasons. First, I ran away from a conservative family. I don't know what you've heard about traditional Italian families, but it's all true," she chuckled. "When I told my family that I wanted to be a ballet dancer or an actress, they cut off all ties with me. Like any other Italian family would have done, they just erased me. From their point of view, I brought shame on them in the village."

"I came to Paris a few years ago," she continued. "I knew only a couple of words of French. The only address I had was one that my uncle gave me in secret, of a friend of his who could help me. It's not easy to be in my situation, in a world completely controlled by men, where women are comfortable being obedient, content in their comfort and wealth, occasionally escaping from their reality to find the attention that they're really looking for, the attention that gives them real happiness..."

"I hope I really understand what you feel," Annette hurriedly responded, as though she knew what Helena was talking about. "Even though we don't have money, and it wouldn't hurt to have a bit more, Marek and I have been lucky enough to have each other. For Marek, our love is an escape from the hard work and from the way his colleagues treat him; sometimes, he needs me to give him strength to keep moving forward. For me, it's an escape to a safe, happy place. An escape from managing the household, and from the full-time job that has been added to my duties two years ago— even though I don't get a salary for it," she laughed.

"You're describing a dream that I once had, though it is no longer mine," Helena said. "I'm not complaining about where I am today, I've learned to live the best in any situation!" she announced. "My dream is to be strong enough and have enough money to immigrate to the United States, and there to finally start the career that I long for."

"Okay, I need to go," Helena concluded, "but really, Annette, thank you for seeing me to fit the dress. Sometimes, little actions mean a lot. I've told you before, and I'll say it again: make use of me. I'm sure I can offer you something from my experience in the French capital. Now, I have to run. I'm getting picked up to go to theater rehearsal," Helena said in an attempt to gloss over the fact that the theater was, in fact, a nightclub. "Tomorrow is the new show, and there are dozens of guests invited. We'll talk next week."

Annette kissed her cheek as was common in Parsi, thanking her. Helena turned to go just as Olivier stood up and drew her attention with his energetic movements, holding out his little arms for a hug.

She swooped him up.

"Nana," he said to her, and she kissed his forehead.

"My little one, I'll come visit you next week. Take good care of Maman!" She put him down and walked out, closing the door behind her. Annette's pulse was racing. This woman who had just opened up to her was a woman of great contrasts: on the one hand, she was alone and fragile, while on the other hand she did not mourn her fate, but instead turned every situation to her advantage.

5

Evening arrived, and with it, Marek. During supper, Annette could not refrain from recounting the day's gossip. This was a kind of therapy for him, allowing him a momentary escape from preoccupation with work and fears about the volatile situation. This time, Annette told him about Helena.

"Today, I really felt close to her. She is a fascinating woman."

"I'm sure she is. I would like to be with you when she comes here," he answered.

"Stop it, Marek. I'm serious."

"I'm also serious," he answered with a smile. "Okay, I promise to listen without laughing."

"She's a very gentle woman, who has experienced a lot of hardships and made many courageous decisions in her life. She is one of the most genuine women I have met, more than all the others that come to me for dresses. She actually dreamed of becoming a ballet dancer. That was her whole world. Only because she was forced to come to Paris did she end up where she is now, a cabaret dancer… She has developed a thick skin. She just shuts off everything that does her harm, and lives the good even in the bad. That's what she explained to me."

Marek felt a sense of empathy towards the woman whom he did not know, but whose beauty he could not help picturing to himself.

Annette could always read his facial expressions. "Just for a minute, forget about her beauty, her body, her stature. Just concentrate on her story. It's heartbreaking. It's true that we also ran away, but we have each other. She has nothing, and she's surrounded by greedy men."

"You're right. But I think that if she really wants to fulfill her dream, she has to get up and keep going, otherwise she's going to get stuck here with fake sparkles and lots of money."

"She said the exact same thing. That not a day goes by when she does not try to find an opportunity to pursue her dream. But wherever she goes, when people hear what she does for a living, they drag her back down, and the dream fades away. In the end, she's a cabaret dancer who titillates men."

"I would suggest that she try to sail to New York. There are plenty of playwrights there, and opportunities to enter the real theater world."

"Strange, that's just what she said to me, that she wants to be strong enough, with enough money, to emigrate to the US and pursue the career she dreams of," Annette said wonderingly.

Suddenly, the sound of a police whistle from outside rippled through the air. Annette and Marek got up and looked out the window. They saw dozens of people marching in the street, waving French flags. They were nationalists, those who were in favor of war and advocated heading to the front to fight the Germans.

Perhaps it was the sight of those warlike crowds, but all of a sudden Annette hunched over, clutching her belly. "I think it's time."

Marek turned abruptly away from the window, knocking over his cup of coffee, and she, with a cool head that only a woman can show in the moment of truth, said, "Marek, go down to the neighbors, Helena's not home. They said they would come up when we need them."

Marek ran out of the apartment and knocked on the door of the Dubois family, owners of the neighborhood bakery. The father of the family, Aubert, woke up his wife, Monique, who immediately got up and prepared to go up to their apartment and watch Olivier.

Meanwhile, Marek returned to the apartment and followed Annette's instructions: "Run to the midwife who lives in the building over the florist shop. I showed you her apartment just before."

Marek ran out, not before managing to trip over the stairs in his hurry. Panting and sweating, he reached the apartment of Mrs. Gomez, a French-woman of Portuguese extraction who was an experienced midwife. They had neither the time nor the resources to go to an official clinic. Half an hour later, Mrs. Gomez appeared clutching her midwife's bag. They sent Madame Dubois home. "I'm at your service if you need me," she told them as she left.

Within less than an hour since the had midwife arrived, Annette gave birth to Laurent, an infant with delicate features and a head full of black hair.

Marek sat on the edge of the bed. Laurent was laid on Annette's belly and Mrs. Gomez cut the umbilical cord. She wished them a happy life and said that it was a blessing to bring a child into the world, and even more so when it was a boy. "I hope that he'll grow up in a good world," she added.

Olivier slept the whole time, and only in the morning awoke to the sound of unfamiliar crying. He ran into the living room and saw his mother, with his new baby brother suckling at her breast. His response was not long in coming: he climbed onto the adjacent chair and tried to nurse too. Marek, exhausted from emotion and lack of sleep, shouted, "can I join too?" He scooped up Olivier in his arms and explained that Maman was tired, that she had just brought his brother into the world. Now his tiny brother needed fuel to grow, and the mother's milk was only for the infant to get big and strong so that Olivier would be able to play with him.

"Let's go down to Helena and surprise her and say hello," Marek suggested.

Olivier ran towards the door, completely forgetting about the new addition to the family. They went down the stairs with Olivier in Marek's arms, and knocked lightly on Helena's apartment door. A moment later, she cracked the door open slightly. Before they had a chance to say a word, Olivier squirmed out of Marek's arms, pushed open the door, and burst inside. Marek felt embarrassed, as Helena was wearing nothing but a see-through robe.

"I-I'm really sorry," he turned away to protect her privacy. "We just came to tell you that Annette gave birth to a boy."

Helena hugged and kissed him. "Don't be embarrassed, every night I perform for dozens of men who are much less polite than you are. It's okay. You don't know how happy I am to hear that she is all right. I'll just get ready and come up."

Olivier, who had already caused considerable embarrassment, now tugged at Helena's robe by mistake, causing it to drop to her waist. Marek pulled Olivier to him and picked him up, half-jokingly apologizing again, "please, forgive me..."

Helena saw Marek's eyes roaming over her body. She took it as a compliment. It was a different kind of gaze from the one she was used to getting at the nightclub. She had always seen him as a different sort of man: she saw how he stood at Annette's side, caring for Olivier, investing time to fix up their little home. He was not a man of impressive outward appearance, but he was special in her eyes. Helena pulled up her robe, placed her hand on his cheek and said,

"It's okay. I'll be up in a minute to visit Annette." "See you soon," Marek said with an embarrassed smile.

Olivier reached out his arms to her and got a big hug.

6

The first week after the birth was full of light. It was also the first week of spring, and Paris once again adorned itself with leaves on the trees and flowers everywhere.

Annette and Marek focused on their expanding family. They sent a telegram to Annette's cousin, Olga, who lived in England, telling her about their newest addition. Olga had also fled to France with her family, but continued on to England rather than settle there. Their financial situation was good; Olga's husband was a successful diamond dealer, and they had managed to save up a handsome sum of money before leaving Poland.

Helena drew closer to Annette and Marek following the birth. She helped Annette, who had gone back to work sewing dresses within a mere few days after giving birth. Being free in the mornings, Helena would take Olivier, leaving baby Laurent by his mother's side. Marek would return in the afternoons, whenever he was able to free up a couple of hours, to pick up Olivier from Helena and bring him back home for a short break; later, he would return to his work at the printing house.

On Monday, when Laurent was exactly two weeks old, Marek returned in the afternoon as usual. He crossed the boulevard with a small brochure in his hand, then stopped at Helena's door and knocked quietly. She opened the door with tears running down her cheeks.

"What happened? Is Olivier all right?" Marek asked in some alarm.

"Yes, yes, everything is okay, don't worry. I visited Annette in the morning and Olivier fell asleep, so I left him in his bed."

"But what happened? Why are you crying?"

"My ex-boyfriend joined the militia, visited my parents, and threatened them that if I do not return to serve the country, they will be considered traitors and they will be hurt... It's all an excuse to force me to go back and be with him. He's gone completely crazy... He has spread rumors to make people think my parents oppose the regime. My parents left everything behind and fled to my cousin in a neighboring village... They're okay for now, but who knows what might happen to them... For a moment, I felt like this is all my fault."

Marek put the brochure down on the dresser and hugged her while she sobbed on his shoulder. He thought about the terrifying situation she was in, and was reminded of his and Annette's escape. At the same time, deep inside, he could not ignore the pleasant fragrance of her hair and the closeness he felt to her.

She rested her head on his shoulder and cried as he stroked her hair in an attempt to console her.

"They'll go into hiding; it will take time for the militias to reach there. At the moment they're focusing on the big cities, they won't get as far as the villages. And even if they get there, they still need working hands for supplying and producing food..." Marek was still in the middle of a sentence when suddenly he felt the touch of her lips on his mouth. Helena, a few inches taller than him, leaned in and kissed him. They kissed in a passionate frenzy, almost without taking a breath. Marek was swept into a world he had never known, a feeling he had never felt, a dream coming true; he had fantasized about this moment countless times, and now, at this moment of crisis, it suddenly came true... He dreamed of her often, but today she was actually at his side. He grabbed her and lifted her up, her legs coiling around his waist.

In a flash, they found themselves with their clothes off, wound around each other; Helena leaned against the wall while Marek kissed her body passionately. She did not hold herself back and he did not stop, and thus they became one body.

Everything happened so quickly, as though the urge had been bottled up for a long time and had suddenly burst out into the open.

They looked at each other.

"Marek, I'm sorry, I don't know why it happened now of all times."

"You know, it happened to both of us, not just you. For a long time, I have been dreaming of you, deep in my heart, but it seemed impossible, something that could never happen. And look, now it's happened... As if the power of my thoughts made my dream come true."

"Marek, you two are my best friends, the only ones who treat me with respect. Annette must never be hurt by what happened here. I feel guilty, she doesn't deserve this. I'm like a member of your family, it makes me feel terrible, it tears my heart out..."

"Helena, we must not tell her. I don't believe that I'm saying this, but what one doesn't know can't hurt him. The fear and pain will be our punishment. It's important to me that you know that I wasn't thinking about you just because you're a beautiful woman. Your story is so similar to ours...You're a model for us. I understand everything you did, but what's more, you did it all alone. That takes a lot of courage."

Helena kissed him firmly.

"I have to go home to Annette. She's waiting for me."

Helena put her clothes on and helped Marek fix himself up so that nothing would give away what had happened a few minutes earlier. She kissed him, saying, "Let's let time do its work. Time has its own wisdom, it heals everything. It doesn't matter what happened, I wanted you so much... Leave me the moment that we had together, it's something I'll never forget."

He picked up the brochure and climbed rapidly to the fourth floor. When he entered the apartment, Olivier jumped on him, trying to wrest the brochure from his hand. "Sorry, darling, that's for work. I'll bring you a new picture this evening."

Annette sat in the armchair, glowing, a mother with her tiny baby nursing at her breast. Marek felt his pulse racing; his cheeks blushed as he recalled the scent of Helena's skin, her hair falling over his face, her statuesque body bending over him ... He became entangled in his thoughts, pulled back to reality only by Annette's voice. "What's wrong, my love?" He sought refuge in the brochure he had brought home, which he handed to her.

"What's this?" she asked, half smiling, hoping for something good. She opened it up and saw the headline by the Ministry of War: "Call for General Mobilization."

Annette let out a soft cry and gasped, "no, it can't be! Is it really true?"

"Yes, they brought it from the government publicity office. They guarded me the whole time it was being printed, and they're still there, making sure that no copy got out. I snuck out a draft copy without them noticing."

"Will they draft you?" Annette asked fearfully.

"No, dear, I won't get drafted. I'm lucky that at this stage, they're only drafting Frenchmen who were in the army. All other citizens will have to serve in other roles, at the government's discretion. I've already read the whole thing."

"What does this mean?"

"I don't know. It's not war yet, but the winds are blowing strongly. I hope France will be smart enough to come to a better agreement with its neighbors on pacts and defense, and not put itself in the sights of this monster."

Tears ran down Annette's cheeks. Although she was sitting in Paris, images of her past in Poland, of her family and what they went through, flashed before her eyes. Without noticing, out of fear, she squeezed Laurent so hard that he began to cry. Marek came up to her, stroked her hair, and held her hand until she calmed down.

"What will we do? I don't want to see our families' histories repeated."

"I'm telling you again, I don't know. Let's see what they announce, and by that we'll know where we stand. And at the same time, we'll start making an escape plan. This time, we'll be more organized; we have time to get ourselves together. We're together." As he said that, he could not help but think of Helena and what had happened a short while earlier.

"I don't know how I'll cope; you know, I may collapse at any second... Last time, the day before we left, you saved me from falling apart... Do you remember how you found me the day we left Poland?" she began to reminisce. "Some thugs followed you back from work and by the time you got home, you were already all bloody, bruised all over your body. The neighbors didn't offer us any help and our families were far away... I fainted, and didn't come to until you slapped me in the face and splashed water on me... You yelled at me, 'pull yourself together! We can't stay here, and you have to be strong. The only way we'll survive is if we stick together...'" Annette delved deep into her memories. "I don't know what I would do without you."

"I'm here," Marek tried to soothe her. "I'm not leaving. We know what we decided, and our family will survive. We'll manage, we'll find a way to escape. We won't let anyone hurt us again. Let's leave it for now. Let's get supper on the table. I still have to get back to work, I have a long night ahead of me."

After supper, Marek put Olivier to sleep, then came back to the living room and hugged Annette.

"You must promise me that you will be strong. Tomorrow we will plan what we are going to do." He kissed her and left for work. On his way down, he stopped to look at Helena's door, before remembering that she was not home at this hour; she was dancing nude before the patrons of the cabaret. His mind in a whirl, he continued on to the printing house to print out the war brochures.

7

Marek returned home in the dead of night. He entered quietly, gazed at Annette and his two sons with a sorrow-tinged smile, got undressed, and climbed in bed to hug Annette. Half asleep, she murmured, "slow down, you'll wake them up."

"With you, I do everything slowly, so that it will never end." He kissed her neck, held her and drifted off to sleep for a moment.

"Keep kissing me," Annette begged, "it's the best thing for us." He kissed her again. He really did love her, but his encounter with Helena had shaken up everything he thought he had known up to that moment. She was now planted firmly in his consciousness.

They embraced. He kissed Annette's neck, sending a shiver through her body. When he kissed her breast, drops of mother's milk flowed from her nipples. "Don't eat your son's food," she laughed.

"Don't I deserve it? I also contributed to it," he joked.

Olivier opened the door and jumped inside, ignoring what was happening in front of him. They laughed, caught unprepared, and he climbed up on the bed between them, taking his place like a little lion cub.

Around eleven in the morning, Marek awoke to see Annette in the living room, fitting a gown for an overdressed lady. They were discussing the war, of course. The lady opined that nothing was going to happen, that it was all just rumors, and that everyone would soon calm down.

Olivier was not there; Marek assumed that Helena had taken him. He was happy that he didn't run into her; he didn't know how to respond to her now.

He sat down on a chair in Olivier's little room and tried to focus his thoughts on what they should do if something really happened. He calculated their savings; Annette had managed to increase their income significantly in the past year. Women spent not little money on their appearance in order to be able to fill the hours of gossip afterwards. It brought in cash. He thought of fleeing west or south and from there by boat to England, to Olga, Annette's cousin. Surely, she could help them start again there.

As they had agreed, Marek informed Annette that he was going out to buy tickets for their vacation, their cover story. The lady said to her, "I really must ask that you finish my dress before the event, which will be in a month."

"Don't worry, we're only going away for a short vacation, just three days. I'll have plenty of time to make you the most beautiful woman at the event," Annette promised.

"I don't have to be the most beautiful, I just have to attract the attention of a certain person," the lady winked.

At the train station, Marek got information on all possible routes and their prices; they hadn't left Paris in a long time, nor taken an internal train in France for years. He obtained all the necessary information, feeling confident in his ability to lead the family in their departure.

When he got back home, he was supposed to pick up Olivier from Helena, but he was afraid to enter. Finally, telling himself that "life goes on," he knocked on the door. Helena opened it, more beautiful and glowing than ever. They kissed cheeks with French politeness, and she asked him how he felt.

"Confused," he answered. "Everything is happening so quickly— us, the situation in France… There's no time to digest it all. Where's Olivier?"

"Annette already picked him up."

"If so, then I'll go up to her …"

She pulled him inside and closed the door. "I didn't have time to think about you."

"You're in my head with everything I do, when I embrace Annette, when I think about fleeing from the war…" They kissed passionately.

He stopped her and said, "I have to go up. I promised Annette we'd eat lunch together. I'll come by before I go to the printing house."

"If I'm here, so much the better for you. If not, then you'll have to re-strain yourself until you find me. Are you capable of that?" she teased him mischievously.

Marek kissed her and hurried up to Annette.

When he went into the apartment, Olivier and Annette were sat at the table, with Laurent in his favorite position, latched on to his mother's breast.

Marek sat down next to Annette. She immediately smelled Helena's per-fume, and did not hold back. "Did you stop by Helena's?" she asked him directly.

Marek struggled to keep his expression calm. "Yes, I was looking for Ol-ivier, but she said that you had already taken him upstairs."

"Just from opening her apartment door, you already picked up her scent..." she mused out loud.

His heart lurched but he kept his tone light. "You know, every time I have the chance to kiss her hello, I take it."

"Tell me what you found out today. What do we have to do?" "Look, I was at the station. It seems possible to me. We just have to get ourselves organized and do it. We can leave on a day's notice. We can take the Dou-ville train and from there, carry on by boat. It's even advertised at the train station. It's not cheap, but with a few more days of work, we'll have enough money. As more people start trying to escape this place, prices will go up, so we should hurry. The problem is that when we get there, we won't have any money. What we have will be enough to live on only for a month or two.

We'll need Olga's help. Perhaps we should warn her in advance...

We have to be prepared for this."

"I'm scared, Marek. I feel paralyzed. If you want, let's leave tomorrow, but I really think that it's too early to make a decision."

"In my opinion, we have nothing to fear from the past, we were in a much more dangerous position, remember? I was almost killed for being a Jew!"

"We have not yet had to experience any hatred directed at us. People here are more real; they judge you for who you are. True, the fact that we are immigrants has come up a few times, but nothing connected to our religion."

"Let's believe that some good can come out of this. Ever since we left Poland, only good things have happened. Look at what you are holding in your arms! Look at Olivier."

Olivier, as though he understood his parents' conversation, interjected with a "yes," to emphasize his father's words.

Annette stroked his head and said, "Marek, I'm scared. Deep inside, I feel something dark and terrifying."

"Annette, you have nothing to be scared of. It will take time for anything to happen, and even if it does, it's not necessarily going to be in Paris. I'm sure it will stay along the borders between the countries." He bent over to her, kissed her neck as he always did to soothe her, and sat down to eat. Olivier quickly climbed onto his lap.

Just before five o'clock, he headed out to work. He kissed Olivier's head, telling him to "take good care of Maman. And if she's sad, tell her a story." Marek kissed Annette and went out.

Olivier, as always, understood what was going on. He acted like an adult, standing close to Laurent and his mother in a protective way, and said, "don't worry, Maman. I'm here."

When he reached the second-floor landing, Marek knocked quietly on Helena's door. He turned around for a moment, to make sure that no one saw him.

The door opened and he was quickly pulled inside.

"Are you afraid to knock on the door? And what if I hadn't heard?" Helena was dressed in tights and a half-open robe, getting ready for her show at the nightclub.

He helped the robe open all the way. She embraced him and leaped onto him with her legs wrapped around his waist. They were becoming addicted to each other's touch and to the sensual intoxication that enveloped them. A few minutes later, they were cuddled together on the bed, embracing, as though they were a single being.

A moment later, he began to doze off. She kissed him and said, "go. Your real life goes on."

He left, but not before Helena checked to see that the stairwell was empty.

8

In the following weeks life went on as normal, although the tension in the air was palpable. Annette and Marek packed their bags, careful to hide them from the women who came for fittings. Only Helena was in on the secret, though she hid this from Annette. Marek and Annette had prepared their escape route, the money, bags for themselves and the children… Everything was ready for their escape to freedom.

At the same time, they began corresponding with Olga, letting her know their overall plan. Olga's response was rather cool, as if she were trying to say, "don't come here. It's hard enough already." At any rate, she promised that when they got there, she and her husband would help them as much as they could.

"You know it's not a very good situation for us. I always told you that Olga thinks about herself first. Everything she does is for her own benefit. If we become a burden to her, she won't be shy to tell us not to come. She would only take us in against her will if something truly bad happens. And still, she's the only relative I have left…" Annette felt powerless to do anything.

"If only your cousin was our biggest problem. But it's true, she does always think about herself," he mused, adding with a smile, "especially after you met me. Remember how jealous she was that you had found a treasure like me?"

Annette relaxed a little, laughing, "Really, a treasure … All in all, just an average guy."

"Oh, look, I see that your cynicism has come back a bit. It doesn't matter what your cousin does, at least your smile came back." Marek was pleased with himself.

It was the end of July 1939, and the possibility of war was looking more certain than ever. The concentration of Nazi forces at points along Germany's borders left no room for doubt. But Europe's leaders, turning a blind eye and seeking reconciliation, just encouraged the Nazis to continue in the direction that they were headed.

Evenings out in the French capital became more and more rare, turning instead into pre-war evenings of worry. Marek finished a month of intensive work alongside the stormy secret life he was leading. Annette's fears grew with every rumor that spread, and he spent a lot of time holding her to reassure her. He would seek out Helena as a refuge. They would share their feelings about the situation, dream about what would be when everything was over, and, when there was time, they would steal a few long minutes of sensual passion.

On the morning of August 31, 1939, Marek had just finished the night's print run and was making his way home. He walked away slowly from the printing house, and stopped by the news seller to pick up a newspaper. Suddenly, his eyes widened at the red headline that jumped off the page. He froze. Although they knew it was going to happen, deep inside, they had not expected it. Standing by the newsstand, he read of the Nazi army's bombing of Poland, of the armored columns rushing forward, of the French army's preparations.

He broke out in a run towards the apartment.

As he rushed up the stairs of the building, he stopped at the second floor and knocked quietly on the door. It opened a crack, and Helena peeked out, surprised.

"War has broken out."

"What?!"

"Yes, just what you heard. War has broken out."

"What does that mean?"

"It means Poland has been invaded and France is making preparations. It will most likely be announced that France is joining Poland's side again the Nazis, in accordance with their defense pact…"

Suddenly, he heard a voice from within the apartment. "Helena, are you coming?"

Marek fell silent, stepping backwards.

"I-I'm sorry, it's the director of the cabaret, Jerome. He asked to speak with me, and I couldn't refuse. You know I'm dependent on his word … Marek, don't think it's anything else, really. It's just a conversation that he has to have with me."

Marek said nothing, taking another step backwards. He turned around and began climbing the stairs to his apartment, breathing heavily. The amount of information spinning in his head fogged his thinking: the war, Helena, Annette… At that moment, he felt only a heavy discomfort in his chest that made it hard to breathe. He took a deep breath and opened the door.

He went over to Annette, still deep in slumber, and stroked her face until she began to wake up. Always awaiting his gentle caress, she turned to him with a loving smile, but met a worried face. Bringing her eyes into focus, she saw before her a frightened man.

"What happened, Marek? You don't look good … Are you okay? Tell me!"

He sat down on the edge of the bed and handed her the newspaper.

"No!" she let out a shriek and then froze in place.

He placed his hand gently over her mouth and stroked her hair. "Don't frighten the children. Let's keep our heads. We really should not be surprised."

She hugged him, paralyzed with fear, her fingernails unconsciously digging into his back. She had told Marek so many times about this nightmare of hers, how the war was pursuing her, and he had always tried to soothe her, saying, "stop, you're only hurting yourself." But now, her terrifying dream had become reality.

He tried to get up, to free himself from the clutch of her fingers, but she would not let go until he finally managed to break her hold, leaving red marks on his back.

"Annette, wake up. War has broken out, but nothing has happened to us yet. It won't help us at the moment for you to be in hysterics. You're a mother, you are responsible for two children. We both are," he said calmly.

"I don't know what I'll do, how I'll keep them safe… Let's run away from here!"

"We don't have to run away yet. The war, even though it has started, is still far away. The French know the Germans, they beat them in the last war, and they'll beat them again now. Their fortification line is impenetrable.

And besides, there are other countries who won't sit idly by. They'll stop this monster." He spoke monotonously, trying to diminish the power of this terrifying moment, but within him a storm was raging. He knew that nothing was guaranteed, and that no one really knew what was going to happen. Despite that realization, he played the game, but Annette was not the type of person who could function when she was terrified.

They were preparing breakfast for themselves and the children when they heard a knock on the door. Marek opened the door, only to find Helena on their doorstep.

Trying to act naturally, he kissed her politely on the cheek and invited her in. Meanwhile, Annette looked at her, still horrified by the news of the war.

Helena told them that the director of the cabaret had asked to meet with her the previous evening and told her that he was thinking of leaving for the United States. "He doesn't feel safe here, and he has an invitation from a big cabaret in New York. He wants me to leave with him."

"And what was your answer?" Annette stood up and asked.

Marek looked at Helena with surprise.

"I said no. I don't feel threatened. Everything will work out for me, I'm already the lead dancer. I have to stay near my parents and try to get them out of there. So, I'm staying!" she declared.

"But why?" Annette responded. "You finally have an opportunity to develop your acting."

"I don't know why suddenly, when the opportunity comes, I'm not ready. I can't explain it…"

Marek glanced at Helena wordlessly, only his eyes expressing his gratitude.

Annette sat down, lost in thought, not noticing their exchange of glances. "Would you like to sit down and eat with us?" she said weakly.

"No, thank you, I have to go rest. I haven't slept a wink since I got back from work."

Deep inside Marek relaxed, realizing that although the cabaret director only saw her as an escort girl, Helena was caught up in their stormy affair. Today, she had given him an indirect reply: she did not want to leave him. She passed up her opportunity at a real career, not because of her parents, but because of their relationship.

9

Two days after the Germans invaded Poland, France, together with England, declared war on Germany. The French army made several forays against the German war machine, but in the end decided to retire behind the fortifications along the French border. Poland fell, and all the defense pacts with France and the British Expeditionary Force turned out to be meaningless.

What resulted was in effect a standoff between two armies, the German army together with its Italian allies in the East, facing the French army with the remnants of the Polish army and the British Expeditionary Force.

The madness of the Phoney War, that is, the standstill between the armies, advanced with frightening speed and power. Marek and Helena's affair developed with the same ardor. As fear mounted in both of them, they escaped more and more into their intimacy, trying to neutralize their thoughts and live, for a moment, in a dream.

Olga wrote that her husband was ill, and therefore that she would not be able to help them, advising them to seek other solutions. She promised that the moment she could help, after her husband's treatments end, she would let them know. She closed the letter with words of concern that were unlike her:

"I beg of you, do not endanger yourselves. Try to find a place as far as possible from the borders. Move south or west, even though the channel is closed to the passage of ships."

Helpless, the two remained in Paris. As the weeks passed, the French capital was mainly given to a storm of rumors, fed by stories of soldiers from the front about what was happening and what kind of war machine they were facing. Everyone was waiting for the Nazis' next steps and to see how France would respond.

Annette and Marek, surprisingly, felt relatively safe, despite the rumors and stories. Marek persuaded Annette that they should not take any complicated steps nor run away at this stage.

The situation caused Olivier to mature suddenly, transforming him in the space of a moment into a little man. He liked to play the man of the house. When Marek was at work, he would help his mother tidy up and take care of Laurent, and he made sure to hug her when she sank into worry and fear.

The Phoney War continued for a little less than a year, until May 1940.

During this period, Annette and Marek hoarded their francs, in order to be able to carry out their escape plan and get to England on their own. Olga promised them that if they made it to England, she would be able to help them start setting up their life there.

In May 1940, several battles occurred along the French-German front, breaking the stalemate: the Germans attacked the French army on two fronts. The first attack was designed to attract attention and the second, primary one, led to breaching the French army's fortification line. These events made Annette and Marek realize that what they had feared was finally coming to pass. They were determined to leave France. Their plan was to take a southerly route towards western France, moving as far away as possible away from northern France and the border with Germany.

On the afternoon of May 10, Marek returned home full of fears which he tried to hide as he considered how best to begin the conversation with Annette. How was he going to tell her that the French army had been crushed. Finally, he told her to get everything ready. It was time to put the departure plan to motion, as they had discussed many times.

Olivier overheard them and immediately asked, "where are we going?" without understanding the reason for the journey.

"We're going to a cousin in England. We'll sail on a boat. You'll see, it'll be fun…" Annette answered him with a pale face that emphasized her fears. Wise Olivier immediately understood that this was not a vacation trip.

The French army was outflanked and its fortification line breached, with the German forces already deep in French territory. In such a situation, the French army had no capacity to defend itself. Within a period of six weeks, all the French defense lines were dismantled with one fell swoop. Western Europe had been swallowed up by the conquering Nazi machine.

10

This was the moment to put their departure plan into action. They decided that Marek would go the following day to work, collect his pay from the Cremieux brothers, and then come back in the afternoon to pick up Annette and the children. They would board a train for western France and from there continue to London.

"We have to leave early," Marek told Annette. "After the German blitz starts, there will be lots of French and others seeking to escape, and the trains will be full."

"I'm with you, like we agreed." Annette surprised him by the calmness she exhibited.

"Tomorrow, I'll go to the brothers and ask for the money as an advance. I'll say that we need it for some important purchases. Let's hope that it will pass quietly, that they won't ask questions or try to get out of paying. After all, they promised me full compensation for all the hours they haven't yet paid me for."

The next day, Marek went to the printing house but, to his disappointment, they asked him to wait until the end of the month for the payment. The change in fortunes in the French campaign against the Germans was affecting everyone. Customers of the printing house had not yet paid their bills. Everyone claimed that their lateness was due to the war that had just started, that they needed more time to transfer the payments.

The stress of this news was too much for Annette to bear. When she found out that their departure was postponed and that they were forced to wait until the end of the month, she collapsed again. Marek soothed her, all the while trying to convince himself that nothing was going to happen in the last three weeks of the month of May.

Over the years, Annette had developed panic attacks that caused her to disconnect from her surroundings. She would be physically present but detached from what was happening around her. Marek took on himself all the housework in addition to his job, hoping that everything would work out and that they would be able to leave with enough money to enable them to reach England.

Helena offered to lend them money, but Marek categorically refused.

The whole time that Annette was not able to function in her role as mother, Helena helped him in caring for the children. Between rehearsals and shows, she devotedly cared for the two little ones.

Olivier was her little helper and reported what was happening with his mother. "Today, Maman feels better. She fed Laurent and gave him a bath." Sometimes, he would take advantage of the fact that Helena was with them and ask her to tell him a story. She understood Olivier's request, thinking to herself that he understood very well what was happening around him, but that he was still a child who wanted to experience a bit of his childhood.

The Cremieux brothers paid Marek an advance only in the first week of June, and even then, it was only a partial sum, not sufficient for them to leave as they had planned. Although they promised to pay the rest in a few days, the brothers did not keep their word.

In the second week of June, when Marek came to pick up his last payment, he discovered that the brothers had fled Paris and locked the printing house behind them. At a loss for what to do, Marek decided that he and his family would join the hordes who had begun fleeing Paris, streams of refugees making their way on foot. He hurried home and told Annette that they had no choice and that they would have to depart on foot. Many of the trains were full and others were stuck in place. Besides, the tickets cost a fortune and they had neither the money nor the time.

He brought out the bags they had prepared and told Olivier to help Maman and Laurent pack. Suddenly, Marek realized that Annette was not with them; she was frozen in place, not moving. He took a deep breath and put down the bags, knowing that he would not be able to handle everything by himself while taking care of her too. He sat down on the floor next to Annette and Olivier joined them, huddling close to Marek as though asking for his protection.

The boy sensed that something had changed.

Marek collected himself, realizing that they would need to prepare themselves for the coming period. His optimism encouraged him. We'll continue living here even after they come, and later it will be possible to escape southward on the train, he thought to himself.

He said to Olivier, "I'm going to the market, I'll bring back something for breakfast. I'm on vacation from work." "So, when are we leaving?" Olivier asked.

"In a few more days, after the vacation," answered Marek with a smile that tried to convey calmness.

Marek kissed Olivier, then got up to bring Annette's medicine. "Give Maman her medicine," he told Olivier. "I'll be back soon. Please help Maman the way you know how." He wanted to prepare Olivier for any situation that might arise.

Marek took the keys to the business and ran to the printing house. The streets were full of people with suitcases, the roads bustling with luggage-laden cars. Everyone's face was turned southward, some in vehicles, others on foot.

He reached the locked printing house, opened the gate and went in. The place was as neat as always, but without a living soul. He walked towards the door of the office. Taking out the bunch of keys, he cautiously let himself in. He began rummaging through closets and drawers, trying to see what he could take that might help them. The office had been completely emptied out except for the bar. Suddenly, he heard the sound of airplanes and faint explosions. He went outside and saw airplanes flying southward, diving and shooting. He understood that they were German planes firing on the hordes of refugees, despite the fact that the roofs of the buildings prevented them from seeing the ground clearly.

He returned to the office, opened the bar, and took out a bottle of whiskey and a shot glass. He sat down on the armchair and poured himself some of the whiskey. A storm raged in his body and his mind was filled with only one thought: "Everything is lost."

A few minutes later, he pulled himself together. Olivier, Annette, and Laurent are waiting for me at home, he thought, I have no time to get lost in my thoughts. We'll hide out for a few days at home, until we can escape. It's possible, he told himself.

11

Almost a year after that Thursday when Marek came home bearing the newspaper announcing the outbreak of war, on 14 June 1940, columns of German tanks rolled into Paris. They advanced rapidly, with German efficiency, along the main boulevard of St. Germain des Prés. On their way, they passed the Folies Bergère nightclub, on down the Champs-Élysées to the seat of the French National Assembly. Marek was walking along, steeped in determination to get out of Paris, when he turned a corner and caught sight of the columns of German armored corps. He turned pale.

He hurried away, making his way to the Latin Quarter, to his home. *I have to get everyone organized and try to get out this evening*, he thought to himself, when suddenly he saw German soldiers beating a bystander who was holding a French flag.

A German officer in immaculate uniform climbed out of the leading tank and stood in front of the man who had been beaten. The officer said in heavily-accented French, "now, do you understand that we are in charge? The French flag doesn't belong here anymore!"

Speaking with difficulty, his face bloodied, the wounded man tried to speak …

"I can't hear you!" the officer mocked him. "Are you trying to insult me? If so, I am obligated to treat you with the utmost severity! You French are arrogant. You thought that you could go on insulting us this time too." He turned around to the crowd that had gathered, standing frozen in place.

"Let me give you an example, so that you'll understand." The officer pulled out his pistol and shot the wounded man in the head. From behind him came an anguished wail, and a woman collapsed to the sidewalk. *That must be his wife*, Marek thought.

Marek, together with the dozens of people around him, took off in fear. As he ran, he threw glances over his shoulder, and every time he heard a car engine, he ran to hide in the courtyard of the nearest building, feeling like a hunted animal.

It took him the better part of two hours to finally get home on foot, having given up on public transportation, which was entirely paralyzed. Panting, he entered the building and sat for a few minutes on the steps, catching his breath, before hurrying up the stairs. Helena, hearing the footsteps and guessing that it was Marek, came out to the hall.

"What happened, Marek? Why are you running up the stairs in such a hurry?"

Still panting and in shock from what he had witnessed in the street, he answered, "everything we have fled from has come here. Where can we go now?"

"Don't worry. Just act normally, no one knows that much about you. You have been living here for several years now, and everyone thinks you are Poles who emigrated to France, so what are you worried about?"

"Helena, you know that I'm Jewish. There have been rumors going around about what happens to Jews in any place the Germans get to."

"Look at me," she smiled sweetly. "In the next few days, we'll try to figure out what's going on, and then we'll decide what to do. I can help all of you: Annette, you, and the children. I know that you were planning to escape today. Don't do anything extreme right now, we don't know how they are planning to behave," she said in a voice that tried to sound soothing.

"Helena, you don't understand, they're beasts! They just shot a man who was holding a French flag! He was no threat to them. I think his wife was standing next to him and saw everything. Who does something like that?!"

"I don't know." She sat down next to Marek and hugged him, and for a fleeting moment, he forgot about the terrifying reality unfolding outside the door, feeling only Helena's protective tenderness. A moment later, he stood up suddenly and said:

"I have to get Annette and the children out of here! I promised her, and I'll do anything to get them away, perhaps to the south."

"Listen to me. Jérôme, the director of the cabaret, sent me a message that the supposed new leadership of France, together with their German allies, are coming to opening night of the new show some evening this week. Marek, I know how to handle people, I will try to find out what is happening without arousing suspicion."

"No, please, Helena, don't do that! What if they try to interrogate you and find out who you're seeking the information for? This is no time to make mistakes."

"Don't be scared, the people I'm thinking of are willing to do anything for me, just to be with me even for a second. They won't ask any questions as long as they're getting what they want."

Marek felt relief mingled with repulsion. How could she even think of being with them? How could this woman, who he dreamt of being with, give herself away like that?

"Marek, I can see in your eyes that you're repelled by what I'm saying, but you have to understand that a Folies Bergère dancer is, after all, a woman who attracts men in order to get them to spend their money. It doesn't matter how glamorous I look on your posters." He was embarrassed, and immediately recovered his positive view of her, not as a "work of art" but as someone who was showing responsibility and a desire to help and risk herself for others' sake. He saw Helena before him, giving everything she had for an important goal that she believed in. She did not have to offer anything at all; after all, they were just neighbors.

He kissed her cheek. "I'm sorry. I'm worried about you. I'm afraid of what might happen to us… Everything is confusing and scary."

"I understand, Marek. We'll manage, and we'll cross the bridge together. Let me take the lead this time," she reassured him.

12

France was taken over rapidly after the collapse of the French army and its retreat to England. The occupation was partial, such that the country was divided in two: the occupied zone, under full German control, and the zone left to the French after their surrender, later known as the "French State". This part, which included the whole southern section of the country, was ruled by French collaborators who were allied with the Germans. The capital of the French State was the city of Vichy, which became the seat of the country's new government.

Marek opened the door to find the house dark and the windows shuttered. When he turned on the light, he heard a scream and spun around, terrified. Annette, pale as a ghost, was huddled under the table, fiercely hugging Olivier, who was almost strangled in her grasp. Marek turned off the light, bent down and crawled under the table, sitting down next to Annette and embracing her. "Relax, honey, I'm here. Everything is alright." Olivier wriggled free of Annette's hold and held out his arms to Marek. Continuing to hold Annette with one arm, Marek hugged Olivier with the other.

"I've been like this for hours," Annette told him. "I heard the noise and saw people running around helter-skelter… Marek, I'm scared. It's a good thing Laurent fell asleep."

"We'll postpone our departure for a day or two and then move like we planned. But we'll do it in a smart way, without attracting any unnecessary attention. In a few days, we'll already be in the warm south, and if they get there, we'll go further. We've promised that we'll keep getting farther away from them, and that's what we'll do. We'll keep dreaming our dream together."

"Marek, stop it! You're just saying that to try and calm me down. I know that any minute now they're going to knock on the door, and the stories we've heard will come true. What has happened before will happen again!" she protested, terrified.

Olivier finally managed to free himself from her grasp and hugged his father. "Papa, are the bad people coming? When will we leave here?"

"My precious son, you amaze me ..." Marek sighed. "Yes, the bad people are here. We'll pack up and leave here in a few days." He pulled the boy into a tighter embrace, then turned to his wife.

"Annette, stop thinking so much and let's pack. It's not too late, we'll figure out a way to escape, and we'll get out of here, you'll see. Helena will help us find a few things out..."

"How is Helena connected to this whole thing?" Annette broke in. "She's a Christian! She'll know that we're Jews! Marek, what have you done?"

"No, my love, please. Relax. She doesn't know a thing, but she has connections with people who can help."

"Are you out of your mind? She'll report us!"

"Enough, Annette! You're scaring Olivier, and you're scaring me. I need you to be strong by my side, we're in this together ... If we let fear rule us, we'll never make it. You have to believe, even a little... No one knows that we are Jews. Our names are Christian, we changed our documents when we came to France, only you and I know the truth. We can get by; they won't suspect us."

"Marek, you are so naïve. How can a pair of immigrants arrive without anyone knowing? I want to believe, but it's impossible. Let's run away tomorrow. We won't wait, and we won't tell anyone."

"I would like to believe that we can do it tomorrow, but everything has to be checked carefully. Everything we've planned up to now has changed. We need one more day to organize everything more precisely, to know how, where, and why we are leaving. We need to be very clear with our story. If they arrest us, we'll be in real trouble. You must know that we'd be in more danger than staying here. I promise I'll do everything I can so we can leave tomorrow. Now let yourself relax. Try to sleep a little. I'm here at your side."

Annette rested her head on his shoulder and, as Marek tenderly stroked her curls, she gradually fell asleep in his arms.

Marek asked Olivier to bring him a pillow and got to his feet slowly, placing the pillow under Annette's head. She continued sleeping, crumpled on the floor.

He took Olivier and seated him on the couch, then covered Annette with a blanket and returned to sit next to the boy. He smiled at him and hugged him, then began singing to him, all the while stroking his head, until they both fell asleep on the couch, wrapped in each other's arms.

A short while later Annette awoke to Laurent's hungry wails, and Marek and Olivier woke up soon after. Annette and Marek exchanged looks, both understanding that this was going to be a fateful day. They tried to keep up the morning rituals for the two little ones, forcing themselves to smile and make funny faces.

"I'll go down to Helena and see if managed to get any information from her meetings, and from there I'll go to the train station again. Be ready, if the train is running today, it leaves at 4:30 p.m. Maybe we'll manage to board it. If not, we'll try some other way."

Marek took a quick shower. Afterwards, while he was still getting dressed, Annette came into the room, holding Laurent with one arm, and caressed his back with her free hand. "Be careful. I say that to you all the time because I have a bad feeling that I can't shake off."

"Don't worry." He turned around to kiss her on the forehead and then Laurent as well. "I'll be back in the early afternoon, if everything goes smoothly. I won't take any unnecessary risks. Get the children dressed in their nicest clothes, so it will look like we're going on vacation and not running away."

After he finished getting dressed, he kissed Olivier and went downstairs and knocked on Helena's door. She opened it with eyes still coated with the night's makeup.

Marek kissed her gently, saying, "Helena, I'm sorry for what is going to happen, though I'm happy about what has already happened. I have to get Annette out of here. Every day that she stays here, she's a danger to herself and to us. She can't handle the stress."

"I know, Marek, I didn't expect anything different from you, that's what makes you so brave and that's what attracts me to you. Listen, I asked around, on the pretext of planning a vacation, and I found out a lot. It's possible to leave. What we have to do is walk towards the station. We'll go in as a couple buying tickets for a vacation, or, if there's danger, I'll go in alone and buy tickets for a whole family who is planning a vacation at a beach in the south."

"How will you go there alone? As a couple, I understand, but alone?" Marek worried.

"This is my profession. I know how to make men do what I want. It's terrible to say, but it's the truth. Give me a minute to get ready, I'll dress more casual and less attractive, then we'll go there together."

Marek sat down on the armchair. Without hesitation, Helena took off her dress, standing before him in her stockings and bra. "Every time I see you like that, knowing what a good-hearted person you are, who gives everything of her whole self, I think that you are just an angel. I love every limb in your body, and I love your good heart and your courage, your ability to get carried away but still remain level-headed… I'll be so sorry to be far away, but sometimes one has to make tough decisions. I have to save Annette and the children. We'll find our way back some day."

"You will always be in my heart," Helena said, putting on a plain flowered dress. "We will find each other very soon." She turned her back to him and signaled him to zip up her dress.

Marek got up from the chair, came close and hugged her from behind, kissing her neck; she reached up to cradle his head in her hands, before they suddenly broke off their embrace in tears. He zipped up her dress and the two headed out into the unknown.

They decided to go on foot, avoiding public transportation, which was sure to be watched. The train station was a forty-minute walk from their apartment building. They walked along hand in hand, Helena wearing a broad-brimmed hat that would hide her identity if she passed any acquaintances along the way. They looked like an ordinary Parisian couple, even if she was a bit taller than him. No one could tell that something else entirely was going on within them. A French police car passed them, announcing through a loudspeaker that from now on, all citizens would be required to carry passports and identity cards. They decided to stick to side streets, walking a long way around, in order to avoid German patrols or Frenchmen loyal to the German occupation.

As they approached the train station, they noticed more checkpoints and German army vehicles. Just before they reached the station, they saw from a distance that there were black cars parked next to the station and three German soldiers standing there talking. They did not appear to be regular soldiers, but rather officers in charge of the army's operations.

Helena held Marek by the elbow and told him quietly, "Turn right into the alleyway." They walked into the alleyway as though it was their natural route.

"What happened?" Marek asked.

"My hunch is that they're looking for someone. They'll stop us if we go together. I'll go there and do it myself."

"Are you serious? You're going to risk your life for us? For me?"

"No, Marek. First of all, I'm doing it for myself, because that's the way I am. Besides, I'm not doing anything serious, I'm just buying tickets. Don't make such a big deal out of it. You head home and wait for me at the corner café, where we had coffee last time. We'll go back together from there." She kissed him lightly and turned back to the main boulevard.

Marek walked back along a side street, passing the nearest building, and then returned to the main boulevard. As he was walking along, a group of youths suddenly burst out from another side street, sporting swastika insignia on their shoulders. They belonged to the nationalist groups who, fed up with the old French regime, supported the German occupation and its policies, particularly regarding hatred of foreigners, hoping that it would change France. They appeared to be drunk. Marek turned pale with fear but, making an effort not to attract their attention, continued walking.

The group came up behind him. As they passed him, he looked at them locked eyes with one of the gang members. They stopped and demanded his papers.

Marek froze in place, then responded, "Just a moment," trying to gain some time. He knew that his identity card would reveal that he was an immigrant.

He tried to stall by pretending to look for the certificate. Then it came to him that if he showed them his worker's card from the printing company, claiming that he had forgotten his identity card, that might satisfy them.

One member of the group, who appeared to be the leader, asked him where he was coming from.

"I'm going home from my work at the printing house."

"Where is it located?"

"The Cremieux Brothers printing house, in the Artists' Quarter," answered Marek.

"Yes, I know it, you served the government, you printed the leaflets announcing that France was going to war, isn't that right?"

"Yes."

"Good to know. Where is your identity card?"

Marek pulled out his worker's card from an inner pocket. "Sorry, I don't have my identity card on me."

"Your accent doesn't sound French, where are you originally from?" the gang leader went on to ask. "Why aren't you following the instructions of the new regime to carry your identity card? Where did you say you're from?" he asked again.

After a moment, Marek decided to say Italy, since he spoke fluent Italian.

"I'm originally from Italy, we came to France a few years ago." "Where do you live?" the gang leader asked.

"I live in Brady Passage, not far from here."

"If so, why are you here?" the gang leader demanded.

"I decided to walk. After working all night at the printing house, I need to stretch and get some air," he answered with a smile, trying to lighten the tone of the conversation.

"You're lying!" the head of the gang declared. "I know that printing house well, and this isn't the way from there to the Artists' Quarter. There's no reason to pass the train station. Now, answer me: what are you really doing here?"

13

Meanwhile, Helena made her way towards the train station. With her aristocratic bearing, she approached a vehicle that was blocking the entrance to
the station, passing three Germans who stood at attention there. They were
wearing black uniforms, different from those of the other soldiers.

"Halt!" a voice suddenly called out behind her. As she turned around,
she directed a sultry gaze at them, as she had learned to do over the years,
knowing that her gaze was a useful tool when dealing with men.

The three Germans were left open-mouthed, lighting up with joyful
smiles as they discovered the beauty of her face revealed under the broad-
brimmed hat.

"Mademoiselle," one of them hurried to explain, "we are checking the
population around the Paris train station for assassins or nationalists who
refuse to submit."

"And do you think I am a nationalist, or that I refuse to submit?" she
bantered boldly, playing up her Italian accent that many found so sexy.

"Ah… by your accent, I understand that you are not a pure Frenchwoman,"
the soldier continued, as she noted that his rank was higher than that of the
others. He was tall, with blonde hair and blue eyes.

"I am pure, though not a Frenchwoman," she chuckled, "I'm in Paris for
work." She broke the ice and introduced herself, "I'm the principal dancer of
the Folies Bergére. Are you familiar with that cabaret?"

The German soldier nodded, stamping his right foot in the manner of a
salute, "I would be lying if I said that I only know of the place. I was there

for the premiere... now I remember you. Allow me to introduce myself and my companions. We are members of the leadership committee for Paris, and we are meant to accompany you and this wonderful city on its first steps into the Empire of the Third Reich. I am Colonel Helmut Schmidt. Lieutenant Schultz Kuhn and Lieutenant Markus Fritz are my assistants." Helmut was the senior aide to the German general, Dietrich von Choltitz, commander of the German garrison in France following the surrender agreement.

"Look how fate arranges meetings for us," he went on. "Just yesterday, I was talking about that wonderful evening when I saw you leading all those graceful damsels on the stage. I could not help but be excited by the dancing, but even more so by your beauty. How can I help you?" From an interrogator Helmut slipped instantly into the role of a friendly public servant. Helena's beauty was indeed an icebreaker.

"Ah, you can definitely help me. First of all, you should know that you've ruined my vacation," she chuckled. "I was supposed to go with some friends to the south of France, to the sea, but you've cancelled all the trains. The only free weekend we have was also cancelled. Couldn't you have thought of that before you came? That we, the French, go on vacation in June?" They laughed, as she tried with all her might to be friendly.

A few hundred meters away, the gang leader who had stopped Marek demanded a satisfactory answer.

"You're lying!" he berated him. "This is your last chance to tell me the truth."

Marek tried to pretend that he had been just satisfying his curiosity. "Look, I've been buried every night at the printing presses, I haven't had a chance to see Paris in the past few days. I always have coffee at the Etoile, not far from here." This was the truth; he was a regular customer at that café.

"Even if that's true, I still want to know where your identity card is. Search him!" the gang leader commanded the other members of the group. Two of them grabbed Marek's arms and the third, a hulking figure, rifled through his clothing. The bully began to empty Marek's pockets: wallet, a small, folded poster, keys, and a red ribbon inscribed with the words "Folies Bergére." He handed his findings to the gang leader, who opened the wallet and, to his surprise, disclosed Marek's identity card.

"What's this?"

"Oh no, I didn't notice, I'm sorry."

The burliest of the gang members, studying the card, immediately fixed on what was written under the title "Place of Birth".

"You're from Poland? Why did you say you were from Italy?"

"I'm originally from Italy, I was born there – I emigrated to Poland and now I'm in France," Marek answered in all seriousness.

"You're lying!" he shouted at Marek, signaling with a nod of his head to the thug next to him.

Taken by surprise, Marek felt all the air rush out of his lungs from the force of a fist in his chest. He fell silent, crumpling to the ground like a rag doll. He lay there for several minutes before he managed to get his breath back and pick himself up.

Helena had no idea of what was taking place so close by. If she had known, surely, she might have been able to change the fate of the man who was so dear to her. But meanwhile she went on flirting to gain what she wanted.

"I'm planning to go with a couple of friends to the south of France for the weekend."

"I can help you get there," Helmut responded, "but only on the condition that you come back to us."

"Do you think I'll give up on Paris so easily?" Helena smiled at him sweetly.

"I'll be generous and help you out by issuing a special permit. It will be my pleasure. Come, I'll take you to my office."

Helena knew that she would have to give identifying information for Marek and his family. She thought that if worse came to worst, given that she had already told the Germans that she would be travelling, she would travel south with the family to avoid suspicion and then come back.

"I'd be happy to join you, it's my privilege. I'm sure we'll see each other around," she smiled at him. They walked to the station and entered one of the offices.

When Helmut entered, everyone in the office stood at attention. It seemed that this man emanated an aura of respect mixed with fear.

Helmut leaned over to one of the soldiers and said something quietly in his ear. The soldier hurried to the adjacent room and returned moments later carrying a certificate with the insignia of the Reich. He approached Helena and asked for her name and the names of her friends.

"Helena, of course, Fotticelli. And my friends Annette, Marek, Olivier and Laurent Oppenheimer." "Are you all Italians?" asked the soldier.

"In one way or another, yes, all of us came from Italy to France."

The soldier directed a piercing gaze towards Helena, as though he knew that she was hiding something. Luckily for her, her own gaze worked to soften him up somewhat, and he did not ask any more questions. He took a piece of notepaper and wrote in German the names that she had given him, then passed it to another soldier who typed the information on a typewriter.

Helmut's eyes met Helena's as they waited for the certificate, and a shred of fear passed through her, along with a shiver of excitement. She was shrinking with terror inside, a terror that she had not felt for a long time, as though her whole life was about to change. Marek came into her mind, and she was thrilled at the very thought of him. She reflected on what he meant to her, how she had been swept into his world and had allowed him to penetrate hers, her deepest feelings, something that had never happened with anyone else before.

The soldier finished typing and handed the permit to Helmut with a salute. Helmut examined the certificate, then handed it to Helena. "Have a nice vacation," he told her. "If I may, and it's not asking too much, I know you're performing next Wednesday, aren't you? I will be away for a few days, but I promise to come to your show on Wednesday. I would be happy if you would set aside the evening after the show for me. For a drink or, perhaps, a late dinner?"

Helena knew that this was a proposition she could not refuse, for she had already given away her freedom for Marek's sake. Helmut struck her as an aggressive man, someone who would get what he wanted by making the other person surrender, or by force. At this stage, she preferred to submit. Anyway, she was committed to helping Marek, Annette, and the children. After all, she had also been a refugee. Then, she had been thinking of her family; now she was thinking of Marek and his family, of what they had experienced over the past few months. She had to save them.

"I would be happy to give you a ride to your house." This sentence frightened Helena, but Helmut, as much as she had managed to figure him out, was not the type of person one could refuse. She remembered the story Marek had told her, of the man who was shot in the street. She understood that human life had no value for the German conquerors.

"No, please, you don't need to put yourself out," she tried to refuse politely. "I'm sure you have enough tasks to fulfill in Paris before you are free to be my chauffer," she laughed with forced lightness.

Helmut laughed aloud. "I like your sense of humor, I'm sure we'll have a good time together. Come," he said, in a command more than an invitation, "I'll take you." He opened the car door for her with a flourish. A cloud of fear enveloped her as she climbed into the back seat. Helmut came around and got in from the other side.

The second officer opened the front door and got into the driver's seat. They pulled away from the station and headed towards the Latin Quarter.

After a short way, out of the corner of her eye, she noticed a group of people who looked like nationalists of the French fascist militia, with armbands bearing swastikas. She saw that they were beating a man who lay on the ground. Helmut reached out his hand to her face and turned her head away. "Don't look at such sights. Those are people that have to be treated with an iron fist. They are a menace to the public."

Her breath caught in her throat, but trying to hide her distress, she smiled at him. Deep inside she felt oppressed, as though a heavy stone had been pressed against her chest. She thought about the man who laid helpless on the ground while a gang beat him up. She remembered what Marek had told her. For a fleeting second, she thought that perhaps it was Marek lying there, but she immediately pushed the thought away. *Marek is already home*, she thought, *he left a long time ago.*

The car pulled into her street and she asked the driver to let her out in front of the bakery. She didn't want people to see her arriving in the official car of Nazi officers. She knew that if Marek or Annette saw her now, they wouldn't believe a word she said, and would fear that she had turned them in. Everything had all of a sudden become so fragile. *I don't know what's happening or what I'm going to do*, she thought. But, in her usual way, she focused on the good deed she had accomplished, on the fact that she had managed to get them what she had hoped to get.

It was the first time she had come face to face with the German conqueror, and she had used her magic and beauty to obtain the much-coveted travel pass. Now, their trip to the south would be safe, and they would finally be able to run away, to escape the fear seeping through the streets of Paris, the madness overtaking power-hungry Frenchmen.

Before getting out of the car, she turned to Helmut and asked, "where can I find you?"

"It would be my pleasure if you would come back and visit me in my office, now that you know where I sit most of the time. But you can always ask one of the officers in the area to find me. They will know how to get the message to me, and I will find you." She had asked out of politeness, and to exhibit her submission, but his answer contained a threat too: "You should know that I can find you anywhere." In her desire to help Marek, Helena realized what a honey trap she had stepped into. She pondered once again the freedom she had sacrificed, the freedom she had sought when she decided to leave Italy.

"You can also call the switchboard and ask for me," Helmut's voice broke into her thoughts. "I will leave them instructions in case Mademoiselle Fotticelli calls."

"I am honored." She held out her hand and he kissed it.

Helena got out of the car. She rejoiced at her achievement, but at the same time feared the obligation she had taken upon herself. She went into the bakery, so that Helmut would not see where she lived, even though she was sure that he would soon find out anything he wished about her, including her apartment number, her neighbors... She hoped that he would not crosscheck the information against the names on the travel permit. Surely, he would find out everything about her today... She would have to push Marek to leave as soon as possible, and she would need to think about how to get into the train station with Marek and Annette without running into the soldiers or Helmut.

Helena waited in the bakery until Helmut's car drove away.

"I see you have some new friends," said Monique, Monsieur Dubois' wife, with the French contempt for the immigrants living among them.

Unable to restrain herself, needing to release the pressure bottled up in her from the events of the day, Helena broke her usual composure. "You know, Madame Dubois," she turned to Monique, "I have connections in high places. It's useful if I want to help someone, and also to use against someone who I don't really like... But usually, I use it to help people." Madame Dubois turned pale, understanding the hint, and fell silent.

"How can I help you?" she finally asked.

Helena, not wanting to carry on the conversation, said, "please pack me up five butter croissants and a small *pain au chocolat.*" That was Olivier's favorite pastry and she, in the midst of the stormy thoughts and feelings of the day, suddenly remembered the little angel she loved so much, her heart expanding at the thought of him.

Over the years, Helena had been the object of contempt from Madame Dubois, both for being a cabaret dancer as well as for being an Italian immigrant. But the hardest thing for Madame Dubois to take was Helena's beauty, which captivated the Frenchwoman's husband. More than once, Monique had called her husband inside when Helena came into the store, going out alone to wait on her. Monsieur Dubois tried to flirt with Helena whenever he had the chance.

"Have a good day, Madame Dubois," said Helena, walking rapidly towards her building.

Not far from the train station, just before Helmut's car passed by, Marek picked himself up after the powerful fist had landed in his chest. He felt that his lungs were bursting; he felt some of his ribs were broken from the force of the blow. He tasted blood with every breath.

He stood up and tried to speak but could not get out a word.

"Where are you from and what are you doing here?" the gang leader kept asking.

Marek, his strength gradually returning, managed to say, "I'm really on my way home from work, I don't know why you're harassing me. I ask you to leave me alone so I can get home…" Before he could finish the sentence, a resounding slap landed on his right cheek. He felt that one of his teeth had broken; blood dripped from his mouth.

"Take him to the militia headquarters! Let's see what they'll do with him there. Anyway, I don't think he's telling the truth about his history." They dragged him a few meters along the sidewalk. Realizing that he had to take some action, he began struggling to get away and begged them to let him go.

The torture was not long in coming. The leader of the group landed another fist which knocked Marek to the ground, his head thumping against the cobblestones. Out of the corner of his eye, he saw a black car passing by; he knew he must be imagining, but in a blur, he thought he saw Helena in the car. A second later, a kick to his head knocked him out.

14

Helena reached the entrance of the building with a sigh of relief. Underneath her collected, aristocratic exterior, a storm was raging. Everything she feared was now on her doorstep, right next to her. She had walked right into a trap and knew that there was no escaping the tie that had just been formed at the train station. She was ready to do anything for Marek, for Annette, and the children.

She stopped for a moment, feeling her leaden legs, her heavy breathing, her racing heart. She sat down on the stairs to catch her breath. A tear ran down her cheek. She grabbed the railing to pull herself to her feet, her head spinning.

As she climbed the stairs to Marek and Annette's apartment, she felt a surge of joy at the success of her mission. But when she reached their apartment, she was met with silence. When she pressed her ear to the door, she heard the children laughing, and breathed a sigh of relief; *they are here, and the children are laughing.* She pictured Marek and Annette sitting together with them. She longed to see Marek and tell him in private what she had endured in the past hours, but she understood that this would not happen. She had done what she had done for him and for his family. She had already made peace with the dream that would never come true. Annette, Marek, and the children would be leaving today, and they would probably never see each other again.

Helena knocked softly on the door, and a moment later it opened to reveal Annette standing there with Laurent in her arms. The two women loved each other and shared a common fate. Helena struggled with the complexity of her stormy affair with Marek, but it overpowered her.

She entered with a triumphant smile. "Hello, my dear. I've brought you some croissants for breakfast, and there's a surprise for Olivier in the box," she added, whispering a secret.

Olivier heard Helena and came hurtling towards her, almost knocking her down.

"Sweetie, what do you like best?"

Olivier answered with great excitement, "*Pain au chocolat!*"

Helena kissed him and took the chocolate roll out of the box. She turned to Annette and asked, "Where's Marek?"

"He left for the station and hasn't come back yet."

The blood drained from Helena's face. "I expect he'll be back any minute..." she said, summoning all her strength.

"Helena, he promised me he'd be back, that there was nothing to worry about... Do you think something's happened to him?"

"Let's wait. He probably took a detour, so that he wouldn't draw attention to himself on the streets." Helena understood instantly that something terrible had happened, for Marek should have already returned home to Annette a long time ago. She pulled herself together and told Annette in a confident tone, "we went together to the station to buy the tickets. He didn't go into the station with me because there were Nazi officers there. We agreed that he would take a detour home and I would stay and get the tickets, and then later we would meet up here. I got delayed..." She pulled out the travel permit and the tickets from her little bag. "Here is the permit and the tickets. I got into the very innermost offices and managed to do what I promised. You will be leaving here today, going south to start a new life together."

"Helena, where is he?!" asked Annette in terror, ignoring Helena's last words.

"I don't know. He'll be here any minute. Let's wait for him a little longer, everything will be alright," Helena said confidently, even though inside she was gnawed by fear. She went to the door and opened it a crack to listen for sounds in the stairwell, imagining— or wanting to believe— that he was already appearing.

Annette was becoming distraught. It was clear, even without checking, that her pulse was racing. She was breathing rapidly, and her face was pale. She suddenly emitted a scream: "Marek!" Helena quickly closed the door so that the neighbors won't hear the screaming. Annette, without noticing, almost dropped Laurent, and Helena lunged forward to catch him at the last second. She held onto Annette with her free hand and pushed her inside to the little room, closing the door behind her. She set Laurent on the floor, turned to Olivier, and said calmly, "Olivier, dear, watch Laurent like you promised me."

He told her, "I'll watch him. Maman isn't well again, I know." Helena opened the door and took the children out of the room. She then came back and laid Annette down on the bed, stroking her head, ready to put a hand over her mouth if she tried to scream again. With a finger to her lips, she signaled Annette to be quiet, then took Annette's head in her lap and stroked her.

After a moment, she said, "Annette, we must be strong. Let's wait a little longer, surely he'll come back."

Annette was breathing rapidly, and tears flowed down her cheeks. "Where is he? What did you do to him?"

"Annette, my dear, I don't know where he is, but he'll be back soon, I'm sure of it. Maybe he just took a big detour in order to avoid Nazis and get home without attracting attention…"

"Where is he? What did you do to him?" She repeated the sentence as though she had not heard Helena at all.

"Let's wait a little longer, he'll be back, you'll see." Helena hugged Annette close to her breast and stroked her hair.

"What did you do to him… What did you do to him…" Annette muttered.

"Olivier!" Helena called. Olivier opened the door and ran in.

"Can you help Maman? She doesn't feel well. Where did she put her medicine?" That was a secret that only Marek knew, but he had told Helena that Annette took medication when she had panic attacks. He even told her that he had taught Olivier how to give his mother the medicine in case Marek was not home.

Olivier went to the bathroom, climbed up on the stool, and took a small bottle out of the cabinet, then brought it to Helena.

To make sure that there was no mistake, Helena asked, "where is this medicine from?"

"It's the medicine in the cabinet that Papa gives Maman when she's sad."

The boy then looked at her and asked with innocent eyes, and asked: "Do you know where Papa is?"

Helena held his hand, slowly opened his little palm, and stroked it. "I know that Papa is okay. We'll wait for him. He'll be back in a little while."

She then went over to Annette, who was lying on the bed staring at the ceiling; she opened her mouth, poured in a few drops and closed the bottle.

Annette grabbed Helena in a painful grip, mumbling, "what did you do to him...? What did you do to him...?"

They sat in the little room and waited together: Helena, Annette, who had fallen asleep in the meantime, and Olivier, who kept his little brother occupied as if he were the baby's father. Although only an hour had passed since she arrived, it felt like forever to Helena. She was happy that she did not have to go to the cabaret; it was her day off and the cabaret was closed. She nodded off.

Suddenly, the faint sound of shots came from outside, apparently from somewhere nearby, which was enough to wake her. Annette, under the influence of the strong medication, slept on.

Olivier asked innocently, "Are there fireworks today?"

Helena answered him, "No, sweetie, that's the sound of the Germans who have come to Paris."

Olivier's eyes opened wide. "Germans?"

"Yes, darling, they've come from Germany, which is the country next to France. They fought with some of the French people. Other French people, who are friends with the Germans, are with them," Helena tried to explain. "We'll have to be very, very careful, because they are dangerous people. We'll try to help Maman with whatever she needs," she said, thinking of the possibility that Marek would come in the door soon and they would have to begin their journey southward. Deep inside she was still pushing away the apprehension which was becoming a real fear for Marek's life …

Annette began to stir. her eyes red, her pupils enlarged, and her head heavy and dizzy. She lifted her head to look at Helena, who was sitting with the children, and suddenly announced with startling clarity: "Helena, I want you to get out of our house. You drove Marek away from me. He's disappeared because of you."

Taken by surprise, Helena thought to herself that perhaps Annette knew of her affair with Marek, and that now it was all coming together. Despite her discomfort at knowing that she had indeed hurt Annette, even if she never meant to, Helena answered: "Annette, my dear, you can get angry at me for anything you'd like, but I did not take Marek away from you. You are the most important person in the world to him, and I promised him that if, God forbid, something happens to him during this crazy period, I'd look after you and help you and the children. He just asked this of me a few days ago, when we were talking about your options for escaping to the south. I promised Marek I would help you, and I do it with great love for you and the children. I brought you this permit from the Germans' Paris headquarters, from the lion's den. I had to come in contact with the intelligence commander responsible for all of Paris in order to get this permit for you.

"I'm sure that the French will not take it well, and they'll accuse me of being a traitor," Helena went on, "but I did it out of a desire that you should manage to escape this place and get all the good that the world has in store for you. I'm not leaving you, Annette, you're important to me, Olivier is important to me, Laurent is important to me, Marek is important to me. You're the only family I have here."

Marek didn't just disappear, Helena's thoughts were racing. *He should have been back a long time ago. I'll go out and try to find him, maybe I'll use my connection with Helmut, if there's no other choice.* As thoughts continued to race through her head, she caressed Annette and soothed her.

Annette finally fell asleep under Helena's caresses. Eventually, Helena got off the bed slowly and covered her with a light blanket. She shut the window and pulled down the blinds, gesturing to Olivier to follow her.

Olivier left the room on tiptoe, making Helena laugh for a moment. He was such a darling child, this boy who was becoming an adult against his will.

Laurent slept the sleep of the just, lying on the floor where he had fallen asleep. Helena picked him up and put him in bed.

"I'm going to find out where Papa is, I'll be back with him in a little while."

Olivier stood erect and declared, "I'm coming with you. We'll go together."

"You need to stay here to watch over Maman and Laurent," Helena replied softly. Someone needs to be here to help them when they get up." She caressed him and added, "after I leave, lock the door, and don't open it to anyone until I come back with Papa. I'll sing you our song from outside the door, that way you'll know it's me. Don't make any noise and you don't leave the house."

Olivier nodded, his eyes serious, all the while tugging on Helena's hand, as though pleading, "don't leave me...are you going too?" he asked tearfully.

"Don't worry, sweetie, I'll never leave you, Maman, Laurent, and Papa. You're my family."

15

Marek awoke to find himself lying on a hard surface. From the shaking and the bumps, he understood that he was in a moving vehicle. He looked around and saw other people, some lying on the floor in the middle and others sitting on benches around them. The smell of urine overwhelmed his nostrils; groping at his clothes, realized that he must have wet himself. He couldn't make out see the faces of the others around him, covered the truck bed was covered by tarpaulin, allowing in only occasional flashes of light. He managed to discern that most of the people lying down were wounded, their clothes and bodies stained with blood. On the benches were men sporting brown armbands adorned with swastika insignias. Marek raised his head and tried to sit up. He reached up to touch his head and felt something wet. It was clotted blood.

Suddenly, the truck lurched to a stop with a squeal of brakes. On the bench, Marek identified one of the men who had beaten him up earlier. The men wearing swastikas got up and started kicking the wounded who were lying on the floor, hurrying them out of the truck. All the people who had been lying down started making their way out of the truck; some of them were actually thrown out. Finally, they were all on their feet, outside the truck, faced by a group of French people with swastikas on their arms, a sign that they were Nazi allies. From there, they were led to the adjacent police building. Marek couldn't tell where they were but guessed that it was a Parisian police building in one of the quarters near the city center.

They were herded into a long line which began advancing towards a policeman who was sitting and writing things down. The line moved slowly. After registration with the policeman, the prisoners were taken into a side room; Marek estimated that they were about thirty in all. He stood in the middle of the line. His mind was racing; he decided he would speak only about himself, and not refuse to answer any other questions. He had to protect Annette and the children. He knew that Annette was registered in his papers, but not the children.

He reached the policeman, stood and waited. The policeman lifted his head, called him by his full name, noted his address and his place of employment. Marek was surprised that they knew his workplace and his home address; he deliberated feverishly whether to lie about the children or not, since they seemed to know everything about him anyway. He decided to try to lie. If they knew, they would do what they were planning to do anyway, and the lie wouldn't change anything. After all, they had already wounded him. He hoped that perhaps, in the meantime, Helena had managed to get to his house, understood that something had happened, and perhaps even managed to hide Annette and the children. His head was bursting with thoughts.

"Yes ..." he answered in a quivery voice to the policeman who read out his personal information. He then gathered the courage to ask: "Why am I here? When can I go home? Can I let them know that I'm alright?"

The policeman lifted his eyes from the papers and said, "you are here because you are a harmful element, and no, you can't notify anyone of anything!"

"But..." Marek tried to insist, before feeling a fist driving into his ribs. He realized that he had attracted too much attention. Gradually he caught his breath again.

"Are you married?" the policeman asked.

Marek could not lie, seeing his papers spread out in front of the policeman. "Yes."

"What is your wife's name, age, and profession?"

Marek drew a breath and tasted blood in his mouth, realizing that his rib was broken, and he was bleeding.

"Her name is Annette," he managed to answer in a feeble voice, "she's twenty-eight, an independent seamstress."

The policeman wrote something down, lifted his eyes again and asked, "how many children do you have?"

Marek tried to look as believable as possible. "We have no children."

The policeman looked into his eyes. Marek thought that he knew he was lying...

"You were not born in France, where did you come from?"

Marek could not lie any more. "Poland."

"Why did you come to France?"

Marek hesitated for a moment and then answered in the most truthful tone he could muster, "I wanted to move to France to develop in the printing profession in which I am a specialist."

"You know that you and others like you have hurt the French economy, stolen jobs that belong to French people. You'll pay dearly for this!" snarled the policeman in rage and hatred.

"Are you a Jew?" the policeman asked. "Is your wife a Jew?"

Marek was taken aback by the direct question. His last name was not identifiable as a purely Jewish name, and he wanted to avoid the truth, but he knew that if they demanded to see whether he was circumcised, he would not be able to hide it. He remembered what they had gone through in Poland before they escaped... "Yes," he answered frankly.

"You Jews have destroyed our country. You've taken our jobs, stolen all our money. You'll pay for that. I'm about to ask you questions about your fellow Jews, and I advise you to tell the whole truth. Maybe if you're honest, you might see your family again. Do you know any others of your ilk? Any relatives, perhaps?"

"What do you mean, *of my ilk?*" Marek couldn't refrain from asking.

The policeman snickered. "Are you trying to trick me after all? You're a Jew. You look like a Jew. You stink like a Jew. Now think hard and answer my question!"

Marek thought to himself that he had to supply the policeman with some information, but at the same time he understood that any information he provided was likely to incriminate him, for the person he turned in to the police would be likely to tell them about his children. He decided to gamble again.

"I am indeed a Jew, but we came to Paris alone, me and my wife. There are no Jews at all in the Latin Quarter, most of the Jews I've met live in the 19th arrondisement."

"I know that you Jews live together in your communities and know one another. You are seeking to gain control over France. But I'll leave you for now. Anyway you will barely survive the night. Go join your friends the Jews and the immigrants in lockup. Later, we'll interrogate you some more. In the meantime, think hard about all the information you need to give me. I'm warning you, if you don't cooperate, you'll regret the day you were born."

The policeman's words calmed Marek a little, for he realized that his end had not yet come. He was surprised by the Germans' efficiency: they had just entered France and were already busy cleansing it of the non-French. He thought that in fact, the French had been waiting for this moment for a long time, and it was likely that some French had maintained contacts with the Germans even before France was conquered.

"Move ahead with everyone else to the next room," the policeman broke into his thoughts.

Marek entered the side room, passed through it, and reached another detention hall where all the prisoners were packed together. Night was beginning to fall, and with emotion he recalled that morning, how he had gone out with Helena in hopes that they would get their travel permit, and how everything had gotten derailed. *What is happening now with Annette and the children?* he wondered to himself. *Did Helena return? Will she really keep her promise, to help Annette and watch the children? Will I ever see them again? I must be strong… Somehow, I'll manage to survive these days and return home.*

In the detention hall, most of the people sat on benches. Others sat on the floor, while some even lied down and went to sleep. There was an air of suspicion in the room; no one really understood why they had been arrested, nor why the person next to them was there. Most of them preferred to sit in silence. Some offered help to those who had been wounded in the beatings they were subjected to, while others hid their faces in shame.

16

In the afternoon, Helena went back out to the train station, where Helmut's headquarters were located. Inside, she was churning with guilt and fear that Marek might no longer be alive. She recalled the sight of the helpless man being beaten, lying like a rag doll on the ground. Unable to dispel that image from her mind, she was determined to find out what had happened to Marek.

Helena walked rapidly towards the station, along the same route that she had trod with Marek that morning. She cast about for any hints, hoping to find Marek hiding in the courtyard of one of the buildings. Walking quickly, she passed street after street, searching for clues. She occasionally stopped by a shop window, trying to unobtrusively observe what was happening in the street.

She crossed the road to the opposite sidewalk, not far from the station where she had parted from Marek. Glancing in the direction of the station, she did not see anything unusual, other than cars going in and out. She then turned on her heels and started back along the route that they had agreed Marek would take to get home. A few hundred yards down the road, she froze in her tracks. On the sidewalk, at the entrance to one of the courtyards, she spotted Marek's wallet. She identified it immediately, having bought it for him herself. Next to it, she saw a newspaper, the same newspaper he had been holding in order to avoid attracting attention. As she bent down to pick up the newspaper, a silent scream escaped her lips— she immediately clapped a hand over her mouth as if to silence herself— the newspaper was soaked with blood. Looking around to make sure no one saw her, she bent down and grabbed the wallet, which was empty and covered in bloodstains. She stuck it in her bag and hurried back home.

Helena now knew that her fear, that something terrible had happened to him, had come true. Her breath was ragged, and her pulse was racing, as though she had just finished the *pièce de résistance* of her dance show.

When she reached the entrance to the building a couple of minutes later, she sat down on the stairs and burst into tears, unable to hold back the flood for another moment.

Just when everything had looked so promising, when she had found love, even if forbidden, everything had gotten violently derailed. She was now left without her beloved, without even knowing what had happened to him, while at the same time found herself all of a sudden responsible for two little children and an ill woman, who would not make things easy for her. She asked herself why she had not left France when she had the chance, and then answered herself: *Marek! I promised him, and myself. Apparently, this is the fate I chose for myself.*

From her bag she took out a small mirror and a handkerchief and began fixing herself up before meeting Annette and the children. She proceeded to climb the stairs to their apartment, knocked lightly on the door, and waited. From the inside, she heard little running steps, and Olivier quickly opened the door.

Helena greeted him with forced cheerfulness. "What did I tell you, Olivier? Who do you open the door for?"

The boy smiled, embarrassed, and said, "I knew it was you... And I was waiting for Papa."

She hugged him hard, as though trying to comfort him. Olivier, not understanding why she was almost strangling him, tried to wriggle free.

"Where's Papa?" he asked a bit nervously.

Gathering her courage, Helena answered, "he won't be back tonight. He's talking to the policemen."

Annette awoke at the sound of conversation at the door. She stood up unsteadily and began walking towards the door, holding on to the wall. When she reached Helena's side, she grasped her hand and hugged her hard. Then she backed off a bit and looked into Helena's eyes with a penetrating gaze.

"Where is he?"

Helena was skilled at pretending and hiding her emotions in front of men. Facing her lover's wife, it was infinitely harder. She breathed lightly, trying to hide her feelings, and said simply, "most likely, he won't be back tonight." Wanting to earn Annette's trust, she told her what she guessed had happened. "Today they arrested people to carry out interrogations, and he's apparently detained at the police station in the city center." Helena felt positive that this is what had happened, even though she could not know for sure.

"How do you know?" Annette asked.

"I don't know exactly. Annette, tomorrow morning I'll try to get more information. For now, we have no choice but to wait."

Holding Annette's hand tightly, Helena made an effort to appear trustworthy. In her years at the cabaret, she had learned that credibility comes with power, by keeping a steady facial expression, by measured movements and breathing, by concealing the storm raging inside.

Annette's eyes filled with tears. She believed Helena and was crying from fear of the unknown. "Where's Marek?" she wept.

Helena reached out a finger and wiped away the tears running down Annette's cheeks. They hugged once more.

"I'll put Olivier to bed. Sit down and rest. I'll come back in a minute to make us tea and something to eat. We have to be strong and give strength to Olivier and Laurent as well." She seated Annette by the small dining table and went to Olivier. She picked him up and gave him a motherly embrace and a kiss on his forehead, while he held her cheeks and pulled them lightly to the sides, making a smile appear on her face. She melted with affection for him. Letting go of his fears and his defenses, Olivier laid his head on Helena's shoulder. He didn't ask a thing, even though his little head was buzzing with questions. Helena took him to the shower to brush his teeth, then sent him off to sleep with caresses. He fell asleep with a smile on his lips.

Helena then went to the kitchen, poured tea from a teapot into two small cups, for her and Annette, and toasted a few slices of bread.

She took a seat at the table. "Let's think about what to do."

They sat facing each other as Annette sipped her tea slowly. It was the first thing she had put in her mouth since the beginning of this endless day. At least she seemed calm, Helena mused.

"Annette, we have to figure out what to do with you. I don't know what is going to happen to Marek, but he certainly wouldn't want you to get hurt. He would want you to get away from this area for a while. He loves you, and that's what he would want for you."

Annette looked at her. "Do you really think I would just get up and run away? That I wouldn't do everything possible to find Marek or at least find out what's happening to him? Look, I believe that you're acting sincerely. I know that you were close to him. I don't know how far it went, and that is not of interest to me right now. Marek is a part of me and I'm a part of him. I'll do everything in my power to find him. Only then will I know what I'll do with myself. I feel strong now, but I know that it's possible I won't be able to hold out, and that I'll break down again. I don't want anything bad to happen to the children, and I don't know if I'll manage to handle whatever happens."

"I had a thought…" she paused briefly I thought of asking Monsieur and Madame Dubois to look after Olivier and Laurent. They've done it very willingly several times already, and they'd be happy to do it again. It would also be natural for Laurent and Olivier to stay with them…"

"I've already spoke to Monsieur and Madame Dubois a month ago," Annette pressed on. "I told them that if something should happen to us, that I would ask them to take care of the children. Olivier and Laurent like them, they see them as the bakers of the most delicious bread and croissants… They'll be okay, right? I promised to give them money from our savings, and they agreed."

Deep inside Helena was hurt, for she was ready to do that without payment, purely out of love. But she understood that Annette would not want her as her children's caretaker. As a stripper, she couldn't be a guiding figure for them, and besides, she had never taken care of children.

Annette burst out, "I know that I rely on you for a lot of things, but I can't leave my children with you. You're young, you have no experience taking care of children. Please forgive me."

"Annette, I understand... Even so, I'm a little disappointed. After everything I've done for you and your family... Olivier is the dearest thing in the world to me. But I'll accept whatever you decide. You're their mother." Feeling wounded, Helena finished her tea in silence, then told Annette coolly, "I have to go to my apartment and get myself organized. I have rehearsals at the cabaret early tomorrow morning. At the same time, I'm going to try and find out where Marek is. I beg of you, don't do anything in the meantime."

Annette held her hand and said with a grateful look, "I'll wait for you." She sensed that she had hurt Helena, who was the only one who could keep them afloat.

Helena went out, descended the stairs, and entered her apartment. She kicked a chair in anger; she then picked up a glass from the table and threw it as hard as she could, shattering it against the wall. Finally, she lay down on her bed, only to pass a sleepless night.

At first light, she climbed out of bed and got ready to go out. In the meantime, she had gone back to being emotionally numb, pretending, a stripper who sold her body. She didn't wait until the cabaret opened, but left home early, intending to pass by the German headquarters to try and find out what had happened to Marek.

Marek awoke to excruciating pain in his ribs, after an almost sleepless night filled with blows from the guards. It was the foot of one of the French policemen, waking up anyone who was lying down by kicking him. Once again, Marek felt the pain from the previous day. His lungs could scarcely hold air, his ribs were broken, and every breath sent him sky high with pain. His mouth was full of clotted blood, his eye was swollen; he felt like he had been run over by a train. Bruised all over, he got himself off the floor with difficulty and stood up.

"Human scum, march! Get into the reception hall!" The prisoners proceeded towards the door to the large hall where they had assembled the night before. There they were lined up in rows.

The interrogator from the previous day stood before them. "If I call your name, go out the left door. If I didn't call your name, remain where you are. I'll remind you that anyone that tries to pull a fast one will suffer for it!"

The interrogator began calling out names. One after another, people went out the side door and climbed into the truck. Marek waited for his name to be called, but finally saw that he remained behind, together with three other people whose names had not been called.

The interrogator went up to them and said, "You're going home." He then sniggered, "you're going to bring the rest of your family!"

Marek turned pale. He did not expect this, and he certainly did not want to be the one to lead them to his home. Suddenly, with no warning, he lunged at the interrogator and began beating him in a frenzy. The interrogator fell to the ground, his eye wounded and gushing blood. Two policemen immediately jumped on Marek and began beating him with the butts of their rifles. Marek fell in a pool of his own blood, a wound on his head gaping open. The injured interrogator, seething with rage, stood, pulled out his pistol and fired two bullets. Marek did not stir again.

PART 2

1

Annette pulled out of a suitcase an envelope that she and Marek had pre-pared in case of need, stuffed with dozens of franc bills. This was their emergency savings, which had been set aside for their escape journey. As she slowly descended the stairs, she was suddenly beset by vertigo and felt as though her heart had skipped a few beats. The pain she felt was an ex-pression of what was happening in that same moment across the city, in the central Paris police station.

The Oppenheimer family, as it had been up to now, had ceased to exist. Their dreams had been washed away. Marek had left the world, and his promise, that everything would be alright, that they would figure out how to relocate to a place with no wars and no persecution, would not come to pass. Annette stood, holding onto the railing in the stairwell, and caught her breath.

She went down the stairs and opened the small door set into the main door of the building. The doors of the ancient buildings in the old quarter were all fitted with a smaller door set into the main one, through which pedestrians passed. The larger doors had once served to admit horse-drawn carriages into the courtyards of the buildings.

When they had moved into this building a few years ago, Marek explained to Annette about the architecture, so different from what they were used to in Poland. Annette remembered how Marek would open the large door, since Olivier loved that; Marek had convinced him that it was the entrance to the castle.

Annette left the building and walked towards the Dubois family's bakery. The bakery was virtually empty, with only one customer at the counter. Annette approached, looking like a walking skeleton, and Madame Dubois signaled to her to come around the back.

Annette went in. "Madame Dubois, the time has come. Marek didn't come back last night, I don't know what to do. I'm trying to reach some acquaintances who have connections and will try to find out where he is. I have to find him. We're lost without him. I came to ask your help, to watch the children for a short time, until I find him."

Annette's request made Madame Dubois uncomfortable. She admired Annette for her professional skill as a seamstress, and secretly envied the Oppenheimer family who represented a dream that she too craved— a loving husband and wife with sweet children. But taking care of their children was an altogether different proposition.

"Annette, first of all, I must advise you not to wander the streets of Paris like that. You know that Paris has become an unsafe place. Try to make contact with your friends without wandering the streets, especially given how you look at the moment. You'll attract attention, and I'm not sure you'll be able to handle the things lurking in the streets of Paris these days."

"I appreciate your concern, but I have to take action and find Marek," Annette replied defiantly, "that's the only chance we have to leave together and escape from here. That was our plan. Marek was on his way to the train station to buy our tickets. It was all planned; tomorrow morning we were supposed to be away from here, but then he disappeared."

"If so, I'll be happy to help you. I'll take the children for a couple hours, until you get back."

"Thank you, Madame. I know there are problems in the streets of Paris and that many people have disappeared. There are also rumors about expelling Jews; I'm not blind. I'd like to ask one more thing of you: if I don't come back in a few hours, please take care of them and find a solution for them, like Marek and I spoke about with you a while ago. I know that it puts you in danger, but we have no one here who will look after them." She took out the envelope from her bag and handed it to Madame Dubois. "Here, please take this envelope. If I don't come back or, God forbid, something happens to me too, I beg of you— take care of them. They've never done anything to anyone," Annette implored her.

Madame Dubois looked in the envelope, and the contents made her forget her fear a bit. The money was in fact a consideration.

"I'll watch the children and I'll try to find a solution for them," she said coldly, as though she knew that there was no chance that either of them would return.

Monsieur and Madame Dubois were a typical French couple, two patriots who had little patience for foreigners. But they liked the Oppenheimer family, Marek, Annette, and the two children, and especially Olivier, who was very polite and mature for his age.

Annette looked into her eyes, thinking how fast things had developed. One event brought about another. *Marek didn't come back, Helena got insulted and left, I'm leaving my children with a strange woman and going to look for Marek. I'll try going to Marek's boss; surely, he has influence and will try to help*, Annette thought to herself.

The grasp of a hand pulled Annette out of her reverie and back to reality. The Frenchwoman was trying to pull Annette aside so that no one would see the money she had given her.

"I'll get the children ready and bring them down to your apartment in an hour," said Annette.

Madame Dubois nodded. "Annette, I beg of you, before you enter my house, check carefully to make sure no one sees you."

"Don't worry, I'll do that."

Annette exited through the side door of the bakery and walked home. She mounted the steps in silence and went into her apartment. She woke up the children, dressed them carefully and combed their hair as though they were getting ready for an important party. She then brought the two small bags that had been prepared long ago. She seated the children in the kitchen and made them hot chocolate. She sat down next to them with a forced smile, as though everything was normal.

"Sweetie, you know that Papa's not here and that he didn't come back last night," she turned to Olivier.

"I know. Helena told me that he stayed to talk to the policeman at night."

"Yes. In a little while I'm going to look for him. In the meantime, you'll wait with Madame Dubois. She'll watch you and your little brother until I get back. Olivier, I'm counting on you not to leave Laurent even for a moment. You're the big boy and you must watch him at all times. I'll be back later," she said, knowing that the worst might happen, that she might never return. But she had to be sure that she had done everything possible to find Marek, or, at the very least, to find out what had happened to him.

They went down the stairs, Annette holding Laurent with one arm and Olivier holding her other hand. Before going out into the street, she peeked outside, but the street was quiet.

They crossed the street and walked towards the Dubois family's house, located right behind the bakery. Annette knocked on the entrance door and waited. After a few minutes, the door opened, and they disappeared inside.

To make it easier on the children, so they wouldn't get scared, Madame Dubois had made two of the *pain au chocolat* that they so loved.

Annette bent down and kissed Olivier. "Take care of your baby brother, I'll come back after I've found Papa."

Madame Dubois glanced at Annette with pity, then hugged her and walked her to the door.

Gathering all the strength she could muster, Annette went out.

2

Annette started down the sidewalk, took a deep breath, and suddenly everything went black.

She woke to find an unknown woman trying to help her up. Not knowing where she was, she sat down on the curb and mumbled, "my children, my children..."

"Annette, what happened? Annette, do you remember me? I'm Geraldine, you sewed me the evening gown ... Annette?"

Not understanding what was happening to her or where she was, Annette just continued murmuring, "my children..."

Geraldine was the wife of Dr. Gerard Gaston, a well-known psychiatrist who lived in the Latin Quarter. She was considered one of the leading women in the bohemian society of the quarter. Geraldine helped Annette to her feet and led her to her home, not far away.

Her husband, who opened the door, asked, "what happened?"

"Something is wrong with her, she just keeps mumbling, *my children, my children...* Something must have happened to her."

From outside, they heard a sudden shrieking of brakes. Geraldine and her husband cautiously peeked out through the curtain and saw a police car, followed by a car bearing swastika flags and a truck, all stopped in the middle of the street. Policemen jumped out of the truck and scattered, running towards houses in the area. From their vantage point, the couple could not see everything that was happening. They went into the darkened bedroom, Geraldine holding Annette, while Gerard continued watching through the window.

The policemen and soldiers who had jumped from the truck returned, clutching and forcibly dragging people towards the truck. They lined up the people they had apprehended in a row in front of the truck bed. A soldier in a German army uniform got out of the car, leading the cavalcade, passed by and examined the row of people, then signaled with his hand to the French policemen, who began pushing the people onto the truck with blows and shouts.

Although his view from the window was limited, Gerard was sure he had seen at least one woman there. He pulled the curtain closed and began to speak. "I think it's connected to whatever is causing Annette's condition. We never asked, but we know they're immigrants, and the police are now rounding up all the immigrants."

"Gerard, they have two small children, what will happen to them?"

"I don't know, but I don't think we can help them. What I can do is try to help her, maybe I can hide her at our sanatorium under a false name. They won't look for her there. I'll try to sedate her with tranquilizers, also that way they won't be able to interrogate her. I've heard rumors, I can't even begin to describe what someone like Annette might go through in these times."

Geraldine looked at Gerard and asked, "but why take a risk? Nothing will happen to us."

Gerard stared back at her, shocked. "You're right, nothing will happen to us. We could also join them and help them find other people, if you want. Nothing will happen to us."

Geraldine fell silent, understanding immediately how selfishly she had spoken. She looked at Gerard, deeply ashamed.

"Thank you for reminding me that we are not like that, that the fear that came out of my mouth doesn't have to control me. You're right, we'll try to help her."

"I have to help her right away," said Gerard. "She won't survive very long like this. I'll go to the sanatorium and see what I can do. In the meantime, try to find out what happened to her children.

Ask at the bakery, they know everything that happens around here."

Gerard left the house in the direction of the sanatorium, about an hour-and-a-half's walk from the Latin Quarter. Geraldine put Annette to bed and called Brigitte, the housekeeper, to watch over her.

"I'm going over to the bakery for a minute to buy a baguette and a few cakes," she told Brigitte.

"Good day, Madame Dubois," Geraldine went in and greeted the shopkeeper.

"Good day, Geraldine, how are you this morning?" asked Madame Dubois.

"Perhaps you know what happened? What was all that shouting we heard in the street? Earlier, I also heard a volley of shots. Gerard explained to me that it happens before they make arrests. It's safe here anymore, no one knows what could happen tomorrow..."

"I'm sure Gerard will have lot of work now, with all the people collapsing from fear," observed Madame Dubois in despair.

"Do you know who they rounded up?" Geraldine casually inquired.

"I don't know," answered Madame Dubois, not wanting to add another word. She certainly did not want to reveal that the Oppenheimer children were hiding at her home.

Geraldine did not manage to gather any new information at the bakery, as she had hoped, but it was clear to her that something had happened. Marek had disappeared, and the children too, while Annette was left alone, having experienced some trauma that had left her unable to function. She decided to go home and wait for Gerard.

Gerard, meanwhile, investigated what he could do to help Annette. In the end, he decided to bring Annette to the hospital and admit as "Maria Keller," the name of a childless patient who had died in the sanatorium not long ago, leaving no relative to seek her out.

A few hours later, Gerard returned to the sanatorium, this time with Annette. She was still not communicating, just staring blankly at the ceiling, apathetic. He proceeded to fill out the forms himself, using the new name, and recording the date of admittance as a month previously.

Towards evening, after he had finished admitting Annette, Gerard went home. He decided to try and find out what was happening at Annette's home; he knew the building from having once brought his wife for a dress fitting there. As he approached the entrance to the building, he saw objects lying in the stairwell. He did not come any closer, not wanting to arouse suspicion.

As he walked by where the trucks had stood earlier, he saw discarded on the ground pieces of clothing, hats, shoes… A shiver went through him, and his pulse began to race. His heart skipped a beat when he suddenly noticed bloodstains on the sidewalk, on the spot where the people had been lined up a few hours earlier. He kept walking, looped around, and then went back to his house by another route.

"Geraldine, what we're experiencing now is the Germans' cruelty and revenge over the Great War" he told his wife back at the house, shocked to the core by what he had seen. "We must be very careful. I don't know exactly what happened to Annette's family, but I assume that all foreigners are in danger now, from the French on one side, and the Germans on the other.

He paused briefly. "We have to keep Annette's story a secret. Try subtly to make sure that Brigitte doesn't leak a word of what she saw here. She doesn't know who Annette is, and it's important that she doesn't make a big deal out of it."

Geraldine nodded. Despite the late hour, she decided to go check Brigitte's loyalty.

Brigitte was a young Frenchwoman, graceful and buxom, a working-class girl who had taken the job of housekeeper in Geraldine and Gerard's home. She lived in the attic of their house, in an apartment reached by a separate entrance.

Geraldine climbed the stairs to the attic, rang the bell, and waited.

Brigitte did not delay opening the door, but Geraldine noticed that her hair was mussed, and that the top buttons of her blouse were undone. She decided to make use of that information, smiling mischievously as she asked, "am I interrupting?"

Brigitte blushed. "I didn't expect you to call me at such a late hour."

"I'm sorry," Geraldine apologized amicably, "I wanted to ask if you found my pearl bracelet." She had in fact been looking for it that morning. "I'm sorry, I didn't know you were here with a boyfriend..."

"I have a new friend, a German," Brigitte told her. "We met at the train station, at a café, when I was with some girlfriends. He's very good-looking. I hope it's okay that he comes to visit me in the apartment..."

"Oh, no problem," answered Geraldine, her heart pounding. "But I beg of you, for the protection of Gerard's patients, you must keep strict confidentiality. I ask that you make sure not to give away any information about Gerard's clinic and his patients by mistake."

"Of course, I understand very well how important that is."

"Did you find the bracelet, by the way?"

"No, ma'am, I'm sorry, I'll look again tomorrow."

Geraldine smiled to put her at ease. "Thank you, you can go back to your friend now, have fun."

Brigitte closed the door after her and returned to the attic, to the arms of an S.S. officer.

Geraldine was stricken with fear. A German soldier was in her home, on intimate terms with her housekeeper, who knew almost everything that went on in their home. Panting, she burst into the workroom where Gerard was sitting.

"What happened? You look like you ran through the entire building," Gerard observed.

"We have a problem. Not only do I have doubts about Brigitte's loyalty to us, but I'm also scared of the fact that she has brought a

German soldier into our home without our knowledge!" "What do you mean?" Gerard jumped to his feet.

"It seems she's met a German soldier. He's right above us as we speak, up in the attic!"

"Do you know what that means? Now she can squeeze anything out of us, and if we don't meet her demands, we can fall into German hands..."

"Yes, yes, we're in trouble!" Geraldine worried.

"Alright, we have to stay cool and behave as though everything's normal and nothing is bothering us."

"That's just what I did, just that I pointed out that since you work with patients, she has to keep strict confidentiality. I tried to seem as believable as possible, as though your clinic is the most important thing. I didn't show any fear."

"I understand. Let's wait and see how things develop."

In the attic, Frank the S.S. officer held Brigitte by the hips and lifted her onto him. She wrapped her legs around his waist and her arms around his neck. Frank ripped off her blouse and she surrendered to him. As they lay on the bed afterwards, Frank asked, in heavily accented French, "What do you think of your employers?"

"They're nice, real Frenchmen. The husband is a psychiatrist, works at a home clinic and also outside of Paris. The wife likes me a lot and gives me a free hand with the housework. The truth is, she's sort of a snob. She's busy all day with her rich friends, but overall, I'm comfortable here, the salary is good and…"

"Good, sweetheart, I have to run," Frank cut off her prattle. "We have a lot of work to do here. Your city is full of people who shouldn't be here, and a few Frenchmen, not the brightest, who don't understand who we are," he sniggered.

"Yes, I couldn't agree more. Just two days ago a woman like that was at the Gastons'. She must have collapsed or something like that. Gerard treated her and apparently transferred her to the sanatorium."

"My tiger, I'm off. I'd like it if you could help me in my job and tell me anything you hear. It will make my work easier and that way I'll have more time to spend with you."

Brigitte had not expected such a request from him. She blushed, surprised; for her, it was a great compliment.

A few kilometers from Paris, Annette, dressed in a hospital gown, sat motionless by a window. The medication had its their mark: her mouth was dry and slack, and she was staring blankly out into the hospital garden.

Annette had become completely detached from her surroundings. It happened following the attack she experienced immediately upon her arrival at the hospital, when she talked about her children who had been kidnapped from her and her husband who was waiting for her.

The attending physician had given her the pills that had been prescribed for her. They seemed to him to be too strong for her condition, but he didn't argue with the institution's director, who had the highest professional authority.

Gerard had decided to give her high doses of medication in order to make it easier for her to deal with her loss, and also to make sure that she did not talk— something that was likely to give her away and, very likely, give him away too in such times.

Through the window, Annette saw Marek waving to her with Olivier and Laurent in his arms. She waved back to them. A small smile crept over her face, as though her world was at peace and her loved ones were here at her side.

The attending physician watched her waving through the window to a deserted garden, understanding that she had apparently lost those dearest to her and was struggling to cope with the loss.

3

The day-to-day reality of war settled over the French capital. Dozens of incidents occurred in which people disappeared, families were separated, businesses were nationalized and closed. The Nazi terror became routine, as part of their war against the French underground and opponents of the French collaborationist regime.

The French police, run by the collaborationist regime, took vigorous action to eradicate the opponents to the French capitulation. This included passing on names of Frenchmen and foreigners to the German Gestapo, organizing deportations by lists of resisters, and sending people to labor camps, all done hand in hand with the Nazi conqueror.

The lists also included the names of Paris's Jewish residents, both those who were already known and those whose names were given away by informants.

Meanwhile, Parisian cultural life flourished: the numbers of patrons swelled with each passing day, among them German officers who were amateur connoisseurs of art and culture, as well as Frenchmen in the Vichy regime.

In these days Helena was a star, the lead dancer of the cabaret, and much sought after by its patrons. Her entanglement with Helmut deepened, and she became the escort of the senior S.S. officer of Paris. Her standing rose among the upper echelons of the regime: the senior Nazi officers saw her as an ally, and the Frenchmen of the Vichy regime saw her as loyal to France's capitulation agreement; in contrast, friends from her past were afraid of her and kept their distance. Deep inside, Helena moved through her days with a wounded soul and a broken heart. One morning, she had left with her lover for the train station, and a moment later, he had disappeared as though he had never existed. Her world had been turned upside down, and in his place, she had let the cruel enemy, Helmut, into her life. Rumor had it that Marek had been shot that same night, but it seemed she would never know for sure. Annette, whose traces she had lost, had apparently been taken to a hospital, but there was no way of knowing where or under what name. Olivier and Laurent were in hiding with the Dubois family. She had not met up with them, having distanced herself from the Dubois family, but made sure to keep track of them from afar. She had not forgotten for a moment the promise she had made to her beloved Marek.

During this period Helena moved to a large, spacious apartment, closer to the cabaret. She detached herself from all her familiar surroundings and tried to go on with her life.

She would go to meetings with the Germans only when Helmut brought her with him; he treated her like a beautiful object that he was showing off to his commanders. For her part, she tried as much as possible to avoid contact with German officers and French collaborators.

She refused to accept the loss of the family that had been dearest to her, and, most of all, the loss of Marek, whom she had loved in a way that she had never felt with anyone else. It was even harder knowing that the person now at her side, in some way or another, held responsibility for Marek's fate.

Helmut, for his part, made it abundantly clear that she belonged to him. She had no choice but to excel as a convincing actress in her new role: the S.S. officer's devoted and loving escort.

It was 1942. Two years had passed since the German invasion. Europe had fallen at Germany's feet, and thus Helena as well. She was part of defeated Europe, her body no more than occupied territory.

Helena maintained her pride, even though her body had been conquered. She encouraged herself that every day that passed brought her closer to regaining her independence. But the world had other plans; in those two years, Germany's power only grew. In contrast to Germany's swelling strength, the opposing Allies were just beginning to get themselves together to fight, with only a few isolated successes, still in shock from the power of the German army and the fall of the free world.

Helena was skilled at playing the game during her encounters with Helmut and the team of officers he commanded. She radiated grace, frequently flashed her submissive smile, and gave Helmut cause to be proud of his Italian girlfriend.

Helmut's wife lived in Berlin. She was a woman with deep roots in German society, the daughter of an aristocratic German family who lost their property when the Nazis came to power; but she herself was active in the Nazi party, where she had first met Helmut. A short while later, they married and had two children.

Helmut lived a double life, one in Berlin and one in France, where he had spent the past two years. His stay in Paris had become more interesting and more pleasant since meeting Helena on that fateful afternoon. Unlike most of Germans, who suffered from homesickness, he felt the opposite: he had no desire to leave Paris. Helena was important to him, and he felt deeply connected to her, first in a gentlemanly way, but over time becoming increasingly jealous and controlling.

One day, when Helmut was recalled to Berlin for a round of consultations, Helena played the game, portraying the broken-hearted lover whose boyfriend was leaving her— even though she had longed for that moment. Helmut's command staff obeyed his orders, most of which concerned the administration of the city, but some included clear instructions regarding Helena. He demanded that they provide for all her needs and keep a close watch over her. Helena knew that she would have to shake them off to obtain some of the freedom that was so precious to her.

"My dear, I'm leaving Schultz as your personal escort, to make sure you have everything you need."

"You can't be serious— an officer of his rank will serve me in your absence? He has to be available for anything that might be needed in the city, particularly when you're gone; he's the most senior commander after you. Besides, he's not the kind of person I want at my side," she embraced Helmut. "I already have exactly who I want," she poured on the flattery.

"Don't worry, I promise he won't bother you. He'll just stick close by. We have information on French rebels who are going to attempt to damage everything we have achieved, including with our allies. Promise me that you will keep him apprised of how you are doing, and if you need anything, just ask. He'll be available to you at any time. Remember: I can find out everything that's happening, even if no one is with you," Helmut added coldly.

"You know I wouldn't hide anything from you," Helena answered, trying to melt the ice.

He embraced her a bit too forcefully, and she let out a little moan, whether from pain or fear, no one could say. He began kissing her neck, and she detached from her body. As she let out the requisite number of fake sighs, she was on the theater stage, playing her role.

A short while later he brought her back to her apartment and continued on to the airport.

Helena went up to her apartment and hurried into the shower, standing for a long time under the flow of water, washing away the filth, disgusted at the very thought of what she had been through. At that moment, she wanted to end it all, end the shame and the feeling of revulsion that flooded her, but she cut that thought short. *I'll survive. My life will change. That's what I've decided will happen.*

She came out of the shower and picked up her robe, the robe that Marek had loved so. As she put it on, she felt the touch of Marek's hands. She remembered Annette, Olivier, and Laurent, and she again promised herself, but this time speaking to Marek: *I'm here, with no strength left, but I will keep my promise. I'll be strong for Olivier and Laurent.*

The following days felt to her like a vacation. She took advantage of those moments for herself, feeling like a bird who had just been freed from a cage.

One morning, she got up as usual and went to the cabaret for rehearsals of the new show. The world went on living. On her way home in the afternoon, she decided to go by the Dubois' bakery. She did so only after making sure that no one was following her, knowing that she was tailed most of the time. Of necessity, she had become expert at identifying Nazi secret agents.

When she spied Monsieur Dubois from a distance, she tried to change direction so as to avoid meeting up with him, but a moment later heard a man's voice behind her. "Helena?"

She turned around and found herself face to face with Monsieur Dubois.

"Helena, I'm so happy I found you."

Helena tried to appear surprised, but at the same time kept her cool, taking care not to let slip any information about her own life. It had been more than two years since she had left the building where she used to live.

"How are you, Monsieur Dubois? I hope everyone in the family is well."

"Yes, yes, everything is fine. Thank you for asking."

"You look worried. Is something wrong, after all?"

"Yes, Helena." He grabbed her hand and tried to pull her into a side street, but she pulled back slightly.

"Don't be scared, I just don't want to stand in the middle of the street. People are looking, listening, you don't know where it will end up." She knew he meant the Germans.

She pulled out of his grip but followed him into a side street, meanwhile making sure that they were not being followed.

"Listen, you must know of the decrees and restrictions that the Germans have issued regarding Jews and those who help them…?" he asked hesitantly.

"Yes, I've heard, but there's nothing I can do," she responded apologetically.

"No, I'm not asking you for anything like that, but you surely remember the family with the two children— Annette, Marek, and the little boys Olivier and Laurent?"

Her heart pounded in her chest. "Of course, I remember," she answered with a slight smile, but unbidden tears filled her eyes. She tried to pretend that she didn't notic.

"So, you must know that they have suffered a great catastrophe since the invasion," Monsieur Dubois went on gravely. "First the father disappeared, then the mother disappeared… They say she was hospitalized because she couldn't bear the loss of her husband. Rumor has it that he was murdered by the Germans when they tried to get to the rest of his family. One of the Frenchmen who was arrested with him, and afterwards released, recounted that they tried to interrogate him, and when he refused to talk, they just shot him on the spot."

Helena had not been prepared for this. She felt the ground slipping from under her feet and everything went black.

The next thing she heard dimly was someone calling her name, "Helena, Helena, are you okay? Get up!"

She opened her eyes and saw Monsieur Dubois leaning over her, trying to lift her up.

"Helena, sit up, take a deep breath, are you okay? You scared me for a moment. The second I started talking about Marek, you fainted dead away." Monsieur Dubois had no idea what that piece of information had stirred up in her, how that glimmer of hope, however miniscule, that she might see Marek again had suddenly disappeared like a puff of smoke.

When she came to, she was burning with rage and hatred, boiling mad at the Germans and their collaborators. She was furious at the xenophobic French, at all those who had attacked what was most dear to her and turned her world upside down in the space of one night.

"Thank you, Monsieur Dubois," she rose to her feet. "I'm feeling a bit weak… Too much work and not enough sleep."

"I can imagine it's hard to hear something like that, they were such a good family. I felt I needed to share this with you, since you used to live in their building. You were in this neighborhood, you knew everyone. There are rumors that you've befriended the Germans, but I remember that you were a good friend of Marek and Annette's…"

He paused, hesitating. "So, you should know that their children have been with us for quite a while already, but now it's starting to get dangerous… My wife, she can't handle it anymore, and I'm growing scared for those children. I have to get help, to find them another hiding place or a family that will be able to take care of them… I promised Annette to take care of them, I'll do everything I can to make sure they survive, but with us, it's starting to get dangerous! A lot of people are talking, including my wife. It hurts me to say this, but unfortunately, I cannot count on her if push should come to shove. I don't know who to turn to, and when I saw you here in the street… I remembered that you were a good friend of that family. I hope I'm not mistaken and that you really can help me…"

Monsieur Dubois concluded his flood of words with a great sigh, as though he had just let go of the burden he had been carrying ever since Olivier and Laurent went into hiding with them. He had acted on his gut instinct, taking a great risk during such an uncertain time, when anyone could be the one to report you and send you the German torture chambers. He gazed into Helena's eyes with despair. He spoke the truth: his wife had threatened to turn in the children to the Germans since Annette was no longer paying them any money. Eventhough Monsieur Dubois was suspicious of Helena, since she was considered a collaborator with the occupation, he admired her and remembered how close she had been to the Oppenheimer family.

Helena gazed into Monsieur Dubois' eyes, examining him, trying to read his body language. His face was beaded with sweat, perhaps out of fear that he had made a mistake in revealing himself to her, and that it would lead to his arrest. Helena did not know whether his fear was rooted in the prospect of being caught, or whether it sprung from genuine concern for the Oppenheimer family.

"Indeed, that family is very important to me. We share a background as immigrants living in a foreign country, and we have been through a lot together. I would be happy to help, but what exactly did you have in mind?"

"I don't know. Perhaps you could somehow smuggle them out of here to the south and from there to England? I think they have relatives there, Annette once told me about some family in London...

I don't know myself exactly what I was thinking..."

"Where are the children? What do you do with them all day?"

"In the meantime, they are still attending nursery and school as usual, and during vacations they are with us at home. We managed a couple of times to send them to our relatives outside Paris, but lately, they have been reluctant to cooperate with us... The problem is that people at school are starting to talk too, and Olivier's teacher hinted to me that there are rumors that he is Jewish. They live with us in a room in the attic. Olivier works with me. Although he's still very young, only six and half, he really helps with all the baking and in general, with everything I do. Laurent is more of a problem... He has been suffering from fits of crying and rage ever since his mother disappeared. The one who calms him down and takes care of him, more than anyone, is Olivier. He helps us a lot in caring for his brother."

Helena's heart contracted. Olivier really was a special child, so young and carrying all this on his shoulders.

She straightened up. "I have an idea, but I need to look into it a little more. Let's meet tomorrow or the next day, and by then I will have made a plan."

"Helena, I don't think you understand. This is urgent. It's a matter of hours. I'm afraid that people will talk, we're endangering both the children and ourselves."

"I know that, and I understand. I'll do everything I can to find a solution." Again, she was unsure how much he was worried about the children and how much about saving his own skin. One thing that could be said for Monsieur and Madame Dubois, they had taken upon themselves a great risk. Annette could not have paid them that much, so it could not have been only about money.

They agreed to meet again in two days time at the Opera Café. Helena suggested that meeting place because she knew that they would be in a safe environment. She knew the owners of the café and relied on them to provide her a safe, quiet corner for their meeting.

When they parted, Monsieur Dubois held Helena's hand, gazed into her eyes and begged: "Try to help us. Those children have become very dear to me, even if they're not my own. But I'm afraid that in the end both they and my family will be harmed."

Helena responded coldly, straining to hide her emotion, "I'll see how I can help Olivier and Laurent. They've already been hurt enough by this insanity."

Helena had no idea what she was going to do, but one thing she knew for sure: she had promised this to Marek when he asked her to look after the family for him, as though he had known that she would be the only person who could do it.

She cautiously exited the alleyway and walked away, her eyes flooded with tears. She pulled down her hat so that people couldn't see her eyes, afraid of running into one of the agents tailing her. She was aware of her image as the amusing, smiling performer when she was before her audience of admirers, most of whom now were Nazis and collaborators from the Vichy regime.

She made her way back to her apartment, her mind racing. She had known for a long time already, according to all the stories she'd heard, that the children were in danger. Now someone had taken the trouble to draw the authorities' attention to the Dubois family.

Free Paris was at a low point. Most of the residents who had stayed rather than moving south had accepted the new regime and the Nazi occupier. Helena knew without a shadow of a doubt that the alarm bells Monsieur Dubois was ringing were real. The danger to the Oppenheimer children was more tangible than ever.

Helena went up to her apartment, undressed, and went into the shower. As the warm water flowed over her body, the not-so-distant past hovered before her; she felt Marek with her. Her tears mingled with the streams of hot water. More than anything else, she knew that she wanted to keep her promise to Marek and be close to him once again, even if he himself were no longer alive. She wanted to save his children.

Helena thought carefully about the danger the children would face if they were with her, given that she was surrounded by Germans, some friendly and pleasant but others cruel. Being around them scared her. More than anyone else, Helmut scared her. He had been like her patron ever since that meeting at the train station, on that fateful day when she had tried to get train tickets for Marek and his family.

Helmut did not let her out of his sight for a minute, frequently making it clear to her that he expected her to be with him whenever he wanted. Although he addressed her in a polite tone, she could hear its underlying menace: *In the end you're just an Italian immigrant, don't ever forget that.* But at the same time, Helena knew that the colonel was also her security card. *As long as you behave yourself, you'll be safe.*

I'll bring them to me, and I'll see how I can keep them safe with Helmut's help, she mused. *I want to do it.* She was preoccupied with figuring out what she would do, for two days from now she would need to have an answer for the Dubois family. She wrapped herself in the robe that Marek had so loved— a sort of private ceremony that she performed on those nights when she was alone in the apartment— and got into bed.

4

Helena was stirred awake by the sound of a fist pounding on her door. Glancing at the clock, she saw that scarcely an hour had passed. By the force of the knocking, she was sure that it was Helmut's soldiers who had been assigned to escort her. Even with all his threatening behavior, Helmut had never showed up like that without giving her advance notice. She approached the door warily. "Who is it?"

From outside the door came a soft voice in Italian: "Questa è Maria." Helena's face turned white, and she opened the door breathlessly.

The two women fell on each other, sobbing, as Helena pulled Maria inside. Maria, or Mari as she had always called her, was Helena's younger sister. Helena had left her when she was a girl of fifteen, and now she had come to her as a woman.

"Mari…" Helena did not continue, just stroked her hair and kissed her. Then she took a step back and looked at her, "I remember you as a girl, and look at you now— a woman! You're even taller than me now. How are Mama, Papa, tell me -- I haven't heard from them for so long… How did you get here? How did you manage?" She hugged her again, sobbing bitterly.

"Helena, I've missed you so much. You have no idea what I've been through since that week when you disappeared. At first, I had to lie about where you were, so they wouldn't follow your tracks. Since then, I have not stopped dreaming about the moment when

I'd see you again… Helena, don't ever leave me again…"

"I won't leave you. I promise. You're exactly what I needed."

They embraced again and again. Maria was taller than Helena, more buxom, and glowing with beauty.

They sat with their arms around each other and talked into the night, filling each other in on years of events, friends, family, lovers, the whole wide world. At dawn they fell asleep in each other's arms, just as they used to sleep in Italy.

In the morning, Helena awoke first and went down to the bakery below her house to buy some pastries. The bakery immediately reminded her of Monsieur Dubois, and once again her mind turned to the problem of saving the Oppenheimer children.

A few days passed, during which Helena was careful to hide her sister, out of fear that one of Helmut's subordinates would decide to visit her when she was not yet sure what she was going to do. She did not show up at the meeting she had set with Monsieur Dubois but tracked him secretly to see that no dangerous measures were being taken against the children.

One morning, a plan came together as an idea flashed through her head. How had she not thought of it earlier? Of course! It's clear that her sister came to the city with her two children. Yes, that will be the story, she thought – their skin tone is even similar to hers. The only problem is the Italian, but we can solve that too. It was as though God had helped her find the solution. Helmut will help: he'll understand that my sister and her two children came to me because of the tough economic situation at home, in Italy.

Even the vacant apartment under Helena's seemed to have been waiting for Maria's arrival. Helena would be able to rent it so that Maria could live separately, thus avoiding running into Helmut or Schultz too much. Until recently, the apartment had been occupied by a young couple who were arrested by the French police, in collaboration with the Germans. The landlords were looking for someone to rent it to, but ever since it came under police surveillance, no one wanted to live there.

Helena shared her idea with her sister as soon as she had the chance. "I know this is going to sound crazy to you, Mari, since you just got here a few days ago, but I'm about to let you in on a secret. It's what's going to save you, me, and two children who mean a lot to me."

Maria, who had just woken up, did not understand what her sister was talking about. "What children? You have children?"

"Do you remember Marek that I told you about?"

"Yes, the neighbor you had the affair with?"

"He was taken by the Germans one day, or maybe by the French fascist militia, and disappeared without a trace. In any case, it doesn't matter anymore. What's important is that I promised him I'd look after his children."

Maria hesitated a moment, amazed, then burst out, "why do you keep getting yourself tangled up in such things?"

"You'll never understand it, Mari, you'll never understand what we had together and what I have left of him. A dream that I dream every night and cannot get free of. I promised him," said Helena with tears in her eyes. "But that's not all... What's going to happen is that you're going to become a mother who just arrived from Italy with her two children."

"What?!" Maria exclaimed. "Tell me, are you trying to drag me into all sorts of complications? They'll see through that story in a minute. They don't like immigrants here!" Maria raged at her sister.

Helena snickered. "Mari, have you forgotten that you're an Italian? Do you remember that Italy and Germany are on the same side? You need to understand, the German officer responsible for all of Paris is my lover, he's madly in love with me. For lack of any other option, I've become his property."

Maria, taken by surprise again, hurriedly responded, "Tell me, don't you ever learn to pick your boyfriends? In Italy, the fascist who almost killed our whole family was your lover, then you have an affair with your married neighbor, and now you tell me that you're going out with a Nazi officer? What are we going do with you, big sister?"

Helena laughed. "When you put it like that, it does sound bad, but this time I'm serious. Mari, I owe it to Marek and Annette."

"Oh, now you're responsible for Marek's wife's fate too, after you destroyed the family?"

"No, not at all. I'm just worried about the children. Unfortunately, their mother lost it after Marek disappeared. She just collapsed. We have to get ourselves organized as soon as possible. Helmut is returning from Germany in three days. He's already written me that he's coming straight to the new debut at the cabaret to see me dance. We have to arrange everything down to the last detail before he comes. Helmut knows everything. Nothing escapes him.

"This plan will save you and the children, and it will give me the strength to go on. Mari, you'll fall in love with them when you meet them, two angels who have no idea what a cruel world they were born into. We'll have to teach them a few words in Italian; our cover story will be that you spoke French with them from a young age so that one day you could come to your sister in France. Their ages fit with your age. Helmut won't look into it deeply, he'll be inclined to believe me. He just wants me near him, as an ornament, as property.

That's all that interests him."

Maria listened to her sister's plan, trying to understand, to imagine how it would be. The fear of this Helmut, whom Helena had described so negatively, trickled down to her as well. But she knew that she had no choice, and that this plan could actually help her survive here. For if they seriously investigated where she came from, they'd find out about the fascist in Italy who was looking for her, and she did not want to think of what would happen then. She had dreamed of seeing Helena again, and now they were finally together, and she was not going to give up on her sister.

"Okay, Helena, I'll do it. But not because I don't have a choice— because I don't want to lose you. I'm counting on your will to survive, which has gotten you this far."

"Mari, trust me, whatever is in my control, I won't leave to the hand of fate. But you must remember that it's not a sure thing. Life has taught me that even if we think that everything is planned out, that the cover story is real, that nothing will happen— nothing is certain. I want you to remember that. The fact that you got here is not by chance. Like you said, you didn't stay there to weep over your bitter fate. Instead, you took your life in your hands and continued onward, just like I did many years ago. The situation is not ideal, but I'm sure that Mama and Papa, even though they remained behind, would like us to have something better, that we should live our lives out of choice and not out of lack of choice..."

"Okay, Helena, you've tired me out with all your talk… I've been here for less than a week and I've already become a mother of two who is soon going to deal with some German officer, who, according to your descriptions, is scarier than my worst nightmare… Let's calm down, sister, and we'll start the war in a little while." They both laughed, but inside they knew that it would indeed be a war for survival.

"Stay here and rest," said Helena. "I'll go meet the French family and make our plan. I'll be back in the afternoon."

Maria hugged her. "I missed you so much. I also want to see you dancing in the show."

"Don't worry, I'll bring you to see a show, but it's better if you come to a rehearsal and not the show itself. Most of the audience are like those we ran away from. I don't want to introduce you to them. In fact, they can't be allowed to meet you, because the moment that happens, they'll take ownership of you and you'll become their property," said Helena gravely.

"Helena, you sound like Papa's preaching," Maria teased her affectionately.

"It turns out he was right. Everything he said about fascists and Nazis was right."

Helena finished getting ready and went out. She strode confidently in the direction of the old neighborhood, where she had come to know her lover, Marek. She passed the corner building where they once lived, a storm of emotions raging inside her. Memories of their encounters— when she would return from a stormy night of performances and Marek would be on his way out to work at the printing house— were as vivid and tangible as if they had happened yesterday. She remembered how he would storm into her apartment; she could feel his hands on her body… Her stomach clenched, and tears flooded her eyes. *No point in regretting*, she would herself in such moments of grief. *Sometimes a minute of happiness gives enough strength for a lifetime. Because of Marek I have boundless energy and I have a goal.*

She approached the Dubois bakery. It was almost noon, and the bakery had begun to fill with customers. Helena went in and stood in line as though she were looking at the cakes; in front of her stood two officers in S.S. uniforms. When they finished and turned to go, their eyes met hers.

"Madame, we are most honored to meet you."

Helena put on her most captivating smile. "Why, thank you. You always make me blush. How is your commander? He should be back soon…"

They nodded. "Indeed," one of them said, "I suppose, if so, that we will have the honor of seeing you soon at the nightclub."

"Yes, I hope so. When I see Helmut, I will give him your regards."

They were Helmut's operational officers, the people who carried out the cruel assignments of interrogation by torture. More than once, to her dismay, she had witnessed conversations about torture in the interrogation chambers, conversations to which she could not remain indifferent. Helmut understood that it was hard for her to hear such things; he once even banished these subordinates from his table in the officers' lounge. Ever since, they had tried to hurt her in revenge, without incurring Helmut's wrath. She was aware of that, and played the game, but at the same time did not let them get away with too much. Realizing that the game was over for today, they bowed and left the store.

Helena picked up a few loaves of bread and stood before Madame Dubois. "How is your husband? I was happy to see him," she said, smiling.

Madame Dubois was still so shocked by Helena's daring banter with the S.S. officers that it took her a moment to respond. "H-He's well… He should be here at the bakery soon."

"Good, give him my regards. Perhaps I will see him next time." She left a ten franc note on the counter for the bread, saying, "Keep the change, thanks." As she left the store, Madame Dubois picked up the note and, to her surprise, noticed writing on it: *3:30 p.m., corner of Belleville.* She folded it and stuck it in her apron pocket.

Two hours later, Helena met with Monsieur Dubois.

During this short meeting, they agreed that the following day at six o'clock in the evening, outside the bakery, Maria would come and take the children. Before that, in the afternoon, Maria would come by just to pick up the children's bags. That way, when they walked together in the evening, it would not look like she was picking up refugees. Helena thought that if Maria picked up the children rather than her, it would avert the risk of running into S.S. officers who would most likely suspect Helena of something and report her immediately to Helmut.

Helena went back to her apartment to arrange all the details of the plan with her sister, and then straight to the nightclub.

She could barely get through the show that evening: she could not concentrate and almost fell during her solo number. But despite everything, she was as impressive as usual.

At dawn, she finally reached her apartment, after being required to stay at the nightclub as hostess to a group of officers who insisted on inviting her, claiming that their commander had asked them to keep her amused, and that they were following orders. She came in quietly, undressed and went to take a shower. After a few moments, she realized that Maria was sitting on the floor of the bathroom, studying her.

"Having fun?" Helena smiled at her.

Maria laughed. "I'm not just having fun, I'm melting away. Your body is perfect! No wonder everyone wants you to be theirs. But don't give in to them, be just mine."

"Mari, if you only knew how beautiful and radiant you are. Compared to me, you're a real wildflower. I always wanted to be like you, with that black hair, the perfect breasts, the butt... I always wanted to be you."

When Helena came out of the shower, Maria wrapped her in a robe and the two sat down on the bed.

"I'm dead on my feet," sighed Helena. "I have to gather some strength for this afternoon."

"Go to sleep, I'll wake you up in a bit, whenever you tell me," Maria suggested.

"We arranged for noontime. You'll go there alone," said Helena, gauging Maria's reaction. "You need to understand that German officers who know me are walking around everywhere— Helmut's orders. I can't just suddenly be seen with bags or with the children. I have to introduce you to Helmut for the first time when you're already with the children; after that, it will look natural that I'm spending time with my sister's children."

"I need a moment to digest this, Helena. Yes, I agreed to the plan, but it's still hard for me to imagine myself suddenly responsible for two children, just like that."

"I'm responsible for them, Mari. I don't want to lose you, but at the same time I want those children, irrespective of my love for Marek. Olivier stole into my heart long before Marek and me got together. I know what I'm doing, trust me," Helena pleaded. "Besides, look, you'll have two sweet children who need an adult figure to be at their side and save them from this crazy world. Let me sleep a little, and then, when I wake up, we'll go over all the details."

"I can't deal with you... But I'm with you. Go rest, Helena, I'll wake you up." Helena fell asleep as soon as her head hit the pillow.

5

Helena felt a caress on her cheek. "Marek…" she murmured. Suddenly, she heard feminine laughter; she opened her eyes as though still in a dream, only to realize that it was Maria's hand. She blushed as Maria said, "I should have met him. He must have been a very special man."

"He really was," said Helena quietly. "Our few months together felt like a lifetime, with all its complexity." Her eyes filled with tears. She got up slowly, dizzy from her short, troubled sleep.

"Two hours from now, go to the address that I'll give you, to the Dubois family's bakery. I wrote down exactly how to get there. When you're there, go around to the back door of the bakery, and Monsieur Dubois' wife will be waiting for you. She's a heavyset woman and she always wears a headscarf. You'll recognize her right away, she looks like a peasant. She'll take you inside. In the first stage, you'll just meet the children, pick up their bags, and come back here."

"Okay," Maria confirmed.

"I've been following them occasionally ever since they moved in with Monsieur and Madame Dubois," Helena continued. "Olivier is the elder, the taller of the two, with a mature face, and Laurent is the younger one. Monsieur Dubois looks like a typical Frenchman: black mustache, a hat like Papa's. I asked him to wear that hat so that you will recognize him for sure. It's better if you squeeze all their stuff into one bag, making it as small as possible. You can't walk around the streets of Paris looking like a refugee. In the afternoon we'll go out again, the two of us together this time, to pick them up. I'll stand a little distance away from you, in case something goes wrong and the children need to be calmed down. I'll watch from a distance, so I won't show myself and arouse suspicion. If something goes wrong, I'll pretend that I was just passing by when you were out for a walk with your children."

"I see you've thought of every detail."

"I hope so. These are not easy days in this city. You can't trust anyone, you never know what might happen... It's important that we tell them to call you mama."

"Helena, what are you afraid might happen? I need to know everything, even if it paralyzes me with fear."

Helena looked at her sister soberly. "Helmut is a dangerous man. He's good-looking, smart, and a gentleman, but he has no emotions and he knows how to hurt people... He won't hurt me, but I see how everyone around him is scared of him. I overheard the officers talking about things he did in cold blood, during interrogations... Unfortunately, I'm his escort. It's helping me survive, but it also terrifies me. I'm taking responsibility for everything that's going to happen— looking after you, keeping my promise to Marek, and also looking after my own life, not leaving it up to fate."

"You brought me into this whole thing," Maria observed. "I have no one in the world besides you, and suddenly I have to become a mother of two... But your determination is carrying me too. We'll succeed somehow. We have each other."

"Let's go, Mari, it's time. You're going to meet them now. Follow the route I explained to you, and don't forget to get their bags. If you sense any danger, or see Germans in the bakery or nearby, just keep walking and come back later. Enter the bakery from the side door, but only when no one is around. We chose this time specifically because there are usually few people in the bakery at this hour. I'll wait for you here."

Helena and Maria embraced, both trembling; they kissed each other and got up to go out. Helena went first and descended the stairs slowly, with Maria following behind. She cracked opened the door to the building and peeked outside. Everything looked as usual in the street, cars passing by slowly, nothing unusual.

She opened the door wide for Maria to go out.

Maria walked slowly, regally, trying to hide her emotion. Within a few minutes, she reached the square near the bakery, but suddenly could not remember which way to turn. Her breathing quickened and she felt drops of cold sweat breaking out on her forehead. She wiped her brow and sat down on a bench at the edge of the square. *Everything is okay*, she told herself. After taking a few deep breaths, she got off the bench, looked around the square, and remembered where she needed to go from there. A couple of minutes later, she was approaching the bakery.

Despite being on a side street, it was crowded with passersbys.. She stopped a few doors down from the bakery and observed the building but did not notice anything unusual. Although she was not familiar with Paris life, the atmosphere felt normal and safe.

She crossed the street to the sidewalk that led to the bakery, turned into the courtyard, and went around the bakery to the back door. Taking a deep breath and letting out a heavy sigh, she knocked on the door.

The door opened heavily, and an older woman stood before her, heavyset, with a headscarf and a cold expression.

"Maria?" asked Madame Dubois.

"Yes, Helena's sister," she answered in heavily accented French.

"No one saw you come in?"

"No, as far as I could see… I waited for a few minutes to make sure that everything was normal and then I crossed the street and came in."

"Good, come in, don't just stand there." Madame Dubois opened the door wide and led Maria inside. The door slammed shut behind her.

They passed through the foyer. Madame Dubois pointed to a low stool next to the entrance and gestured her to sit, then put a finger to her lips, signaling with her other hand that she should wait, and disappeared.

It was the back room where the pastries were prepared. The aromas of coffee and pastries wafting through the air momentarily soothed Maria's raw nerves. She remembered Helena's stories of the French bakeries, which she had described as paradise.

Maria could dimly hear snatches of conversation, apparently from

customers in the bakery. Suddenly, a man came in. She immediately identified him as Monsieur Dubois based on Helena's description. At his side, so
it seemed, stood Olivier, she guessed by his size and appearance. *His face is
already that of a grown boy, perhaps mature for his age*, she thought to herself. He had an unkempt look and did not utter a word; she felt that he was
scared. Compassion stirred within her as she approached Monsieur Dubois
and introduced herself, "Maria, Helena's sister." At that moment Olivier's
face lit up with a smile at the sound of Helena's name. Maria reached out
and stroked his head.

Monsieur Dubois clasped Maria's hand between two of his own. "Thank
you, Maria. You look like your sister, if you permit my saying so. You have
Helena's beauty, perhaps even more. Laurent is sleeping, so you can see him
but do not wake him. We're in the middle of work right now."

"I understand." She looked into Olivier's eyes, and he spoke with his gaze.
She caressed him again and asked, "do you know who I am?"

He nodded. "You're Helena's sister." *He's only six-and-a-half years old*,
Maria thought, *but apparently the fact that his parents had abandoned him,
or at least so he felt, had made him grow up quickly.* It also seemed to her
that Monsieur and Madame Dubois, who had been looking after him and
his brother, were not the ideal caretakers…

"Right, sweetie, do you remember Hele…?"

"Yes," he did not wait for her to finish her question. "She was my parents'
neighbor, and always helped Maman."

Monsieur Dubois signaled Maria to move into the adjoining room. She
gave Olivier her hand and they walked together. She entered the small room
and saw Laurent, who was just over three.

"That's Laurent, my brother. Maman asked me to look after him, he's
very little… I promised her I would look after him until she returned." In
the same breath he added, "Do you know where my mother is? When will
she return?"

Maria was caught off guard, but quickly recovered her wits and answered
confidently, without knowing if what she was saying was true: "Of course I
know. Maman is in a sanatorium, she was very sick and needed to rest. She

will feel better and come back to you. In the meantime, she asked Helena and me to watch the two of you." She pulled him to her and kissed him on the head.

"Would you like me to come get you and Laurent and bring you home to Helena later?" His sad eyes opened wide. "Yes!" he nodded rapidly. She could ask for no more decisive confirmation than that. He wanted to go with her.

"Monsieur Dubois, I will take the children's bags now and come back later, as we have arranged."

She turned to the boy, "Olivier, I have to go now. I'm just taking the bags now, and in a few more hours I'll be back to take you home. Will you wait for me here?"

Olivier immediately understood the game and nodded again without a word. From behind a door, Monsieur Dubois took out two identical small bags and handed them to Maria. "Here are all their things."

Maria looked at him searchingly. If what Helena said was true, that Annette had given them no small sum of money to keep the children, the children should have had a little more possessions, clothes, toys...

But Maria did not want to embarrass anyone, and she was afraid to linger there any longer. Clutching the two bags, she thanked Monsieur Dubois, then turned to Olivier and said, "you wait here for me and look after your brother when he gets up, okay? I'll be here in a couple hours." Standing by Laurent's bed, Olivier nodded again. Maria kissed him on the forehead and turned to leave when Monsieur Dubois suddenly grabbed her hand and signaled her to be quiet. At first, she did not understand, but then she heard voices in German.

Soldiers had come into the bakery. It was not the time to go outside. Maria sat quietly on the chair and signaled to Olivier to come sit on her lap. Monsieur Dubois went out and closed the door behind him.

She could vaguely make out sounds of laughter, followed by the chime of the doorbell, signaling that the clients had left the shop. They continued waiting in silence. A few minutes later, Monsieur Dubois came in. "They're gone, I checked the street. All is clear, so you can leave now."

They got up from the chair and Maria bent down to Olivier. "Wait for me. I'll be back in a little while." She kissed him again on the forehead and turned to go, but suddenly changed her mind and put down the bags. She had decided to take out some of the contents and stuff them into her bag; she would take the rest with her when she came back. She did not want to attract any extra attention on the street at that moment.

She walked back along the same route she had come, carrying her handbag stuffed with some of the children's clothes. Just before the street where Helena lived, a dark car passed her. It reminded her of the cars of the fascist militia in Italy, and several men were peering out of it. When they caught sight of her, they asked the driver to slow down. One of them shouted, "Perhaps we can help you get where you are going?" in French with a thick German accent. With all her might she struggled to stay calm, despite the storm raging within her. She turned her head toward him and, answered with a smile, trying to produce her best French accent, "No, thank you, I've reached my destination." Her eyes sought a building entrance that she could escape into if they stopped, pretending it was her home, but they just laughed, "Next time we'll come and give you a ride," and careened off.

Taking a deep breath, she changed direction to head towards Helena's street, checking that they were not following her. She walked a few hundred yards further and, when she was sure she was alone on the little street, ducked into the stairwell of Helena's building. She started up the stairs just as Helena was coming down to greet her, and they met and embraced. Only after they went into Helena's apartment and closed the door after them did she begin to speak.

"Well, did you meet them? How are they?" Helena asked eagerly.

"Yes, I met them. Laurent was asleep but I spoke with Olivier. He's sweet. He knows we're coming to get him. They're pretty neglected, from what I can see; let's just say, they haven't been very well cared for. The clothes they're wearing are worn to rags, and Olivier had a constantly scared expression. But all in all, he looks okay. He smiled when he heard your name. It seems that he really remembers you."

"It hasn't been so long since I left the building where we all lived together."

"You're right, but the trauma those little ones have been through could have made them forget everything." "I know," Helena agreed sadly.

"I told him we'd be back later to take him and Laurent. He nodded to show that he understood and that he would wait for us. We only exchanged about three sentences, but I already feel connected to him. He told me that he promised his mother to always take care of his little brother. He also asked me if I know how his mother is doing and when she will be back... I told him what you told me to say, that she needed a vacation because she was very sick, that she will be back when she feels better, and meanwhile asked us to take care of them..."

"Excellent. I hope that even if he didn't believe you, he'll play the game with us. He's such a smart child. I don't know any children with that level of maturity... We'll wait three hours and then go back. In the meantime, let's see what's in their bags." They pulled a few worn-out items of clothes from Maria's bag.

"We'll go out a little early and get them some clothing that's suitable for my sister's children," Helena announced.

6

Helena and Maria went out that afternoon, stopping by a shopping center not far from the bakery. They went into a clothing store and tried to estimate what size clothes to get, Maria insisting that the sizes be just right. They bought two outfits for each child, in two different sizes for each, just to be sure that one would fit. Then they approached the bakery, keeping their distance until they had surveyed the territory. The street was full of the usual afternoon crowd, allowing them to blend in and cross the street towards the bakery without raising suspicion.

They went around to the rear entrance of the bakery and knocked softly on the door. It opened and they disappeared inside. Helena politely embraced Madame Dubois, who had opened the door; there was no love lost between the two, but they played the game.

"I'm so happy to see that you are growing and developing," Helena told her, referring to the expansion of the bakery premises that she had noticed outside. "I understand that the office workers have made you their home bakery," she observed pointedly, hinting at the fact that the bakery supplied the Gestapo headquarters not far away.

"Yes, we can't complain, business is good. I expect it is for you too," Madame Dubois shot back. "You have plenty of fans in those offices."

Helena knew that she needed to stop this game and avoid stirring up animosity in Madame Dubois, who could destroy her entire plan with a single word.

Weighing her words, Helena said slowly, "I am doing what I was doing before, dancing, and I am trying to survive in this insanity." She was careful not to speak negatively of the Germans. "I agreed to help you because I remember the lovely couple," referring to Annette and Marek. "Everything I am doing is for the children, who never hurt anybody; their parents have been taken, and now they are alone. They have nobody but each other," she observed, adding, "you have done wonderful work. You have done a good deed by taking the risk you did. I don't take it for granted." Helena observed that Madame Dubois accepted the compliment, catching a glimpse of humanity under the woman's cold demeanor. In fact, she had saved the children's lives.

"I assume you've already met my sister?"

"Yes, your beauty clearly stayed in your family." Madame Dubois softened a little. "Go ahead into the room, the children are waiting there." As they entered the room, Olivier ran up and jumped on Helena. Catching herself from falling, she dropped her bag and caught him in the air. Just like that, all her love for him came flooding back. She had fallen in love with him when he was still little, with his angelic smile; she remembered how he had called her "nana" when they would meet together with Marek. Tears rolled down her cheeks, and Olivier burst into sobs.

Madame Dubois ordered him to stop crying immediately. "He's never cried like that; I don't know what's come over him."

"It's okay, we don't know what's going on in this little head, how hard it is for him. Come, sweetie, everything's alright. I'm here and we've come to take you home, until your parents come back." Helena pulled him close. Her heart contracted, knowing that his father would never come back, and that there was very little chance of his mother ever coming back either, given all the horror stories she had heard of people disappearing, of expulsion and torture.

Laurent, clinging to Madame Dubois' leg, looked from one to another without saying a word. Maria crouched down and held out her arms to Laurent; with some hesitation he let go of Madame Dubois' leg and allowed Maria to pick him up. A moment later he was already clinging onto her, as though he sensed a warmth that he had not experienced for a long time. Maria hugged

Helena too and for a moment all four were locked in an embrace, tears running down their cheeks, as though such closeness was only natural.

Madame Dubois wiped a tear from her eye. "None of this is their fault," she said. "But how will you manage?"

"We'll do everything for the children's welfare. I think that my ties to your clients may finally guarantee us some peace…"

Madame Dubois surprised her by saying, "I can bring you anything you need from here."

"Thank you, I'll keep that in mind," Helena said, even though in her heart she did not trust anyone and made sure not to tell Madame Dubois anything more.

It was one of the most emotional days of the two Italian sisters' lives. A brew of powerful feelings flooded them: fear of the Germans, worry about the unexpected motherhood, excitement about the children, Helena's longings for Marek and both of them for their parents. They knew how they went into this adventure but did not know how it would develop and what hardships they might face along the way. They were following their hearts.

Monsieur Dubois came into the room and kissed Helena and Maria in the customary French manner. He caressed the children and asked, "so, is everything okay?"

"Yes," Helena answered, "everything is okay, and it will be even more okay." Despite the fears and the irrationality surrounding them, she felt good and was pumped up with adrenaline.

"We'll leave right away; I don't want to delay here. We have a full schedule and the children will be tired. It's better if we do everything while they're still awake." They shook hands, and Monsieur Dubois repeated what his wife had said, even though he hadn't heard her say it: "we'll bring you whatever you need from here."

Helena thanked him but remained strong in her determination not to reveal a single detail of the plan, including where she lived. "Thank you both. I will come by here, if necessary."

Helena and Maria set down Olivier and Laurent and dressed them in the new coats they had bought.

"We're going home now, Give Mari and me your hands," Helena said gently. "I want you to be quiet, the streets are sometimes dangerous, and I need to watch over you like I promised Maman."

Olivier nodded with a serious expression; Laurent looked at him and did the same, without comprehending.

The children looked again at Monsieur and Madame Dubois, then turned to go. Madame Dubois took two rapid steps towards them, bent down, and hugged them. Something had broken in her: these children were not her own, but nevertheless, they had softened her a bit. She also saw Helena now in a different light, almost as a hero, given what she had taken on herself.

Monsieur Dubois went first, peered outside, and then came back in. "The road looks clear."

Helena and Maria went outside. Monsieur and Madame Dubois watched as the two women went off into the distance with the children at their side. They looked at each other, flooded with great sorrow, but also with relief. They went back inside and closed the door after them.

Helena and Maria walked rapidly, with Laurent in Maria's arms and Olivier holding Helena's hand. When Helena saw that Maria was struggling to hold Laurent, they switched. Life in the street went on as normal, with no one expressing any particular interested in their story: an Italian cabaret dancer and her sister, war, German officers, French collaborators, and two Jewish children whose parents had disappeared.

They walked through the streets for a short time, thought it seemed to them an eternity. The children grew tired, but did not utter a word, just rubbed their eyes from exhaustion. As time passed, they both became heavier and heavier.

Finally, they arrived. Maria's legs were trembling. Helena, being more fit, showed less difficulty.

They entered the stairwell of the building and immediately closed the door behind them. At the sudden darkness of the hall, Laurent burst out crying. Helena quickly turned on the light in the hall and his cries eased, leaving just a tear sparkling on his cheek.

Helena smiled at him. "Don't be scared, my little baby, I'm here."

Olivier quickly responded, "but I'm your little baby!" He rushed to guard his place with Helena zealously.

Helena bent down and whispered in his ear, "You're a big baby, my love, and Laurent is a little baby who has to be watched over." Olivier had heard what he wanted to hear.

They climbed the stairs to the third floor, where Helena passed Laurent to Maria and opened the door.

7

The flight was tempestuous in more ways than one: unexpected anti-aircraft fire and a storm that tossed the plane about. Helmut kept his cool, despite the shaking of the aircraft and the explosions echoing around him. They descended down towards the Paris airport, after an absence of almost three weeks for meetings at Berlin headquarters.

Helmut had found time to visit his family in Berlin, and his wife had done her best to make his stay pleasant. The meetings at headquarters were long and exhausting, discussing the details of the "Final Solution" and its significance for the newly conquered territories. He was pleased to have had the chance to visit, but was even more pleased to be returning to Helena. The meetings indicated that the program of the Party and the Reich were progressing well and highlighted the strategic importance of France for the Reich's continued expansion to the British Isles and North Africa.

The plane landed and pulled up by the passenger terminal, which had been converted to serve the member of German command that flew the Berlin-Paris route frequently. A dark Wehrmacht Mercedes swiftly approached the door of the plane that had just come to a halt. Lieutenant Schultz peered out. Helmut came down the gangway and Schultz stretched out his arm in salute, *Heil Hitler*. Helmut smiled at him and patted him lightly on the shoulder. Another soldier brought out the suitcases and Helmut's briefcase.

Helmut stood by the car. "So, tell me what's new. I understand that some more cells planning terrorist attacks were discovered?"

"Yes sir, Herr Helmut, but the news is that we have more and more collaborators with us. We're in the process of eradicating all of the cells in the region of Paris and further north. Our work has not been easy, but in the end, everyone's started singing. The resistance here has been dismantled."

"I'm happy to hear it. Now to what I'm really interested in, what about Helena?"

"I saw her about a week ago in the cabaret. They put on a new show, and your friend was more impressive than ever. During your absence we made sure that she received whatever she asked for, as you instructed me. The agents trailing her informed me that she has been appearing frequently in the company of a woman with two small children. Our inquiry shows that this woman is her sister, and apparently those are her children."

Helmut was surprised by this new development but hid his reaction from Schultz. "Other than that, anything else about her?"

"No. I'm sure that she's waiting for you."

"Good. Let's go to headquarters to a scheduled meeting, and after that I'll go to her. Did you give her the message with the invitation to dinner?"

"Yes, sir. We notified her that you would pick her up at seven o'clock this evening."

"If so, then everything is in order. Let's go." Schultz signaled the driver, who opened the door for Helmut and stood at attention.

Helmut was one of the most admired commanders at Berlin headquarters. Among his successes, he was credited for establishing a spy network before the occupation, managing to destroy French resistance cells in Paris by planting secret agents even before the city was occupied. When the city was conquered, the agents netted all possible resistance cells, and from there it was a short step to getting rid of them.

Helmut's subordinates feared him. It was known that nothing would stop him from getting what he wanted, primarily in operations against enemies. But they also knew that it would be preferable to be Helmut's enemy than to make a mistake in carrying out his orders. Helmut respected his enemies, eventhough it did not prevent him from torturing them, but more than anything, he hated incomplete fulfillment of his commands.

His behavior tended to extremes: he was known for his generosity, as well as for his cruelty. It was difficult to predict his reactions. Helena knew this quality of his very well, and always tried to maintain a consistent line of behavior with him. Routine behavior ensured routine reactions as well. She knew that to refuse a request of his, without what he considered adequate justification, could end in reeducation, as he had once told her. Luckily for her, he was in love with her, but that was also her misfortune...

A few days after Helena and Maria had begun to settle into their new roles with the children's caretakers, Schultz came to notify Helena of Helmut's return date. Entering the building, he met Maria in the stairwell. Her beauty drew him, and he immediately introduced himself in order to engage her. Maria's heart skipped a beat, and she tried to smile a forced smile. When he explained that he was on his way to Miss Fotticelli, Maria seized the opportunity to publicize that she was Helena's sister, in the hope that the news would soon reach Helmut.

"The pleasure is all mine," she said in French with a slight Italian accent. "I am Miss Fotticelli's sister." Schultz acted surprised, even though he already heard about Helena's sister, who had come with her two children. If he had investigated thoroughly, he would have discovered that her children did not appear anywhere in the notes. But it made perfect sense to him that she would have arrived after leaving Italy with her children, considering that Italy was now suffering great shortages, and come to Paris to stay with her sister, who was making money and enjoying the Germans' patronage.

"I see that the beauty of Italian women is not just a fable. Have you come for a visit or will you be joining your sister?" Despite Schultz's pleasant tone, Maria felt that she was under cross-examination. She understood immediately that she had to think quickly and produce convincing answers without showing any hesitation. Those were Helena's precise instructions: "Give quick answers, but ones you've thought about a lot." Helena explained how she would play out conversations in her head with Helmut and his companions, such that she was ready for almost any question that could come at her. Helena told her that a delay in answering indicated thinking, and that thinking before answering a simple informational question cast doubt over the answer, making it seem that one had something to hide.

It would be a lie to say that I came for a visit, Maria thought, and hurriedly answered, "I came because things are so difficult in our village, and bringing up my children there is even more difficult. Helena forced me to come," she finished, smiling. Apparently, that was the answer he expected to hear.

"If so, I suppose she told you about us. Her new friends."

"Of course, that's one of the reasons she begged me to come here," she answered, inwardly horrified at herself.

"Good. I'll go up to your sister to give her a message. I'm sure that we will meet again soon under pleasant circumstances," he smiled and bowed, before continuing on up the stairs. She did not take her eyes off him.

Inside, she took a deep breath. She felt that she was entering the role of a mother. The children, in the few days they had already spent with her, flooded her with deep feelings, like those she felt when she left her parents and fled. She was becoming more and more attached to them.

Schultz knocked on the door and Helena opened the peephole. She was in the process of getting ready to go out to rehearsal.

Schultz could not help gaping at her body, which she tried to hide behind the door.

"How are you, Helena?" he asked in a supercilious tone.

"I'm fine. To what do I owe the honor?" she responded with cold cynicism.

He tightened the noose a notch, answering, "I came to see you."

"Well, that's unfortunate, I'm heading out. Besides, Helmut insisted that I not get friendly with anyone in his absence, and that includes you." She always mocked him, knowing that he was Helmut's watchdog and informer. At moments when Helmut seemed to be sympathetically inclined towards her, she would always try to stick in some disapproving word about Schultz. She did not want him around her and now, having taken custody of the children, she was more afraid of him than ever.

"I have a message from Helmut," said Schultz, cutting the power grapple between them short. "He'll be here a week from Wednesday and has already reserved a place for you at the Maison d'Or." This was one of the most luxurious restaurants in Paris. Helmut, an amateur wine and food connoisseur, considered himself like a member of the family there. He had endeared himself to the restaurant owners who cooperated with him, mainly in order to keep the restaurant intact. The rapid connection with Helmut proved to be sagacious; the restaurant was full every night, even during Paris's lowest moments, at the start of the occupation. All the who's-who of the Nazi and collaborationist leadership were among its regular patrons.

"Helmut asked me to make sure that you were notified of the date, and that you will be ready at seven o'clock in the evening, when he comes to pick you up." He smiled as though what he had meant was, *get ready to serve him.*"

"Thank you, Schultz, for your faithfulness and for being such a devoted postman."

Schultz could no longer hold in the humiliation and rage that flooded him. He shoved open the door, striking Helena in the head, and seized her by the throat. As she was gurgling and struggling to breath, he said quietly, "watch out for me. I may do Helmut's bidding, but I would have no problem making you disappear or framing you, you and your sister who fled from Italy. If I do so, you'll beg for help, but even Helmut will not be able to help you!" With his free hand he grabbed her robe and undressed her, then forced her around and pressed against her from the back, all the while continuing to choke her, leaving her only a tiny opening to breathe.

"Your body is beautiful," he said as he grabbed her breasts with his free hand, "but it won't help you." He shoved her and she fell on the floor, her face stark white. She quickly regained her composure, and resumed playing a role, knowing that what he wanted was to control her. She was in fact terrified, so there no need to play-act. But she had a plan.

She picked herself up off the floor and begged him, "Schultz, I beg of you, I'll do whatever you want, I won't tell Helmut anything, just don't hurt us…"

"I'll think about it," he stood in front of her and snickered. "I'll think about what else you'll need to do for me. In the meantime, go back to your life. But just remember— you won't get a second chance, you'll simply disappear. Think carefully before you utter a sentence when I'm around, and even when I'm not around, because everything reaches me."

"I promise to obey you. I ask your forgiveness … I beg of you, don't hurt us."

He strode out of her apartment and slammed the door behind him.

"Wednesday at seven, don't forget!" she heard him shout outside the door.

Helena finished dressing and hurried down to her sister's apartment. Maria opened the door and Helena burst inside, burning with rage.

"What happened? I just wanted to let you know that I met that German soldier, Schultz, in the stairwell before. He was very polite, and even made a point of saying that we would surely meet again soon..." she suddenly noticed the bruise on Helena's forehead.

"That's it, exactly— a wolf in sheep's clothing," Helena swiftly responded. "You must watch out for him, Mari. He's venomous. I have to make Helmut do something about him. I want Helmut to get him away from us. He's dangerous. He threatened me, and talked about you and the children too." Helena was incandescent with fury. "I'm still trying to figure out how to get rid of him, but in the meantime, we have to take into account that he is capable of doing whatever he

wants to us ... Are the children okay?"

"Yes, they're sleeping."

"Good. Try to be careful if you bump into him again. He's always trying to glean information and get the broadest picture possible. He's always trying to be one step ahead. Helmut relies on him, but is also wary of him. He once told to me that he sometimes feels like kicking him out. So, you understand? We have to make him to do that." Helena gave Maria a kiss and hurried off to rehearsal.

8

Wednesday arrived quickly. In the mirror, Helena saw that the mark on her forehead from her meeting with Schultz had all but disappeared. She went up to the door, pressed her forehead against the doorframe and butted it lightly. The bruise that had almost disappeared became visible again. She was careful not to give herself too bad a bruise, so it would not bleed or leave a scar, but she wanted Helmut to notice it.

At 6:45p.m there was a knock on the door. Helena, dressed to go out, opened the door slightly, and Helmut came in.

Helena behaved as though she were acting on a stage. She turned her gaze slightly to the side as though she were trying to keep Helmut from seeing the bruise. Helmut smiled at her. He was addicted to her: her body, her laugh, her humor and wit, her dance moves. He came closer to her. She moved towards him, again, as though trying to hide the bruise on her forehead, but then he noticed it.

"What happened to you?" he grabbed her head and turned her face to him.

"I'm sorry, it's nothing, I-I had an incident with your assistant…"

"Schultz? What happened?" his tone changed instantly as he grabbed her arm forcefully.

"I-I'm sorry, it was my fault. A few days ago, I heard a knock at the door; I was here in my robe, so I just opened the peephole. Schultz managed to see me in my robe through the peephole and broke in, trying to…"

"Trying to what?!" Helmut asked impatiently.

"He tried to touch me, and I was struck by the door when he burst in. He tried to touch me…" She repeated her words and then began to sob. Helmut held her arm even more tightly, to the point that a bruise began to form. "You're hurting me, Helmut."

He let go and hugged her. "Did he do anything to you?"

"No, I begged him to have mercy on me and to think twice before he did something that he would regret. He laughed while still standing over me and then ran his hands over my body… I can still feel his disgusting hands on me… I wanted you to come back so much! I felt so powerless… And then he told me that you were coming on Wednesday and that I should be ready on time. And I have been scared ever since."

Helmut hugged her again and she snuggled up to him.

"I'm here, nothing will happen to you."

"I don't want to cause a fight between you… I don't want to hurt your work, but I'm scared of him…"

"Don't worry about such things, that's not your business. Everything will be okay. I'm here now," he kissed her lips. She gathered her strength and returned his kiss passionately. He could not control his urges; he had waited so long for this moment. He embraced her, grabbed her forcefully, and took her. Her body was silent as she disconnected from herself and let him have his way with her. Again, she was there but not there. It was part of the script; she had no choice.

They then showered and went out to the restaurant.

It was a festive dinner, attended by many of the senior German army command. Schultz was there too. Helmut opened by saying that Germany was flourishing, all thanks to their great leader and their impressive operations in every country they advanced to, annihilating the feeble regimes and opposition.

"The peoples under our rule understand the greatness and the advantages of a strong Germany, which is for their good as well. According to the plan, we are going to continue to change the face of the world. Europe is almost entirely under German rule. Every place we arrive in, we bring growth. But let us not forget, anyone who is not with us and tries to resist will taste the power of the Wehrmacht." The officers and French collaborationists rose to their feet and applauded.

After the speech, the meal began, with a quartet of French musicians playing in the background. The Frenchmen and their wives at the table were easily distinguishable from the German officers and their escorts. This evening, Helena was there in the role of escort.

Schultz sent her a piercing glance, and she froze. Helmut noticed Schultz's glance and that was enough for him. He believed Helena.

Schultz once said to Helmut that there were lots of women in Paris like Helena and tried to convince him to break off the relationship with her: "They're not Germans and they bring only trouble. Use her, but nothing more."

In response, Helmut made it clear to Schultz that it was the last time he should ever give advice about his commander's personal life, unless he wanted to leave this city and go back to fighting on the front lines, in Africa perhaps.

Schultz tried to defend himself; he said that he didn't mean to pry into Helmut's private life, and that he only said what he said out of fear that Helmut would get hurt and perhaps even endanger his career. A relationship of that kind, and of that power, was likely to be poisonous.

Helmut just stared on him with his cold, penetrating gaze, and Schultz backed off. Schultz was one of Helmut's most loyal assistants, having served under him ever since finishing his officers' training.

Schultz had friends in senior positions in the German army headquarters. Most of his colleagues from intelligence officers' training course had made their way up into key positions in army leadership, and the information they had at their disposal made them centers of power. They even made sure to preserve this power by creating work and nurturing friendly relations. It was this network that gave Schultz the power and confidence to behave and speak as he had. Helmut learned about this network from Schultz himself, and he knew he had to watch out for them so long as he fostered a career in the Reich. Although he valued Schultz's loyalty, Helmut was wary of him and his connections.

The evening wore on, ending only at one in the morning. Helmut gave Helena a ride back to her house. He didn't go in, just saying, "I'll pay you a visit in the next few days."

Helena inwardly rejoiced, but acted disappointed. "When should I expect you? Will you come to the new show?"

Helmut, with a smile that worried Helena, answered, "don't worry, I'll surprise you. I want you just like you were earlier this evening."

His driver opened the car door for Helena, then opened the door of the building for her before returning to the car. Helena hoped that the process she had started would lead to Schultz's banishment from Helmut's presence. She sighed and went up to her apartment.

9

The children adjusted quickly to their new reality, and Maria grew more attached to them with every passing day. She had braved the flight from Italy, but she had never imagined that she would become a mother so soon after arriving in Paris. At the same time, she was afraid of what the future held in store.

The day arrived for the premiere of the new show at the cabaret. Maria helped Helena get ready while the two boys played in the living room. Olivier could not take his eyes off Helena, as it had been since the days when his father would bring him home posters from the cabaret.

Suddenly, he remembered his father. He rose to his feet and asked, "where is Papa? Why doesn't he come already? And where is Maman? You said you talked to her and she asked for your help, maybe she needs us now to help her?"

Helena and Maria were startled. It was the first time that Olivier spoke with such determination of his desire to see his parents.

Annette was still in the same institution, thin as a skeleton, pallid, sitting and staring out the window. Most of her time was spent under tranquillizers. When she would come back to herself a little, she would burst into tears, mumbling Marek's name. Because of the deep depression she was in, and because of the fear that someone might wonder who Marek was, the staff was careful, under Dr. Gerard Gaston's orders, to continue giving her the high doses of tranquilizers that he had prescribed when she was first hospitalized.

Gerard truly feared for her life. He tried to protect her from being asked too many questions, fearing they might lead to the revelation that she was

Jewish, something that would drag her to the terrible places that he had heard stories about. He also knew that if such a thing happened, he was also likely to suffer at the hands of the Nazis.

Maria and Helena gave the children all the love and security that they could. The two women made sure to repeat at every opportunity that this was the boys' home, that they were there for them, and that they would never leave them. Two small children, who had lost their parents less than two years prior, had been turned over to a strange family who merely served them as a poorhouse, who exploited their labor, and were now moved again, this time to Helena and Maria.

"Sweetie," said Helena to Olivier, "I can't tell you exactly when, but you will be back with Maman at some point." She knew that she could not really promise such a thing, but she tried to sound as believable as possible. "Do you know that there are problems in Paris now…"

"Yes," Olivier answered before she had time to finish the question. "I know that the people in uniforms who came from Germany are bad people, and they've taken lots of French people to bad places. I even heard Monsieur Dubois saying that to his wife. And once, when we were in the store and I was helping Madame Dubois arrange the loaves of bread in the morning, a few soldiers like that came in. They took loaves of bread and didn't want to give Madame Dubois the money. There was one man there, the most evil of all the soldiers, who came up to Madame Dubois and pinched her face until she screamed in pain. We were really scared. I took Laurent, and we hid in the storeroom."

"That's right, sweetie. You're smart, you know everything." Helena stroked his hair. "Those same soldiers took Maman and Papa too." She gathered her courage and went on, "But Maman managed to pass me a message, so I'm sure that she will come back the moment those people leave here. I promise you. You want to be here when Maman returns, right? Then you have to be careful and listen to Mari and me. Sometimes there will be people like that with us. You can't be with them and talk to them. If they try to talk to you, you're forbidden to say anything…" She stopped the flood of words, took a breath, and then asked him, "do you remember what you are to say if they ask you who we are?"

Olivier smiled as though it brought him pleasure, "that you're my aunt and Mari is my mother." He really did love Helena like a mother, and though Maria had only entered his life recently, he was very attached to her too.

"Right, sweetie, so always be careful to call Mari *Maman* and me *Auntie*."

Olivier's brow furrowed. "Why can't I call you *Maman* and Mari *Auntie*?" as though it was a game whose rules could be changed. Helena hugged him. "Honey, when no one is around, you can call me Maman. I love you so much, my sweetie pie, but you can't call me Maman around other people. Do you know why?"

"Why?"

"Because people here know me and know that I don't have any children. And how would I suddenly tell them that I have two such sweet children? Do you understand, muffin?" Helena asked, picking him up and hugging him.

"Yes, Maman."

She laughed. "You're so smart!"

She set Olivier down and said, "run along now, go back to your brother. I have to get ready to go out."

Helena was putting the last touches on her make-up before leaving for the nightclub when she suddenly heard knocking at the door.

She and Maria exchanged surprised looks.

Maria went to the door and asked, "Who's there?"

"Herr Helmut!" A steely voice could be heard from outside the door.

Maria looked at Helena, who nodded, and then Maria opened the door.

Helmut's driver peered in, straightened up, and left. Helmut came in as soon as the driver left. He stood in the entrance, studying Maria, then stretched, cleared his throat, and introduced himself.

"Colonel Helmut Schmidt, and you must be …" he paused politely. "Maria. I'm Maria."

"Helena's sister, of course. I could not have imagined you'd be so lovely. . Welcome to Paris."

"Helmut, darling," Helena broke in, "I was just about to leave for the show… What a lovely surprise! You'll have to take me quickly to the cabaret, otherwise I'll be late, and if I remember correctly, you hate it when the show starts late…"

He came up to Helena, put an arm around her waist, and kissed her.

Olivier approached and stood between him and Helena, as though trying to protect her. Helmut patted Olivier's cheek in a friendly way. Maria immediately came to Olivier's rescue, trying to avoid giving him the opportunity to say anything or react in a suspicious way.

"Come, sweetie," she called him. "I was just about to put them to bed," she explained to Helmut with a smile. Olivier tried to resist slightly, but Maria was firm, and he gave in. Maria hugged him, picked up Laurent, and reached out to hold onto Olivier tightly.

"Nice meeting you. I hope you enjoy the show," Maria said.

Helmut stretched again. "It was a pleasure to meet you. I'm sure we'll find other opportunities to meet. I'll make sure you have an arrangement for the children so that you can join us some time in the future. It would be a shame to have a blossom like you hidden away in some inner sanctum," he smiled at her. "And if you need anything, just let your sister know, and I'll be happy to help."

Helmut waited until Maria had closed the door after her and then embraced Helena forcefully. Helena sighed and pulled away from him. "If we start, I won't be able to control myself, and then the show won't go on. I promise to make it up to you afterwards."

Helmut gave her a chilly smile and linked his arm through hers. They left the apartment together and went down the stairs.

"She's impressive, your sister. Exotic, with a beauty the likes of which I haven't seen in a long time. I suppose your parents must be very good-looking people," he said, smiling. "How did she get here? Why did she leave your parents?"

"I persuaded her to come. The situation in Italy is much worse than it is here. Maria had children outside of marriage, and Italy is not the place to bring up such children. Her boyfriend disappeared; she was told the militia recruited him and that he was sent to the front. We haven't heard from him since. A woman of her age, with two little children, unmarried and with no one to take her under their wing... It's hard to live like that in our village. It was easy for me to persuade her to come."

"You did the right thing by persuading her. There's no doubt we can help her here." Helena noticed how Helmut had already taken ownership of Maria. She held her tongue, lest a comment be misinterpreted and lead to more suspicion and investigations from him. She just smiled instead, feigning gratitude for his desire to fulfil her sister's needs as well her own.

Helmut's driver opened the car door for them, and the two climbed in. The car moved through the streets of Paris towards the nightclub, the cabaret.

A long line of official cars of German officers and French government officials stretched by the nightclub. The dignitaries were slowly getting out of their cars; the crème de la crème of the leadership was in attendance. Helmut's car cut to the head of the line and pulled up precisely in front of the entrance to the nightclub. The driver jumped out and opened the door for Helena and Helmut, who got out and stood next to her. The line of people waiting at the entrance made way for Helmut and his escort. She kissed his cheek and disappeared into a side entrance meant for nightclub staff only.

Schultz was waiting for Helmut at the entrance. He stamped his foot and led Helmut to his table. Helmut responded to him coldly.

Before he sat down, Schultz addressed him, "Herr Helmut, I trust everything is in order?"

Helmut looked at him with cold eyes. "Of course. Everything is fine with me; I am in my favorite place. And what about you, Schultz? Is there anything you want to tell me?"

Helmut's response told Schultz that something had happened, but there was no time to go into it at that moment. Helmut took his seat, and Schultz sat down not far from him, at the Gestapo commanders' table.

The lights dimmed and the show began. The dancers took the stage to the sound of the audience's enthusiastic applause.

It was a particularly colorful show. It centered around an African tribal queen and her battle against white hunters, one of whom fell prisoner to her spells. It incorporated exciting attractions, such as two terrifying tigers who stood on the stage with their trainers during some scenes of the show, and rope bridges on which topless dancers climbed, dressed only in lace panties. The queen of the show was Helena, of course, who played the African tribal queen.

Helmut felt proud. *That queen belongs to me*, he chuckled to himself, *so that makes me king.* She was like an ornament of which he could be proud, and he ruled her absolutely. At least, he felt that he did.

The show lasted more than two hours. When it finished, Helmut stood up and all his subordinates rose to their feet to show him respect. He bowed to them courteously and moved away, not before leaving them with his impression: "Amazing dancers. We should recruit them as career soldiers." A cynical smile spread over his face, and the commanders around the table laughed loudly.

Helmut left the table and headed backstage. The dancers were getting dressed, some naked and others still in their costumes. As he passed among them, they tried to hide their bodies while bowing politely before him. He smiled at them, saying, "hey, don't hide all this beauty from me. The show was amazing, good job!"

He reached Helena's room, knocked lightly on the door, and entered without waiting for an answer. Helena was naked, about to put on her clothes in order to leave the nightclub.

Helmut came up to her. "You were wonderful." Helena felt uncomfortable at the thought that someone might come in and see her naked with Helmut, so she went over to close the door. From his pocket, Helmut withdrew a small jewelry box and handed it to her. Helena reached out, opened it carefully, and pretended to be excited and emotional about the gift: a delicate gold chain with a pearl. Like the whole recent period, her life had become one great act. She knew well that in order to survive this dark period and meet her obligations, she had to continue acting. She turned to him and gestured him to put the necklace on her. He fastened the clasp and kissed her neck. She lifted her hand to stop him. "Someone is going to come in…" she said, attempting to avoid what was coming.

"Don't worry, my driver is guarding the door. No one will come in." Grasping the situation, she continued the show as usual. Her body was extinguished from the inside; her soul was somewhere else. She told him what he loved to hear and always made him feel good: "I'm just melt when you touch me." After all, she was an actress. That had always been her dream; she just never imagined that the role she would have to play would be so fateful, so different from what she had fantasized…

10

In 1942, the resistance operations of the French underground increased steadily. Helmut was busy cracking the organization's infrastructure. He was trying to investigate their chain of command, where they were getting their arms, and what their next targets were. He set to work hundreds of collaborators and dozens of expert investigators from the Gestapo.

Those who "merited" his personal investigation did not survive. In most cases, if they possessed any useful intelligence, they were kept alive for a few days, until the information they gave had been corroborated. But at the first opportunity after the information had been revealed, they were executed. The "lucky ones" among them were executed by bullet, and the rest by torture.

Helmut was considered valuable by the German command and was widely admired for his achievements in cracking the fighting mechanisms of the underground, those French who never submitted to the Nazi occupation. He succeeded in handling local initiatives, as well as initiatives organized with the Allies' support.

Helena, for her part, heard a little about Helmut's iniquities in his job, but tried as much as possible to avoid any in-depth familiarity with his dealings. She was afraid that if she found out about Helmut's deeds, she would no longer be able to pretend in her relationship with him. All that she wanted was to manage to bring up Olivier and Laurent and to protect her sister. This was her family now.

Helena and Maria continued leading their new lives, while all around them reigned tumult, pain, and evil. The task at hand was caring for the two small children who had been placed in their care. Maria became a full-time mother, while Helena took care of them whenever she was home, meanwhile maintaining the forced relationship with Helmut and giving herself over to him as part of her survival plan.

More than once, Helmut paid a surprise visit, and every time, Helena had to calm Olivier, who was ready to attack Helmut on her behalf. He sensed the evil and the injury to Helena and was too young to understand why she was going along with it. Sometimes, he became angry that she agreed to let Helmut visit; he saw Helmut as a competitor and feared that Helmut would end up taking Helena away from him.

Helena tried to look into possibilities of leaving— that is, to escape France beyond the area controlled by the Vichy regime, from where she could sneak Maria and the children to England, as Annette and Marek had planned.

But any hopes of such a plan passed quickly, after the southern region was also conquered by the Germans, so that all of France was now occupied. Helena knew that she had to continue the show, but she did not know how much longer she could keep it up.

Helmut called Schultz in for a consultation regarding the activities of the underground. Although relations between them had calmed down for the moment, it was clear to Helmut that at some point he would need to deal with the injury to Helena.

Schultz arrived at Helmut's office, entered with a salute, and greeted him. Then, as part of the friendly conversation that had developed between them, he asked after "the queen of striptease at the Folies Bergère."

Helmut lifted his head from the maps he was studying. "Who exactly do you mean?"

"Excuse me, Herr Helmut, I meant it as a compliment to Helena." Schultz knew exactly what he was doing. He knew things about Helena's sister, Maria. He had not forgotten his humiliation by Helena and had promised himself to hurt her even if it injured Helmut as well. He was sure of his connections. Recently, he had taken pains to obtain details about the past of both Maria and the two children, at first without great success, but then, through friends in Italy, attachés of the Reich, he had managed to obtain significant information about Helena's family.

It turned out that Maria, Helena's sister, had never been married. If so, how did her two children suddenly appear in Catholic Italy? He assumed that giving birth to children out of wedlock was unlikely in such a conservative region.

Schultz waited for the right moment to shake up Helmut's faith in Helena and Maria. That moment had arrived.

Helmut got up and stood in front of Schultz. He was threatening, taller and bulkier than him, and his face was cold.

"Schultz, you are so sure of yourself among your friends that you permit yourself to do things that others would be afraid to even think of. You say things that are intended to hurt me, hurt Helena. So, let's make one thing clear: whether Helena is the *queen of striptease* or not does not interest me; she is here only because she meets my needs. You, on the other hand, are forgetting your place in allowing yourself to speak to me like that."

"Herr Helmut, I am not trying to hurt you," Schultz reddened. "I said what I said out of respect for you, and perhaps also out of envy of your achievements with women in Paris. Helena does not interest me, I honor her only because she is under your patronage, otherwise she and her sister would have been in my investigation

chamber a long time ago."

"Schultz! I see that you are trying as hard as you can to arrange your own retirement. What investigation are you talking about?! I'm the one who decides who gets investigated here!"

"Herr Helmut, there is information you do not know about Maria, Helena's sister."

"And what is it? And I warn you, you better be sure of what you are about to say."

"Maria was never married!" Schultz thought he was detonating a bomb in Helmut's face.

Coolly, without a change in his expression, Helmut played the game. "How does she have children then? Remember, she comes from Italy; they wouldn't let such a thing happen there." He knew that Maria was not married, for that was what Helena had told him; she also told him that Maria gave birth to the children out of wedlock, but the conversation with Schultz played into his hands. "This is indeed important information; I wonder what she is hiding. I will order an investigation into this issue, but under my direction. I hope you are sure of what you are saying."

"Herr Helmut, I am doing everything to defend you and the Reich. I am sure, there is something suspicious about her story and I want to get to the bottom of it. In the end, I wouldn't be surprised if it turns out that she resisted the militia and escaped in order to join their opponents in France."

"It could be, but I demand that you act solely on my instructions, and without arousing their suspicions."

"Would you like me to propose a plan?" Schultz asked.

"No, thank you. That's all for now."

"Then why did you summon me?"

"A minor matter, but it's not relevant anymore. The information you presented me with is much more interesting at the moment."

Helmut knew that Schultz would not let go until he had managed to obtain information that could hurt him, whether directly or indirectly. He decided to put an end to it this time.

"Come back to me later, around 3 p.m."

Helmut had information concerning a meeting of underground leaders in a certain quarter in Paris, in preparation for a major attack. He had originally summoned Schultz in order to consult with him about that, but now, full of anger and hatred, he just wanted to use the information to bring about Schultz's dismissal.

Helmut summoned Lieutenant Fritz, his special assistant, one of the S.S. officers responsible for field operations. He asked him to be present, together with his team, at the intended meeting place and strike at the two conspirators who were known to them, as well as anyone else present at that spot— but without killing them, so that they could be investigated.

Lieutenant Fritz was an enthusiastic officer, decorated by the Reich for operations under his command. He commanded an extermination team and an investigation team, both highly skilled. He studied the classified information, organized his extermination team; they took their places the day before, in the dead of night, camouflaged in key positions. The operation was planned for the meeting time the following evening.

At 3 p.m. that same day, Schultz reported back to Helmut's office. Helmut gave him the information about the meeting. He instructed him to postpone dealing with Maria for another day, and to show up the following day in undercover clothing at the meeting place near the Opera Café, in a store which was used by the underground and was under surveillance. Schultz was surprised by the request but saw it as a sign of Helmut's trust in him.

The following afternoon, Schultz arrived at the meeting place.

The officer Fritz identified Schultz through the scope of his rifle, and it immediately occurred to him that he was a traitor. Schultz sat in the café in civilian clothing. A number of figures arrived there, and two of them went out through the back entrance of the café and took up places opposite the exit door.

The extermination team was located in a position that enabled them to see the figures clearly. Schultz was the third figure to leave, following Helmut's instructions exactly.

What no one knew was that Helmut, disguised as a Frenchman, had passed information to the underground that a high-ranking German officer would try to catch the leaders by himself in a secret operation, in order not to arouse their suspicions.

The people in the café were underground members who were verifying the information, found it trustworthy, and made arrangements ahead of time to catch the officer. As soon as Schultz left in the direction of the store, the underground members burst out. Fritz's team shot at two underground fighters who were already outside, wounding them severely; those two were of a higher rank than the rest of the underground members. Fritz did not manage to kill the rest of the underground members, who shot Schultz to death and fled, exactly as Helmut had planned.

The problem created for Helmut was the wounded underground leaders. What would happen if they gave the information that they had received word of a German officer at the café? He prepared ahead of time for this possibility; he knew how to handle them, that was his specialty. That same evening, after the underground members had been taken care of, Helmut asked them to be brought in for investigation, without taking their condition into consideration. The two were brought bandaged and bleeding to the interrogation chambers of the notorious Fort Romainville.

Helmut asked to be present from the very beginning of the interrogation. His subordinates understood this to stem from his admiration for Schultz, who was his second in command. The interrogation began. Holding their heads down in a bucket of water and administering electric shocks did not suffice to make them reveal any information. And then, without warning, Helmut pulled out his pistol and shot one of them to death.

"Do you want to end up like your friend?! I'll offer you a deal: talk, and I promise you won't end up like that."

The Frenchman began to talk. "W-We were trying to wipe out a Nazi pig…" Helmut, coolly, pulled out his pistol again, pressed it to the Frenchman's head and fired three shots.

"They weren't talking anyway. I'm just sorry about one thing, that they did not suffer more. That's Schultz's revenge. Clean up this interrogation room and dump their bodies next to the store where Schultz was killed. After that, burn the store!"

"Yes, sir!"

Helmut left in great agitation. He had executed the plan to perfection, exactly as he had wanted, satisfied that Schultz had gotten what was coming to him. That same evening, he released both his rage and his victory in a tempestuous night with Helena.

Though Helena did not know it, she had been the one to set the ball rolling. Over the course of the night, Helena learned that Schultz had been killed by the underground, but Helmut did not share the details of his secret plan with her.

Towards morning, when he got up and got dressed, Helmut asked, "what was Maria's boyfriend's name?"

Helena knew that Helmut's questions were meant to gather information, part of an investigation.

"Giorgio," she answered without missing a beat. That was in fact his name. "Maria ran away from him. He became violent when he joined the militia and threatened her and our family when she rejected him," she remembered. The village in Italy where Helena's family lived was a picturesque place in Tuscany, with a heritage of wine, agriculture, and Catholic tradition. Everyone there knew everyone else. For a moment, Helena lost herself in memories of the village. But she returned right away to reality.

"Why are you asking?" she turned to Helmut.

Helmut understood that his question had made Helena uncomfortable. She never dared to ask him the meaning of his questions or decisions. She was always submissive to him. He turned on her a penetrating gaze.

"I'm always thinking one step ahead," he answered, knowing that his response would make Helena even more uncomfortable. She instantly understood that she could not let herself be pulled into a battle of questions, and she changed her approach.

"If you find him, it will be a big achievement for Maria. I hope that what you said about taking care of her will in fact come about." Helmut came to the conclusion that his instincts had misled him— she was not hiding information; she was genuinely concerned for her sister.

Helena was an excellent actress. Inside, fear bubbled up that perhaps there was something she wasn't aware of, that Helmut was preparing a surprise for her, an unwanted surprise.

Helmut left the apartment and went back to headquarters, where he summoned Fritz.

"I want you to do some information gathering among the militias in Italy. Activate your network in the Tuscany region. I want you to find out if there is a militia member named Giorgio, from the village next to *Arezzo*.

This was an unusual demand. Everyone knew that Helmut had thrown himself body and soul into breaking the French resistance, chalking up his recent obsession with eradicating the French underground, among other things, to Shultz's murder.

Fritz addressed his commander, saying that this could be problematic in light of the situation in Italy, the militias' instability in facing the underground and anti-Mussolini operations. It was the beginning of the insurrection in Italy against the tyrant's rule.

"Are you saying that this is a problem or are you saying that you will deal with it?"

The question left Fritz with no doubt: he could not challenge Helmut's request.

"I will do my best; I promise to get results." Without asking any questions, he left the room.

Fritz summoned one of his soldiers and furnished him with the initial information. He instructed him to try and reach the commander responsible for the region. If he managed to speak with him by telephone, all the better. If not, he would need to go to the region in person and carry out a preliminary investigation to obtain the requisite information.

11

Olivier was possessive of Helena, like a child who feels that his mother is his personal property. His questions became increasingly difficult. After all, he was growing up in a sad world. He would bombard Helena with questions: Why was she with Helmut? Why can't they continue to play the game without being in contact with him? When would they be able to escape? Since Helena could not provide him with answers, Olivier withdrew inside himself. Sometimes, he would hide in Maria's apartment in the dark.

Maria was a lifesaver for him. She was "clean", in the sense that she was not in contact with the bad people in uniform. Maria was the image that Olivier dreamed Helena would be. And yet, his love was for Helena. Deep inside, Olivier understood the situation but, despite already being almost seven years old, he was having a hard time coming to terms with it.

Laurent's behavior was problematic; he ran out of the house to the street several times, with Maria and Olivier running to find him, until they figured out that he would hide in the trash room. He did not really want to run away, just to release some built-up frustration. Olivier would soothe him, try to explain things to him, and sometimes was tough with him when he was naughty. At times, when Olivier was angry at him, Laurent would break down out of fear that the figure who was closest to him would leave him.

Maria tried to prepare them for the day in which something would happen that was out of their control. She taught them how to behave when there were people in the house, what was forbidden and permitted in the street, told them the "story of her life" so they would know what to say, told them about her and Helena's parents, their "grandma" and "grandpa," described where they lived in Tuscany. She prepared them well; after all, they were living among S.S. officers, and they had to be ready for their veiled interrogation.

In late 1942, the tide of the war began to turn. The German army's battles became increasingly difficult, both in Africa, where the Allies had landed and taken over the German territories, and in the east, on the Russian front. Meanwhile, as the German campaign was losing momentum, restrictions on Jews and rumors of atrocities only increased. The shift in German fortunes, even if Germany still maintained the upper hand, spurred the French underground to escalate its actions against the Vichy regime and the Nazis in Paris and throughout France. In the circles Helena moved in, she heard the rumors about the Jews which brought her great suffering. The man who ruled her and her life was, among other things, responsible for all those same actions against the Jews.

Helmut, for his part, felt pressure and dissatisfaction coming from the senior command in Berlin. Damage to their infrastructure was steadily increasing, German officers were being wounded or killed, French collaborators were being executed by the French underground, and the German army's control of the region was slipping.

Helmut's special teams were on the warpath, murdering anyone suspected of resistance or caught during an operation against the regime.

An order was given at the end of 1942 to occupy all of France, including those territories under the Vichy regime's full control, spurred by the Allies' advance and their conquering of territories in North Africa. The Germans took control of the "French State" in several lightning operations, which met with no resistance. After the takeover, however, resistance to the Germans accelerated. With the assistance of England and the other Allies, the underground urged the French population living under the occupation to begin to rebel. At first, the operations were extremely amateur; but with time, they picked up in both quantity and quality. Allied fighters joined up with the French resistance to support it.

Helmut was recruited to the *Abwehr*, the Nazi military intelligence organization, because of his special interrogation skills. He was summoned to various regions, mostly in southern France, to lead interrogations of underground members with the goal of obtaining information regarding the Allies' plans. His absence from the capital gave Helena and Maria a little peace.

Helmut and his team were in southern France, assisting in a special operation in which more than a hundred resistance fighters were captured. They conducted interrogations for several days, and then arranged a mass execution of all those from whom they had extracted information. Helmut became a well-oiled, merciless killing machine. The military turning of the tide had affected him, and the frustration brought out a wickedness in him whose intensity surprised even his own soldiers. They tried to please Helmut by supplying him with new and relevant information, information that they had managed to obtain by improving their methods of torture and murder beyond what Helmut had taught them.

The interrogations took place at the temporary headquarters that Helmut had set up on the French-Italian border. Helmut, Fritz, and the rest of the interrogators were interrogating members of the French underground, together with several British agents and Italian fighters who had collaborated with them. After learning that several of the Italian fighters were from the region of Tuscany, Helmut decided to interrogate them, given his doubts regarding Helena.

Fritz knocked lightly on the door of Helmut's office in the villa that had been converted into the Gestapo headquarters. "They're ready, we've brought the four of them to the basement." "I'm coming down," Helmut answered.

He stretched, picked up his pistol lying on the desk, and made his way down to the basement. Before him stood the four Italians that had been captured in Provence, naked, tied up with their hands raised towards the ceiling.

Helmut entered the room and began asking them questions in garbled French. They tried to ignore his questions as though they did not understand French.

"I know you were in the French underground," he went on, and mentioned the name of the Frenchman who had turned them in. "He told me that you spoke among yourselves in French. So, I will ask again. Where are you from in Italy and how were you recruited?" They did not answer.

Helmut approached the youngest among them, who looked more scared than the rest; he pulled out his leather stick and stuck it up the youth's nostril. The terrified youth began screaming and going wild, and his foot struck Helmut's body. Helmut stepped back and directed an icy gaze at the two guards there, who understood that they had erred in not holding the prisoner tightly enough. They immediately stood at attention, apologized to Helmut, and began beating the Italian youth.

Helmut approached him again; this time, the guards held him firmly. He grabbed the youth's head, yanked it back, and shoved the stick into his nostril again.

The youth tried to struggle but the guards, not taking any chances, held him firmly, afraid that Helmut would get hit again.

"Gentlemen," Helmut addressed the prisoners, "you can end the matter quickly or go through a hell that you have never imagined.

What will it be?" They did not answer.

Again, he shoved the stick into the youth's nostril, who suddenly began to bleed from his nose and passed out.

Helmut removed the stick, bent the youth's head back and pressed on his nose to stop the bleeding.

"You see, the blood is now starting to fill the nasal cavities. I can go easy on him, or I can keep going until his whole head is flooded with blood from the inside. Do you want to explain to me how you got here and what were your assignments?" He released his hand from the youth's nose; he came up to one of the older prisoners and wiped the bloody stick across his face.

"You look like a responsible person. You must be their commander, responsible for bringing them home safely. Don't you want to assume your responsibility and end this story well?" He pulled out a small penknife from his pocket and began drawing a swastika on the older man's face with little bloody scratches, but without causing him to bleed excessively. The man's screams got louder and louder.

Meanwhile, the youth regained consciousness. Helmut went back to him, pulled his hair, tipped his head back, and shoved the stick into his nostril again, producing another outpouring of blood. Again, Helmut pressed on his nose and sealed it. The youth had no strength left.

Helmut took a seat on a chair, turned to Fritz with an evil smile and said, "let's see how you extract this information."

Fritz stamped his foot and approached an older man in the back, a cudgel in his hand. He instructed the guards to release the prisoner from his binding and lay him down with only his upper body on the table and his hands tied under the table.

They grabbed him and placed him in this position on the table.

Fritz approached him. He knew enough Italian for the interrogations he was doing.

"Are you ready for a pleasure trip, or are you ready to talk? When I finish with you, you will beg for death!" He waved the cudgel and then shoved it into the man's buttocks. The screams were so loud that even Helmut was surprised.

"It sounds like a slaughterhouse of pigs," said Helmut. "And indeed, that's what you are, pigs."

"W-We're from Tuscany..." wailed the older prisoner. "We know that," said Helmut. "Who recruited you?" Silence.

Fritz grabbed the cudgel and increased the pressure.

"A-Alfonso..."

"What was your assignment?"

"We were supposed to join the French at the border..."

"And do what?"

Again silence. The older man writhed in pain, until Fritz kicked his knee and he stopped moving.

"We were supposed to attack strategic points in the Lyons region..."

"How many were with you?"

"I don't know..." he sobbed bitterly.

Fritz pulled out a knife and stabbed him in the muscle of his knee; he writhed in pain as much as he could, being tied up, and screamed.

"How many were you?!"

"I'm not sure, we were supposed to be a few dozen fighters." Suddenly, Helmut asked, "do you know Giorgio from the Arezzo region?"

The older man, slightly taken aback by the question, asked in response, "which Giorgio? We have a lot of them ..." he mumbled.

"From the Arezzo region, a militia member," Helmut's response was accompanied by a sharp kick to the man's knee, which had also begun to bleed.

"T-The militia commander, he was named Giorgio, h-he's dead."

"How did he die?" Silence.

Fritz jabbed the knife into the man's other leg. His screams filled the room.

"He died in battle. He ran into our fighters."

"Did you know his wife, Maria?"

"No, he had a girlfriend, but she disappeared."

"Did you know his children?"

"No, I didn't know he had children... All we did was find all the militia commanders in our district. Our goal, before we came here, was to kill them, those who weren't sent to fight. I don't know him or his family."

Helmut sensed that the information, while it meshed with what he already knew, was not the whole truth.

"Who was the contact person for the French?"

"I don't know him; he came to us. An English fellow. Told us he was from English intelligence and that his job was to create an internal front against you."

"What was your precise assignment?"

"I don't know. Our first goal was to liaise with the French." "What was the assignment?" Helmut asked again.

"I don't know! T-They don't share that kind of information with us, for fear of a leak..."

Fritz grabbed the man's right foot, held it tightly, and stuck the knife into the arch of his foot. Overwhelmed with pain, the man lost consciousness. Then Fritz moved on to the third man who was tied up and passed the knife over his abdomen, wiping off the blood that was on it.

"So, then. What was the assignment? Maybe you will remember?" the man did not answer. He was the commander of the ring, named Antonio, and he knew the assignments very well. He also knew Giorgio and the history of the family. He was the one who had helped Maria escape to France before they killed Giorgio.

"Well, since you already saw part of the pleasure that your friends earned, we'll start a new game with you." Fritz glanced at the guard, who left the room without saying a word. Silence fell. A few minutes later, the guard returned carrying a red-hot iron rod.

Fritz took the rod and said to the prisoner, "do you know the advantage of hot iron? It hurts but doesn't kill. And it also stops the bleeding, so it can be used every few minutes with different degrees of force. Do you think you're ready for this? Or do you have the information I want to hear?"

The prisoner did not answer. Fritz stood in front of him and signaled to the guards to hold him well. They grabbed him savagely. Fritz came close and pressed the burning iron against Antonio's cheek. He screamed in pain. The smell in the room changed from one of feces and urine to one of scorched flesh. The iron scorched Antonio's cheek as Fritz pulled the rod off and handed it to the guard.

"You understand, we have a fire that keeps the embers burning," he sniggered. "Perhaps now you recall the information?"

Meanwhile the guard went out and came back a few minutes later with the burning hot iron after it had been reheated in the coals.

Antonio remained silent. The scene was repeated with his other cheek as well, until he finally passed out. Fritz poured a bucket of water over him and he came to.

"Well, then? What do you say?" Antonio tried to mumble something.

"I can't hear you," Fritz replied, drawing closer. It seemed as though Antonio could not raise his voice any louder, so Fritz brought his ear close to Antonio's mouth to hear what he was saying. Suddenly, Antonio bit Fritz's ear and would not let go. The guards tried to beat him to release his grip on Fritz's ear; but he did not relent, and as the guards were trying to pull him off, Fritz lost his ear. Helmut pulled out his pistol and shot Antonio in the head. Fritz thrashed around the room in a frenzy, writhing with pain, with his ear hanging off. He was like a man possessed. Suddenly, he pulled out his pistol and started emptying bullets into the older man without cease, until Helmut overpowered him.

"Take him out of here to the clinic and bring in more guards!" shouted Helmut.

Two guards came in the room.

Helmut went up to the fourth fighter with a knife in his hand. "I want you to tell me everything, from the beginning, and don't leave anything out." The fourth fighter looked at Helmut and remained silent. Helmut inserted the knife a quarter inch into his abdomen and began to cut his flesh. Again, screams were heard, and blood began to drip from his body. After he made a deep cut along his abdomen, he pulled out the knife. "Talk!"

The man did not answer; all that was heard in the room was his rapid breathing.

Helmut cut another slit and then another in the man's abdomen, until he passed out from pain and loss of blood. The pool of blood continued to spread, and it seemed that the fourth fighter's fate was sealed; he could no longer be saved.

The young prisoner who still remained alive was Helmut's last hope of obtaining information on the underground, and also perhaps on Maria and Helena. He ordered the doctor to be summoned.

The Doctor was an expert at torture. He focused primarily on fingernails and teeth, and worked thoroughly on every subject, until there was no more information to be extracted. In the end he would leave his victims to bleed to death.

Helmut left the torture chamber. He performed a reassessment on the basis of the additional information that had been collected from the other underground members who had been arrested. When the picture had become clear, he ordered them all to be executed. His exertions had yielded over a hundred fighters who had provided a significant amount of information, shedding light on the intentions of the Allied forces in the region.

Helmut travelled to the Nazi headquarters in southern France, to present a detailed report on the intelligence picture that he had managed to compile.

The intelligence appraisal was that during the coming year, or in early 1944 at the latest, the Allies were planning a massive landing in England. The findings presented by Helmut strengthened the German army's readiness, regarding both its deployment in the field and the fortification lines that it needed to set up. Having completed his job in the region for the time being, Helmut was summoned back to Paris.

On the eastern front, a difficult war was being fought, and the Nazis no longer had the upper hand. The Russian forces had managed to cut the German army off from its supply lines. The first signs of defeat could be seen on some fronts. These events led, among other things, to an order that Helmut received from his commanders in Berlin: make use of the French to carry out the evacuation of the Jews.

Helmut made his way back to Paris on a flight from the airport in the Riviera. He landed in Paris late in the afternoon and reported to headquarters to be briefed on what had occurred while he was away. After a series of emotional discussions, in which the officers began to face the fact that the turning point of the war was coming, stirring fears of defeat, they got ready to leave for their quarters. Helmut, contrary to his usual habit, decided to invite them all to a show.

"If we're on the brink of a difficult period, let's celebrate tonight! I would like all of you to come this evening to the Folies Bergère nightclub. Tomorrow we will begin carrying out plans for eradicating the French underground from Paris and its environs."

"We will also focus on shipping out the French kikes," he continues, "but tonight, let's forget all that for a moment."

12

Somewhere in the suburbs of Paris, she sat by the window. The little psychiatric hospital continued operating throughout the war, although its population changed, and many wards there now were suffering wounds from the war. It was desperately overcrowded, but it was better than the German concentration or labor camps.

Annette had recovered somewhat since her arrival there two years earlier. Physically, she was in a decent state, but on any matter concerning her children or husband— her memory was gone. Only when she was detached from awareness would memories of her family surface to her consciousness. She would sit, staring out the window and mumbling, like a ceremony repeated several times a day.

One evening in early February 1943, an S.S. car pulled into the hospital parking lot. A uniformed officer entered the office and demanded that the director be summoned. The nurse approached him and told him that the director was in Paris and would only be at the hospital the following morning.

"If so, are you in charge here?" he asked her.

"Yes, I'm the manager of the night shift."

"Then I demand to see the list of all the patients here at this moment."

"I am sorry, officer, but we cannot give out the names of patients in the psychiatric hospital. That's the regulation."

Smiling, the officer came up to the nurse and slapped her face with all his might. The force of the blow knocked her to the floor, where she lay in shock from the pain and humiliation.

"Now do you understand what you must bring me?"

She nodded. She pulled herself to her feet, holding onto the wall for support, and caught her breath. "I will get you the list in a minute."

She came back after a few minutes with the list of patients and handed it to the officer.

"What time does the director come in?"

"He should be here about nine in the morning," she lied. Gerard usually came in very early in the morning, but she wanted them to have time to decide what to do before the Germans arrived. Even though the list of wards was already in the officer's hands, it was not complete. She knew that she would not be able to notify Gerard of what had happened, since the hospital was disconnected from the communications network, and sometimes even from the electricity grid.

That evening, S.S. officers and soldiers, accompanied by French police, were dispatched to all locations where people suspected of being Jews resided. After their arrest, the Jews were shoved into trucks for their last journey, as part of the accelerating campaign to wipe out French Jewry.

At the same time, at the cabaret nightclub, the senior German officers were at the height of a celebration. Helena sat at Helmut's side with a smile on her beautiful face, but inside a storm was raging.

When he came to pick her up that evening to go to the nightclub, Helmut had told her that he had caught acquaintances of hers in southern France, who had been picked up together with members of the French underground. Helena did not understand what this meant for her or her sister. What did Helmut mean by *acquaintances of hers* in southern France? She wondered to herself if he was linking her to the underground, but she decided to play the game to the end and continued to act as though it was business as usual.

"Who are they really?" Helmut asked her, repeating that they had been caught together with members of the French underground.

Helena answered coolly, "the underground members are not my acquaintances. Since I left Italy, I have no idea what's going on there."

He smiled understandingly. "I know that you haven't been there for a long time. Perhaps your sister might know them. But let's forget about that for now and celebrate, we haven't seen each other for a long time. I couldn't wait to see you again! Tonight, we'll celebrate, for I'll be very busy the next few days. We have a lot of operations in Paris now," he explained.

"The only thing that I'm interested in, my love, is this night. I hope they won't take you away from Paris again, and that we'll be able to continue meeting even with your operations." She let out a convincing sigh.

"Don't worry, I'll find time for us," he promised.

The party went on into the wee hours of the morning. After they left the nightclub, Helmut instructed the driver to take them to Helena's apartment and they went in together.

Helmut, who was half-drunk, could not wait any longer. The moment the door closed behind them, he grabbed Helena from behind and peeled her dress off her shoulders, leaving her in nothing but her stiletto heels, stockings, and garters. He held her with one hand while he laid her across the nearest table with the other. She bent forward, leaned her head on the table, and closed her eyes. Her thoughts wandered away as she imagined a sunrise, green leaves, but she made sure to let out a moan from time to time …

The police van transporting the patients from the hospital pulled up at the Velodrome, a Paris sports field that was used in normal times for bicycle races. Annette was among the passengers, moving like a sleepwalker shoved along by the crushing crowd, until she came to a stop in a place where no one was pushing her.

The Germans, together with the French police, herded some 8,000 Jews into the arena. The plan was to round up as many as 22,000 Jews from Paris and the suburbs. People were packed together on top of each other like sardines; the stench was terrible.

Not seeing or hearing anything around her, Annette just continued staring into space. An older man, seeing that she was in a bad way, pulled her out of the crowded center to a spot on the side.

"What is your name, madame? Are you alone here? Where did you come from?"

Not hearing what he said, Annette did not respond. Suddenly she muttered, "Olivier… Laurent…"

The man bent close to her and asked, "What did you say? Are you with Olivier and Laurent?"

She repeated faintly, "Olivier… Laurent…" this time adding Marek's name as well.

He sat her down in a spot out of the way of the crush. "Don't move, I'll be right back."

He went to the place where blankets and food were being handed out and managed to get a tattered army blanket and a plate of beans. He pushed through the crowds until he got back to Annette, then sat down next to her and began to feed her carefully.

"I'm Phillippe. Up until a few days ago I was still with my wife and children on a farm not far from Paris. We were hiding with a family who are friends of ours, in a hideout under their house." Annette did not respond, but he went on with his story. "The Germans suddenly showed up, as though they knew exactly where we were. They interrogated the owners, who didn't say anything until the husband was shot to death. Then the wife broke down and told them where we were. Fortunately, the hideout had an opening at the end, and it was possible to escape into the woods. My wife and daughters managed to get out of there and hide under cover of darkness. I remained inside, trying to delay the soldiers. They dragged me out of there, and that's it. From that moment on, I don't remember a thing until I came to when they took us out of the trucks."

Annette looked at the man and continued murmuring faintly,

"Olivier… Laurent… Marek…"

"Who are they, Olivier, Laurent, and Marek?" he asked her again. Annette did not answer.

All the Jews who had been rounded up were placed in the Velodrome arena. When a few tried to escape, shots immediately rang out, making it abundantly clear that anyone who tried to run away would be shot outside. A few days passed until trucks came to transport the Jews to the concentration camps of Drancy, Compiègne, Pithiviers, and Beaune-la-Rolande.

Annette remained with Phillippe the whole time, as though she were under his protection. He looked after her until they reached the Drancy concentration camp, where the two were forcibly separated.

The Drancy concentration camp was built partially from wooden barracks and partially from houses that were already standing. Everything was fenced in according to the best Nazi tradition, and terrifying dogs circled the camp.

Annette was lodged in one of the barracks, together with the rest of the women who had just arrived.

The director of the barrack, a Jewish woman from a Paris suburb, was authorized by the French police to manage the rest of the female prisoners. Her welcome was harsh, accompanied by blows for all the women who had just arrived. Annette, who did not escape her blows, found herself lying, bruised, on the floor.

One of the women in the barrack helped her up and led her to her bunk.

Thus, Annette's saga of torment began.

13

A few days after the deportation of the Jews, Fritz returned to his post in Paris. He had undergone medical treatment in his ear, but his hearing had been significantly damaged. In the days after his recovery, Fritz was put in charge of mapping the underground based on the findings that they had received. Among other tasks, he continued interrogating additional resistance fighters who had been captured. One of them was an Italian who shed light on Helmut's questions.

Giorgio had indeed been the militia commander in Helena's village. Fritz learned that Maria had been his girlfriend, and that they had no children. Giorgio was executed by underground members, the same fighters who had been interrogated in the south of France.

Fritz wanted to tell this news to Helmut privately. He knew that the very existence of information that was kept secret by Helena would make him see red. *And who were those children*, he wondered, *if not Maria's…?*

Fritz went into Helmut's office early in the morning, after having been away from it for a long time. When Helmut arrived, Fritz stood at the entrance to the office and saluted. Contrary to his habit, Helmut patted him on the shoulder.

"Good work, Fritz. I'm sorry you were injured, but we are well on our way to making them pay the price."

"Herr Helmut, I must brief you in person with some information that was not in the report."

"What information?" Helmut was surprised. "Come in, I have a few minutes."

Fritz followed him into the office and closed the door.

"Herr Helmut, the information concerns Helena. Or to be precise, Maria, Helena's sister. The information we had is correct, the commander of the militia was indeed killed by the underground. But there is more updated information on him: he was not married and did not have any children. This came from people from his village, who notified my liaison who was doing the interrogation. His girlfriend was Helena's sister, Maria; they positively identified her. They also said that Maria's parents are still alive and that to this day, they do not know what became of Maria."

"Interesting. And here I thought I knew everything. But they managed to outsmart me." He remained calm, his face impassive. "I'll deal with that later. I will ask you to keep our conversation a secret."

Fritz stamped his foot and left the room.

Helmut began his day vexed with the new mystery. He was in the midst of planning the operations against the underground and its branches in the Paris area, as well as expelling the remaining Jews who were not French nationals; all those Jewish immigrants who had arrived in the past few years, and particularly since the outbreak of the war.

At the start of the day, he summoned all of the commanders who were tasked with the eradication of the French underground throughout Paris and its environs. The meeting opened with news from the Russian front, which was not very encouraging. According to reports, the fighting on the Russian front had not brought a decisive outcome. Moreover, the winter was not making things any easier for the German army, which was not adequately prepared for the cold conditions; there was fear that the German defense line might be breached, something that could bring down the Reich on the Eastern Front.

"I want everything you heard here to spur you on in the next assignment I give you. You have to show the French, the underground, the collaborators with the Allies, and the Jews who is boss here! I don't want to hear anything about mercy! I want you to carry out a hundred percent of the assignment I'm going to give you. Anyone who fulfills his tasks with more than a hundred percent— all the better! Bring me results and return morale to the German people who are looking to us!"

The senior staff stood and with raised arms shouted in unison, "Heil Hitler!"

Helmut was angry, and his personal anger shaped how he gave out the assignments.

"Today we are embarking on an all-out war against the underground, until its very last fighter shall fall. At the same time, we are continuing with the orders to expel the kikes, according to the lists we have received from the French regime. Fritz's force will lead the battle against the underground, according to the plans that have been presented. At midnight tonight, they will begin operations in a Paris suburb. Only those in this room will receive the exact location, to avoid leaks. The French will back us up, but so that information would not leak to the underground, we decided to let them deal only with the issue of the kikes. There, they are more than happy to do the work.

"All of you have worked hard and have built models of what is going to take place, but you did not know the target until the day before yesterday. We are facing a long battle on all of Germany's fronts and here too, in Paris, the high command has their eyes on us. Paris is under our full control and as long as that continues, the Allies will be afraid to engage us in battle in France."

"Set your watches to leave at 8 p.m." he continued. "The operation will start at 10 p.m., after everyone's arrival. I will be in the leading vehicle. Kohl, at the same time, you'll liaise with the French police and be responsible for deporting the Jews from the stadium and the other areas where they have been rounded up. Any questions?"

"Yes, sir." Fritz stood up. "What do we do in the case of civilians resisting, and how much force do we use?"

"Fritz, I told you to give more than a hundred percent. That means, *everything*. Use as much force as you need. If there are losses among French civilians— that's the price they'll have to pay. I'm not interested in anything other than destroying the underground, at whatever the cost, even if it means hurting the civilian population and even our collaborators. I don't give a damn about those French!" Helmut finished speaking and took a seat.

He thought for a moment, then stood up and went out to the lobby of the command headquarters. His driver stretched as he saw him come out. "Let's go," Helmut said sharply, "we have a short trip to make."

The driver opened the car door for him, and Helmut took his seat inside. "Drive to Helena's." The driver hurried to his seat, started the engine, and headed off towards Helena's apartment.

Helena was in the middle of her morning preparations. Maria and the children were in her apartment as well, busy preparing a late breakfast. Helena came out of the shower with wet hair, wrapped in her bathrobe.

There was a sharp rapping at the door. The sisters exchanged glances as Helena went to the door and asked, "who is it?" "Open up!" a command came from outside the door.

Helena recognized the voice and the tone, and opened the door.

Helmut burst in, shoving the door and pushing Helena out of the way.

"Helmut, did something happen? You look all worked up."

He turned to face her with an icy stare, and immediately looked over at Maria. The children clung to her, frightened. Helmut's driver stood in the entrance.

"Maria," Helmut turned to her.

"Yes, Helmut."

"Tell me about your partner, the children's father."

Maria felt her temper rising, but her gut feeling told her to watch her words, for it was possible he had acquired new information about her or her past.

She decided to stall for time. "My partner? Why? Do you know something about him?"

Helmut took two rapid steps towards her and grabbed her chin. "Maria, I'm not interested in your games. Tell me about your partner."

Maria felt her chin being crushed in his hands. "Ow! You're hurting me!"

Olivier climbed off Maria's lap and tried to push Helmut away in an attempt to defend her. Helmut let go of Maria's chin, grabbed Olivier's hand and lifted him into the air by his arm. Olivier writhed in pain and tried to resist and to kick Helmut.

"Enough!" Helena's scream split the air.

Helmut dropped Olivier on the floor, sobbing with pain and fear; Laurent also began to wail. Maria immediately hugged them and tried to protect them.

"What is wrong with you?! I've never seen you like this!"

Helmut spun around to Helena. "There is nothing I hate more than being lied to! I knew that your sister's story was not real, even though I hoped I was mistaken. Indeed, you both lied!" He came up to Helena and gently stroked her neck. "You lied to me."

Fear almost stopped her breath, and a cold sweat broke out on her forehead. Helmut wiped away the drops of her sweat. "Are you hot, dear?"

She gazed into his eyes without looking away, making the decision not to be afraid no matter what.

Helmut looked at her and continued drawing his finger from her forehead down her face. Suddenly he grabbed her hair and pulled it so that her head was jerked backwards. She did not scream, but just let out a faint sigh of pain.

"What is your story and your sister's story? And be good enough to tell me the truth."

"Let go of my hair, calm down, and then I'll talk to you!"

He looked at her. Scarlet with fury, he pulled her hair even more brutally. "You think you can speak to me like that?!"

She let out a scream, feeling her hair being torn from her scalp.

With his other hand, Helmut grabbed her bathrobe and pulled it down. Maria tried to take the children away, but he ordered her not to move. Helena was naked.

"Now start telling me," he said, meanwhile caressing her body.

Olivier tried to get away from Maria and attack Helmut, but Maria held onto him with all her might; she knew that it would end very badly if Olivier came near Helmut at that moment. She tried to prevent them from seeing the terrible sight that was unfolding before them.

"Maria left Italy because her boyfriend was a violent militia fighter. That's not a lie."

"And the children are theirs? Tell me the truth!" He continued running his hand over her body while pulling her hair and intensifying the pain.

"They're the children of my neighbors, their parents disappeared.

That's the truth. I just wanted to help them, to save them."

"Who are they?" Helmut asked in astonishment. Suddenly, Olivier managed to wriggle free of Maria's grasp. He ran to Helmut and began kicking him in a fury. Helmut, taken by surprise, dropped Helena on the floor, turned to Olivier and began kicking him. Helena pounced on Olivier and tried to protect him with her naked body. But Helmut grabbed Olivier's ear and lifted him, almost tearing his ear off.

"Stop!" begged Helena. "He didn't do anything bad to you! I don't understand what's happened to you… Stop it!" she screamed.

Helmut left Olivier, bent down to pick up Helena's robe, and threw it at her.

"Put that on!" he commanded her. "Now listen to me, and listen to me well. I have no time to waste. If you don't want the situation to get worse, tell me who these children are!"

"I'm telling you, they're the children of my neighbors who have disappeared!"

"Why did they disappear? When did it happen?"

"They disappeared when you arrived, when Paris was occupied. I don't know when, exactly. They both disappeared in one day, and all the neighbors got together to help the children."

"Are they Jews?"

Laurent and Olivier glared at him with fear and hatred. They did not know what it meant to be a Jew.

Helena answered, "yes."

She then begged him, "please, leave them with me, I'll do whatever you want."

"You don't have to say that, you'll do whatever I want anyway," he said maliciously. "First, your sister will come with me to pay a courtesy call at headquarters. You will stay here with the children and don't make a move. If I don't find you here when I return, your sister will pay for it. Do you understand what I'm telling you to do? Remember that if you do anything else, you'll be responsible for whatever happens to your sister." He grabbed Maria's arm and handed her over to his driver, who had been watching the whole scene without moving from the doorway.

"Take her to headquarters."

Maria, pale as a ghost, still dressed in her housedress, went with them unresisting, terrified of what was to come.

"You disappointed me," Helmut turned back to Helena, "and you're endangering everyone around you." He turned on his heel and left the apartment.

As soon as the door slammed shut behind him, Olivier and Laurent began sobbing uncontrollably. Up to then, they had been frozen with fear, and only now burst into tears, clinging to Helena.

Helena hugged them hard and told them, "don't worry, everything will be alright. Maria just went to the police station. They're going to ask her some questions, and she'll be right back. You'll see. Come, let's straighten up the house."

Olivier got up and said, "I'm going to watch over you the next time he comes. I'm going to take a knife and kill him!"

Helena immediately put a hand over his mouth. "Don't talk like that, sweetheart. Everything will be alright. Don't worry." Deep inside, she herself wanted to cry. Instead of protecting this child, she had dragged him into a cruel world. Everything she had promised Marek now looked to be impossible. How would she protect this small child who had rushed to her defense?

She tried to think of what she should do, but her hands were tied. Maria was Helmut's hostage. She decided to wait and see how things developed, and when and how Maria would return home.

She hugged the two boys and told them, "Let's make ourselves some breakfast, and then we'll wait for Maria to come back."

14

Helmut's driver dragged Maria to the side door of the headquarters building. He brought her to the entrance of a small room and pushed her inside, closing the door after her.

The room was empty except for two chairs and a table. Maria sat down on a chair and straightened her clothes. Hardly a few minutes had passed before a German officer entered the room. It was Fritz, whom Helmut had summoned specially to interrogate Maria.

His instructions were explicit: do not leave any external marks of injuries. Beyond that, Fritz could go as far as necessary to extract the information that Helmut thought she had concerning the underground, the route she had taken from Italy, and the identity of the children who were with her— every bit of information that she held. In recent weeks, since the underground attacks, Helmut had become paranoid. He didn't trust anyone, and particularly not the French.

Fritz sat down opposite Maria. "Tell me everything you know," he began. "Do you understand what *everything* means?" he asked, pulling on a thick, padded glove over his right hand. The glove enabled a dry blow that did not leave marks on the victim.

"Yes," she answered weakly, looking down.

She did not see his hand flying towards her, but heard a powerful ringing in her ear. The force of the blow knocked her to the floor.

Fritz pulled her by the hair and sat her back on the chair.

"When and how did you get to France?" he asked.

She began to mumble, "I-It was in the summer. I came by way of the south of France. I crossed the border on foot and walked as far as a village not far from the border, St. Paul; from there, I travelled by bus to Marseilles and from there to Paris."

The second slap landed on her. "You didn't understand? Tell me all the details! Where did you leave from, where did you get to, who helped you, how did you get to the border. Everything!" He stood behind her and placed his hand on her shoulder, stroking her while pulling down her dress to expose her shoulder. She trembled, terrified of what might happen to her.

"Early in the morning I left my parent's house, outside a village not far from the city of Arezzo, Vitiano. I got to the village square and from there I got a ride with a peasant who was bringing his produce to the city, to Florence. I arranged this secretly with him ahead of time. From Florence I took a bus to Pisa, in the direction of the sea, and from there another bus towards France. In four days, I reached the border. Along the way I stayed at three inns: the first in Pisa and the other two along the way, I don't remember their names." Then she added, "But the second inn was in the city of Genoa and the third was near the border, next to Sanremo."

He continued to stand behind her. He stroked her second shoulder and exposed it as well. Her dress would have fallen off in another moment if she had not grabbed it with both hands. Fritz suddenly yanked her hair forcefully; when she tried to resist, her dress slid down. She was left naked to the waist, trying to cover her breasts with her hands.

"Who are the people who helped you? It can't be that a young woman like yourself did all this without any help."

"I coordinated everything with one of the peasants that my father worked with. He promised to help me and take me to Florence. He was the only one who helped me leave the village. My boyfriend beat me, and I ran away from him."

Fritz pulled her hair and lifted her from the chair. Her dress fell away completely, and she tried to hide her nakedness as much as she could. Fritz, looking at her naked body, thought to himself, *interesting interrogation...* He was Helmut's protégé and knew his methods of torturing underground

fighters and prisoners. He had already interrogated several women suspected of belonging to the underground, but he had never been as excited as he
was this time.

"What was the peasant's name?"

"Antonio, Antonio Baggio."

"Who else helped you?"

"No one. I even surprised my sister. That's the truth, I'm not making
anything up…"

He stood before her, still clutching her hair. "How did you cross the
border?"

She looked him in the eye. "In Sanremo, I met people who were smuggling people between Italy and France."

He slapped her in the face. "What do you mean, met? How did you meet
them? Tell me who connected you with them!"

"Antonio told me to try and find a man who dealt in smuggling, that
perhaps he could help me."

Fritz stood behind her and forced her arms up in the air, then tied them
to a leather strip hanging from the ceiling. He tightened the strip so that she
was standing almost on tiptoe, completely naked.

"Did you not understand me? I don't want to hear any partial answers. It
will only get worse."

Maria burst into tears. "I'm telling you the truth!" "Do you think I can
find this Antonio?"

"I-I can give you all his details…" she sobbed.

"And you really think that I believe you, that there is a peasant like that,
who you suddenly met, and he managed to arrange a trip for you from Italy
to Paris, to your sister?" He stood in front of her and passed his palm along
her neck, down along her chest, and then pinched her nipples hard. She
screamed.

"Tell me everything! I don't believe you!"

She felt her strength ebbing away, that she could not stand on her tiptoes
any longer. "I'm telling the truth…" He slapped her hard in the face with his
gloved hand. If she had been free to move, most likely she would have fallen

from the blow and been injured, but she remained hanging in humiliation and pain.

She didn't remember what happened after that; apparently, she had lost consciousness. A bucket of cold water brought her back to reality.

"How did you cross the border, and how did you get to Paris?" he asked from behind her. She could not turn to face him, but could feel his breath on the back of her neck.

"I got in a truck that was carrying agricultural produce and hid under some cartons of vegetables." She felt his hand stroking her back and his body rubbing against her from behind. He said into her ear, "go on." She thought to herself that an interrogation like this, with just the two of them in the room, could only go in one direction. Knowing that her life was likely to end in this interrogation chamber, she screwed up her courage and said, "I will do whatever you ask."

He came closer to her. "I can do whatever I want to you, I don't need you to do whatever I ask. Now, go on."

"From the village, I reached, Breil-sur-Roya; I travelled in a truck, hiding for close to three hours. The truck stopped once and I heard voices, but I couldn't understand anything. Finally, they let me out in Lyons and from there I continued to hitch rides in the direction of Paris..." Suddenly, she felt the lash of a leather belt on her lower back. Her skin burned and she felt him pressing even closer to her from behind. Fritz grabbed her hair, so that she could barely move, but she began to scream and thrash around. He grabbed her and covered her mouth, rendering her utterly powerless. He then pressed his hand on her neck, nearly strangling her. At that moment, Maria remembered Helena's description of disconnecting from the body. She released her soul, leaving him her body to do with as he pleased.

Another bucket of cold water brought her back to consciousness. A soldier standing in front of her was unhooking the strip that held her up. He tossed her dress at her and told her to put it on.

Fritz entered the room again with a blood-chilling smile. "I'm sending you home. I hope you know very well that at any moment I can come and interrogate you again."

Maria understood full well that she was now a hostage, just like her sister. "I understand."

"If you want to continue living with your sister in Paris, you have to obey me. If you want those children, you have to obey me." He came up to her, as the soldier held her so she wouldn't move, and pulled her hair back. "Do you understand that?" "Yes, I understand," she answered quietly.

"Take her back to the apartment," he instructed the soldier in German, "and have someone tailing them openly, so that they will know that someone is watching them at every moment." Those were Helmut's instructions, so that the two women could not make a move without his knowledge. The soldier yanked her arm brutally and they left the room.

The operation against the French underground was a resounding success. Dozens of underground fighters were taken by surprise, most of them were killed before they had a chance to retaliate. When they realized that all was lost, they blew themselves up with a grenade blast right in front of the German soldiers who surrounded them. It was one of the highlights of Helmut's career in Paris. In that period, Germany's position on the Eastern Front was deteriorating; the Russian army was pressing its attack. Helmut allowed the senior command in Berlin the fleeting satisfaction of having eradicated the French underground.

15

Maria returned home. Helena opened the door and Maria collapsed into her arms, shaking from head to foot. Helena understood that Maria had suffered the worst of all, that she had lost her soul while her body had become a tool in their hands.

She seated Maria gently on the floor, crouched down beside her and hugged her. They were both sobbing. Laurent stood next to them and Olivier, behind him, placed a hand on Laurent's shoulder. The brothers looked at the two women who were so dear to them, the only two adults they had in the world. Overcome with helplessness, they did not utter a sound, but just stood with tears rolling down their cheeks.

Olivier took Laurent to the inner room, sat him down on the armchair and told him not to move; he then went back to Helena and Maria, held out his hands, and patted each one. Suddenly, he declared: "We'll conquer the bad people together. In the end they'll run away from here. I'll make sure of it. They won't hurt you anymore."

The two women looked at him tearfully, their hearts full of admiration for this small child and his great sensitivity.

They told him not to worry, that they would all be alright.

"We have to be very careful. It's a good thing you're with us, you give us the strength to fight the bad people," Maria told him. Olivier felt proud.

Time went on. Ever since the battle against the underground, fear had seeped into everyone in Paris. Helena and Maria lived like prisoners, feeling the fear every day and experiencing it on their own flesh. They were hostages;

they were responsible for the children and were paying for it with their bodies.

Fritz's success in his assignments earned him privileged treatment from Helmut. One of the prizes he received was Helmut's consent to his owner-ship of Maria, who became his escort against her will. Helmut and Fritz, together with Helena and Maria, became two talked-about couples in oc-cupied French Bohemia. Many of those who resisted the regime viewed the two sisters as traitors, but did not dare open their mouths. Their partners were the most powerful men in the capital.

In response to the constant fear, and out of concern for the children, Helena and Maria instituted a "visit routine," in which Laurent and Olivier would hide when one of the officers arrived. Although Helmut and Fritz knew of the children's existence, the women were worried about Olivier's behavior, since he would burst out in violent attacks of rage when he saw the men. He felt hurt and could not understand how the two women whom he most trusted could be seen with the evilest of men: Helmut, who had beaten him, and Fritz, his malevolent associate, who was hanging around with Maria. He could not accept the situation.

For their part, Helmut and Fritz ignored the two children as long as the men got what they wanted. Everything was done, so to speak, by agreement. Despite the power they wielded, they took into account the women, and did not hand over the children to be deported to extermination camps. Helmut knew that the children must belong to one of the Jewish families that had been deported from Paris, but decided to ignore this, contenting himself with reminding the women from time to time that the children would stay alive as long as the women gave themselves fully to the two men.

Helena suffered from the image of herself as a bar dancer entertaining German officers but could not do anything about it. Life, and the existence of the children, had laid out a different path for her and her sister than the one she had hoped for.

Late 1943 was a difficult time for Helmut. A large part of the German forces was fighting on the front between France and Italy, which had sur-rendered to the Allies. The Italian defeat forced the Germans to direct forces to areas of western and northern France, with the goal of reconquering the

French territory along the Italian border, previously occupied by the Italians.

Meanwhile, the French underground carried out several significant attacks on German command posts in Paris and throughout the territory controlled by the Vichy regime. These highly successful attacks and the losses of German officers hobbled the Nazi war machine, just when it was facing the coming Allied attack. A number of S.S. officers were killed in these attacks, including several under Helmut's command.

Alongside the loss of German soldiers, the infrastructure of the German war machine suffered significant damage. This included attacks on railroads, police stations, and supply warehouses. On the Eastern Front, the German defense lines had been breached, and the Russians outflanked the German forces. The Russians thus decided the terms on which the battle would be fought, and the Germans found themselves retreating from the Russian army and the harsh Russian winter. The icy conditions paralyzed the German army, which suffered losses in battle as well as shortages in winter equipment and food supplies. For all practical matters, the Germans had lost the Eastern Front.

Helmut was planning an attack, making use of the information that Fritz had collected over several months, up to the beginning of 1944. Towards February, Helmut set the date for the attack and gathered his forces, including several army units that were loaned to him for the operation. However, he was not the only one making plans to take action.

The commander of the underground in the Paris region, Pascal André, had learned his lesson from recent events, and had taken into account every possible scenario. Meanwhile, he was planning the main attack on German forces and the German headquarters, as well as the French collaborators. For this operation, he set up an information network which included some double agents— ostensibly collaborators with the Germans but in fact informants for the underground.

The underground was one step ahead of the Germans. Pascal operated his network in compartmentalized fashion to prevent its exposure if its operators were captured. The operators knew only their small part of the picture, so that even if they were captured, they would not know the locations of the other cells, nor the identities of the other operators or their plans. On the one hand, he struck fear in every French person who cooperated with the Germans in any way; on the other, he extorted their cooperation with the underground, as a condition for not getting hurt.

Helena was just returning from rehearsals at the cabaret. As usual, before entering the building, she surveyed the surroundings to look for any uniformed or hidden Germans in the area. She stopped by Maria's apartment, sat down on the armchair, and heaved a sigh.

"It looks like the cabaret is going to close. Philippe, the owner, is getting endless death threats from underground members. But even if it happens, we'll still get by. I've saved enough money for these days. I didn't expect them to actually come, but it seems they're already here." Maria stood behind her, massaging her neck. "The children are not okay— they are constantly asking for their mother and father. It's gotten to the point that, today, Olivier slapped me and called me a liar. He burst out crying like I've never seen him before, hugged Laurent like he was defending him, and yelled, "Maman and Papa are not coming back! They've left us! Now you're both going to leave us too and go to those Germans!"

"We have to be very careful in the coming period," said Helena. "Everybody's talking about the end of the war; the Germans are being defeated on the eastern front, and that affects everyone. I heard that Germany is also being bombed all the time now by Allied planes."

"But especially now," Helena went on, "because everyone thinks this is the end, we have to be more careful than ever. The torture of Jews and anyone involved in hiding Jews has been stepped up. There's evidence that the Germans are executing everyone who's sent from Paris on those trains I've heard about. Together with everything we've heard that the underground has done and apparently will continue to do, the fact that Helmut feels like his back is against the wall makes it impossible to predict that man's behavior. If the children cause problems when Helmut and Fritz come, they will not hesitate to send them off with the rest of the Jewish deportees. They don't even need to look into who the children are. I'm horrified by the thought that this could happen at any moment."

"I feel the same way… What will happen to us?" Maria asked, still leaning over Helena.

"At the moment, we won't do anything. Let's get through the next few days, and then we'll see. I sense that the Germans are extra-vigilant right now, but on the other hand, the underground is very active too. I see what's happening at the nightclub."

Helena sighed. "I'm going to go to sleep now, I'm exhausted. Tomorrow morning we'll try to encourage the children and explain things in a way that will help them make sense of what is happening."

The night passed and morning came. The children woke up and came running into Maria's bed. She jumped up in alarm, then relaxed when she felt the presence of the two little ones who had become, over time, an inseparable part of her.

Maria had come to Paris with the desire to change her life and to run away from her difficult circumstances in Italy. But she had found herself in France deprived of the freedom she had hoped to find, fighting for her life and busy trying to save these two urchins to whom she bound her sister's unbelievable story.

She hugged them and said, "Let's surprise Helena! We'll go up to her apartment and make her breakfast. She's tired out from work."

"She dances for the Germans— I don't want to make her anything!" shouted Olivier. Without intending to, Maria slapped him.

Olivier froze. Shocked.

"I-I'm Sorry, I'm sorry… I didn't mean it…" he apologized.

"You're already a big boy, Olivier. You should appreciate everything that Helena has done, is doing, and will continue to do for you. Do you understand that everything she does, from morning to night, she is doing for you and your brother? I'm sorry that I hit you, but you must understand that you are her whole world. She would rather be somewhere else, but she has stayed here just for you, in order to save you. Can you understand something like that?" Maria said through her tears, hugging Olivier. Laurent, who was already almost five, jumped off the bed and stood behind his brother.

Olivier's body sagged and he burst into sobs. He understood everything

Maria had told him. He knew it already, but he could not stand to see Helena keeping company with Germans; she had been a motherly figure for him from a very early age. He remembered how Helena had taken care of his mother, how she had been there when all the problems began, and how she had taken him and Laurent away from Monsieur and Madame Dubois and created a family for them.

Maria hugged the two brothers. "We're here together. The only way we'll get through this is by staying together. You're a big boy now, and you understand everything. We'll be here for you, but if something happens to us, you'll be the one to look after Laurent. He's little, and he doesn't understand; he'll only feel safe with you. You'll have to help us, because if we don't stick together, we won't succeed. We love you. You're the most important thing in our lives, and you're our family."

The three of them got ready and went up to Helena's apartment. Maria opened the door with her key, and they went in. Before they had time to close the door, however, two men pushed their way in. One of them grabbed Maria and clapped his hand over her mouth, and the other grabbed the shocked Olivier, who began writhing in his grasp. Laurent started to cry. One of the men put his finger to his lips, signaling the children to be quiet, and they both fell silent out of fear.

The two men began searching the apartment, found Helena's bedroom and went in quietly. Suddenly, Olivier let out a shout. Helena awoke in a panic, then froze in place as she saw a cocked pistol directed at her.

"Helena, we've been trailing you for a long time. We know that these are not your children, we also know that Helmut visits you frequently. Now listen to us well…" Helena did not move, merely nodded.

"Tell madame to take the children to another room with my friend; you and I need to have an important conversation."

Helena looked towards Maria and nodded. Maria hugged the children as the second man led them to the adjoining room, the frightened children clinging to her fiercely.

"Now listen well, Helena. Starting today, you are going to have to cooperate with us. Your refusal would cause everyone unpleasantness. We want you to inform us when Helmut comes here."

"I don't know, he always makes a surprise appearance. You're endangering both me and yourselves. He has men observing my apartment all the time—he doesn't trust us and has put us under surveillance. I just know that before he comes here, his office manager, Fritz, goes to my sister. You're playing with fire and you're going to cause unnecessary deaths."

"You've got some nerve! Do you know how many of our members have been killed in this war against the Germans? Do you have any idea what kind of monster you're welcoming into your home?"

Helena stood up and said, "you're not making anything better by bursting in here like this."

The underground fighter swung his hand and slapped her in the face. "We're not playing, and we certainly don't need any preaching from some cabaret whore who consorts with the Germans. Listen, and listen well: first, starting today, you're going to signal us when he comes to visit you. The signal will be a white ribbon on the windowsill, so that we can see it from down below. Second, you will report to us when he comes to watch your shows at the cabaret. Our people will be tailing you everywhere: we'll know everything you do, inside the cabaret and out of it. Do you understand your job?"

"I assume that you're planning something."

He slapped her again. "It's not your job to assume anything! Just do what I've asked you! Remember that everything dear to you is in our sights, and we won't hesitate to strike. War means losses, unfortunately. Be ready that someone will occasionally appear and ask you a question. He will identify himself by a word from the French anthem before he speaks to you. Don't fall into any traps and don't answer the wrong person. Now, you and your sister will sit in the room together with the darling children and count to a hundred before you make a move."

Helena nodded her head. They were serious and had no qualms about murdering French people who had contact with the Germans, even under exceptional circumstances such as their own.

"Gaston!" He raised his voice. The second man came in, holding the three of them almost in one hand, and said, "here's the package."

"Sit here on the bed and count to a hundred together. We're going to disappear. Don't try to go out after us."

Helena and Maria sat on the bed with the children between them. The underground fighters backed out of the room, pistols drawn, and closed the door to the bedroom.

All was quiet in the room. Not one of them— not the children, not Maria and not Helena— dared to speak. They just looked at each other with frightened eyes. After a few minutes, Helena got up and walked over to the door with silent steps, opened it a crack, and peeked out. She widened the crack gradually until the door was fully open. She searched the apartment. They were gone.

Olivier ran over and hugged her, followed by Laurent with stumbling steps. Olivier was confused: Maria and Helena were not Germans, they were against the Germans, but everyone was bad to them… He hugged her tightly and just asked, "why?", his voice choked with tears.

Helena hugged the boys. "They're scared. That makes them behave badly, trying to defend the underground." This was the same underground that Helena believed would be able to bring them to freedom, but as much as she felt empathy for the underground fighters, she was also afraid of their threat. She and Maria now faced double danger: from the Germans, Helmut and his subordinates on the one hand, and from underground members who wanted to use them to reach Helmut and his men, on the other. She locked eyes with Maria; they were both terrified.

"It's not going to get any easier. I don't want to think of what will happen if Helmut… And I certainly don't want to mess with the guests who were just here… We have to behave as normally as possible, Mari. Olivier, you have to be grown-up and help us during this period. You have to be disciplined, and even if you get angry— it's okay, but before you do something out of anger, tell us what's making you angry and we'll solve the problem together."

"It's very dangerous now," Helena went on, "there are all sorts of people around us that we can't trust. Everyone is fighting each other and we're in the middle. Remember that Laurent and you are the most important things to Mari and me, and you'll help us get through this bad period."

16

The following days were difficult for Maria and Helena. Their every step was dictated by fear: when to go out, when to return, how to behave at the nightclub, what to do with the children, how to put on an act in the company of Helmut and Fritz. There was fear of the man who came to Helena's rehearsal room to get information, and fear that she would be seen talking to him and that it would get back to Helmut's men.

The first week passed, and the four of them had already adopted a lifestyle to fit the situation: little signs between them to pass information when they were being followed or their apartments watched, simulations of situations and behavioral training with Olivier and Laurent— what to do and when, what to answer people, etc. Everything with the goal of surviving this dangerous period and the uncertainty about what was going to happen.

Several weeks passed by; rumors increased of a significant turning point in the war and German defeats in various parts of Europe and Africa. Meanwhile, the Germans gained victories against the Allies and the underground in France.

One evening in early May 1944, after some three days in which Helena had not heard from Helmut, a knock was heard on her door. She opened it to find Helmut's driver standing in the entrance. He came in and searched the apartment.

"Helmut will be here shortly," he said, taking up his place outside the door.

"I'm going to get ready for him," Helena told him and tried to lock the door after her. But the driver wedged his right foot in, and she understood that she had to leave the door open. With some trepidation, she went into the bathroom and locked the door, turned on the faucet, and let the water run. She went to the window and peeked through the blind to see if anything suspicious was happening outside, but could not see anything in the dark. She took the small white ribbon, designated as the sign of Helmut's arrival according to the underground members' instruction, and tied it to the window shade in such a way that only a trained eye could notice it.

She came back quickly and climbed into the bathtub which had begun to fill with water. Helmut arrived just at that moment. He tried to open the bathroom door only to find that it was locked. He rapped loudly, and Helena, dripping wet, opened the door for him.

He stood on the threshold and gazed at Helena's body.

"Why did you lock it?"

"The apartment door is open, and a soldier is here; I didn't feel comfortable. Would you like to join me in the bath?" she asked with a sensual gaze.

Helmut was suspicious, but her invitation made him to thaw a bit. He came up and began stroking her neck. Helena let out moans of pleasure. "Oh, how I've missed this."

Helmut continued massaging her body and when the massage turned into something else, Helena entered the role that she so despised. But the show had to go on; like always, she was no longer there, leaving her body behind to respond automatically.

He pulled himself away from her and hurried into his clothes.

"I don't have time. I'm busy now with critical matters, but in the midst of all this insanity I just had to see you." His voice was different, almost frail, and she heard a note of fear.

"Is everything okay?" she asked. "Your voice sounds different somehow."

"Helena, things are happening. I don't know where they will lead, but it's important to me to tell you that you're one of the most significant things to have happened to me in the last three years."

Helena understood that whatever was going to happen might change his life, and thus her life as well. For a moment, she felt empathy for him; but she quickly regained her senses, remembering who he really was, in his moments of power, when there was no uncertainty in the air, how he had used his power in inhuman ways; how he and his men had taken from her the most precious thing of all...

"What happened?" she continued her act. "Why are you speaking in such a worried tone?"

"The situation is not simple. Problems are cropping up in all sectors. We're facing critical days, and I don't know how I will come out of them. I felt the need to share that with you. Even if for a moment I didn't believe you, I know that I'm important to you, and I wanted you to know that you're the best thing that's happened to me in all this insanity." Naked, she embraced him.

He told her, "I'll be gone for a few days. I'll be back at the end of the week and we'll meet then. I want to spend some time with you." Helena understood that some kind of operation was being planned, very likely connected to the underground. She continued embracing him, then kissed him and said, "I'll wait for you." He kissed her on the forehead and left the apartment.

After he left, she hurried to the shower, first removing the ribbon from the window and then performing her usual ritual to purify her body from what it had just experienced. Desperate to remove the contamination that clung to her, she scrubbed her skin until it turned red.

Just as she was finishing her shower, the walls of her apartment shook from a powerful explosion nearby. She pulled on her robe and ran down to Maria's apartment. Maria opened the door for her. The children were already asleep.

"Did you hear that?"

"Yes, I felt it too. It was really close."

"Helmut was at your place before," Maria went on, "I heard noises.

I leaned out of the window and saw that you hung the ribbon." "Yes. Are you thinking what I'm thinking?" asked Helena.

"I don't want to think anything, I'm just scared... It doesn't matter what happened. It's clear that it's connected to us. Now we're in danger, both from the Germans and the underground..."

They sat and waited to see what would happen. Shots rang through the air and cars raced through the streets nearby. They peeked out through the blind and saw people running from house to house.

By craning their necks, they could see German armored vehicles at the head of the street with foot soldiers running alongside them, passing the houses and opening the doors.

They saw two men running into a building across the street. The armored vehicles approached the building; as they stopped in front of the entrance, the gate opened, and a moment later the vehicle exploded. Some of the soldiers standing nearby were wounded, while others managed to open fire on the building. Return fire was visible from within the building; it appeared to have been an ambush for the Germans.

Maria and Helena turned out the lights and went into the children's room. The children, not hearing a thing, went on sleeping. The shooting continued for a while longer, finally giving way to a tense silence.

Maria peeked through the window and saw more people coming out of the surrounding entrances, all with their weapons drawn. They passed by the German soldiers, who lay there dead or wounded, and went on shooting anyone who moved.

Trembling, the two women crouched down underneath the windowsill. About an hour later, they raised their heads and peeked out the window again. The street was full of German soldiers who were searching the houses. They were going from house to house, pulling all the residents out to the street and making them stand with their hands on the wall. Most of the residents there were men.

Suddenly, the door burst open and two German soldiers entered the apartment. They were not Helmut's soldiers, for Helena did not recognize them.

They asked the women if there were men in the apartment. Helena and Maria did not open their mouths, just shaking their heads no. The soldiers searched the apartment and left.

Helena and Maria closed the door and kept quiet until the voices from the stairwell finally faded away. The children were still asleep, unaware of the tumult around them.

The two sisters looked at each other. Without saying a word, they both thought the same thing. Did they have a hand in this? Was the explosion connected to Helmut's visit to Helena?

"What should we do now?" Maria asked.

"I'm not sure. Maybe I should pay a visit to Helmut? Maybe should try to find Fritz and ask what happened next to our building?"

That evening, the underground carried out attacks against targets of the collaborationist French police and against the Germans all over Paris. Some of the attacks were carried out by Jewish fighters, trying to free the people who were destined for the transports to the extermination camps. One of these attacks was a partial success, but many of the Jews in the Drancy concentration camp, on the outskirts of Paris, were shot. The camp itself was not liberated.

"I'll go to Helmut's headquarters to find out how he is," Helena said, "they know me there. I'll try to show that I'm worried. The main thing is to get them away from here, so they won't come and try to interrogate us or even take the children."

That morning, there was heavy traffic of German forces through the city streets. Many men were arrested at checkpoints of the S.S. and the French police in an attempt to track down underground fighters.

Helena walked rapidly past the checkpoints. At one of them, she saw a gang of German soldiers beating a man with the butts of their rifles, with a vicious attack dog biting him. The man was trying to crawl away when one of the soldiers pulled out a pistol and shot him point blank.

Helena was shaking. The thought that Marek might have experienced such an attack a few years earlier made her skin crawl. Her head spun and her heart skipped a beat. She stopped and leaned with one hand on a wall of a nearby building, catching her breath before continuing on her way.

A few minutes later, she reached Helmut's headquarters. She noticed that it was fenced in with barbed wire which had not been there before, and armored vehicles were defending the entrance. Inside the fenced enclosure, she saw handcuffed men sitting on benches, guarded by soldiers with terrifying attack dogs and a large machine gun pointed at them.

She approached the guard at the entrance and said she was looking for Helmut or Fritz. Not recognizing her, the guard sent a second guard into the building.

A few minutes later one of Helmut's subordinates appeared. Helena remembered him from the evenings at the nightclub. "Madame," he said to her with a severe expression, "be so good as to come inside with me."

Helena began playing her role. "I just wanted to see Helmut. Two days ago, he visited me, and during the night there were shots and explosions not far from my building. I have to know that he's alright…"

"Come with me, please."

They went into the building and entered the office. The room was full of officers leaning over maps. When she came in, everyone lowered their voices. The officer accompanied her to a side room and asked her to sit on an armchair and wait.

He left and came back a few minutes later with an officer of a higher rank, in a black uniform: a senior S.S. officer.

The officer turned to her. "Madame, how can I help you?"

"I have to know that Helmut's alright. He was with me the night before last, and he sounded different. He promised me he would return at the end of the week and we would spend the weekend together… All night long, there were shots… Soldiers then came into my house looking for men… I have to know what happened…" She looked agitated on the outside. Inside she felt scared— had her decision been the right one? She tried to push aside her thoughts and play the role convincingly.

The officer took her hand in a gentlemanly gesture, and she felt that her playacting was working. "Madame, I know how close you were to Helmut. Unfortunately, two days ago the underground carried out a massive attack on our facilities in several regions. We managed to curb the attack and catch the underground fighters responsible, but to our great sorrow, we suffered a large number of losses, among them Helmut… I assume that you also knew Fritz; he too is no longer with us…"

Helena held her breath, closed her eyes and fell to the floor. She stayed that way, without taking a breath, until she felt the officer slap her cheek. She moved her eyelids slowly, as though it was an effort, until she finally opened her eyes.

"Are you alright?" Another officer had already gone to bring a glass of water and carefully offered her a sip. Helena sipped slowly, breathing rapidly, as though on the edge of hysterics.

The officer helped her get up and seat herself back on the armchair. "Is there something we can do?" he asked.

"I-I don't know," she answered quietly. "Two nights ago, I was with him. It was so wonderful, and… That's it? Just like that, he's gone? I-I don't understand, what will happen now?" she continued, sobbing.

"Come," the officer said, "let's take you home. Those responsible will get what's coming to them in a few more hours. We've arrested hundreds of resistance fighters in an operation that Helmut himself planned, but did not get to take part in." He held out his hand to her. "I am sorry for your loss. If there's anything we can do to help, please let me know. In the next few days, I ask you to try and avoid leaving your house and be careful, for the underground members are killing people indiscriminately."

She moved so as to create the impression that she was unstable on her feet and the officer tightened his grip to help prop her up. He led her to the car, where two soldiers were sitting in the front seat. The officer helped her into the back seat and sat next to her. The car drove away and within a few minutes arrived at the entrance to her building. Helena secretly hoped that Maria would not open the door and that the children would not make a noise that would cause the officer to investigate and obtain any extra information.

The officer accompanied her up to her apartment and, to her relief, silence reigned in the building. She assumed that Maria had seen her from the window and understood that something was going on. Their agreement was that if something was happening, Maria would make sure to keep the children quiet and hide with them in the storage room of the apartment.

The officer seated her on the armchair in the foyer of her apartment and asked if there was anything else that he could do to assist her. She shook her head.

"Once more, we are sorry for what happened. We will be in touch. He was our much-admired commander, and we knew how much you loved each other." He stamped his foot and left the apartment.

She took a deep breath.

Only after a few minutes had passed, when she was sure that they had driven away, she went down to Maria's apartment, and noticed two German soldiers sitting in a car opposite the building that had not been there earlier.

She knocked softly on the door four times, followed by two more rapid knocks; that was the signal that they had agreed upon to indicate that everything was normal.

Maria and the boys opened the door. Helena bent down and hugged them with a motherly embrace, protective and loving. "How are my boys doing today?" They were all smiles.

"Let's eat a late breakfast. I'm not going to work today, we'll all stay together."

Maria was a bit taken aback by Helena's vivacious air and signaled her with a questioning glance, as if to ask, *what happened?* Helena signaled her back to wait a minute. She went into the kitchen and called the children to come help her. They mixed together flour and eggs to make pastry for profiteroles, like she used to make for Olivier when he was little and lived with his parents upstairs.

The boys finished helping her and began playing together. There was a sense that the tension they had been holding the past few days was beginning to ease a little.

Suddenly, Helena said to Maria, "they're gone. Both Helmut and

Fritz, and a significant number of other German soldiers with them. Do you understand what that means?"

Maria stood still, burst into tears, and hugged Helena. Helena returned her embrace with hands covered in pastry.

"Mari, we're still in danger. We have to hope that no resistance fighter will break under interrogation and link us to this attack. At the moment, we're staying home. If you look out the window, you'll see that they have assigned security or guards so that we won't run away. I gave a serious performance there at headquarters and I think that it worked. I'm Helmut's broken-hearted girlfriend."

17

The days passed. Many resistance fighters, as well as innocent civilians, were arrested by the Germans and subjected to brutal torture in an attempt to extract details about the attack that had taken place. Gaston, one of the two fighters who had dragged them into this adventure, felt the need to tail Maria and Helena, keeping an eye out for anything that might happen with the Germans. The underground had acted wisely by forming no links between the fighters involved in different events, and the select few who knew of the overall plan were not caught, so the Germans were struggling to piece together the whole picture.

At one of the interrogations, in late May 1944, one of the captured fighters, unable to withstand torture, revealed that they had followed Helmut and Fritz's girlfriends. They knew that the Nazi officers were visiting the women, and the plan had been to kill the men while they were still in Maria's and Helena's apartments, and after that the women and their children— the collaborators. The interrogating officer continued torturing him to extract all the details, but he could not hold out, becoming an unidentifiable hunk of bloody flesh, until he finally breathed his last.

The information that the fighter gave confirmed the act that Helena had played, but also set off a warning light in the interrogator's mind. A few days later, on the morning of June 6, the interrogator asked the officer who had accompanied Helena home to go back and bring the two women for interrogation.

But that morning brought a guardian angel, an angel who arranged the start of the Allied invasion on that very day. The interrogating team was distracted from Helena and Maria, focusing instead on their orders to eliminate the Jews who were still in the concentration camp in Paris.

The Germans operated police and S.S. squadrons around the clock to round up any Jews left in the capital and imprison them in the Drancy concentration camp, in preparation for transporting them to the extermination camps.

News of the Allied invasion spread rapidly among the residents of Paris. There was a feeling of finality, and the French understood that the Germans would soon be leaving. Most of the residents who had been collaborators began fleeing from the operations of the underground, operations that were steadily increasing with the backing they received from Allied forces parachuted in.

The guards next to Helena's building were called away to join the battle for the roads leading to Paris from Normandy, where the Allies had landed.

Helena and Maria feared that the underground members would try to hurt them, just as they had executed a significant number of collaborators. Helena moved in with Maria and the boys, since Maria's apartment was not as widely known as hers.

Leaving the building was extremely dangerous. They tried to have only Maria go out, since she was less likely to be recognized than Helena. She would go out to the corner of the street just to get a bit of food such as bread, milk, and vegetables.

One time, when she went out to shop, several underground fighters who had been hiding in the entrance burst in after her when she came back into the building. They covered her mouth and dragged her up the stairs to Helena's apartment.

"Knock on the door normally and open it." Maria knocked and tried to open the door but knew that it would not open. One of the men grabbed her hand forcefully. "Where is she, the whore?" He pulled out a knife and began slicing it into Maria's shoulder. A drop of blood welled up from the thin cut that was formed, then spread into a blood stain on her dress. Unable to stand the pain and fear, Maria signaled with her hand to indicate downstairs.

They went down one floor and Maria knocked on the door with a warning sign so that Helena could prepare herself.

Helena took the children and hid them in a camouflaged closet, whispering to Olivier to look after his brother, no matter what happened. She then went back to open the door.

The gang burst in and made the two women lie down on the entrance mat. One of the men, apparently the ringleader, stood over them. "You are accused of collaborating with the Germans, and you'll soon stand trial!"

Fortunately for them, Gaston, who had been keeping surveillance on the two women ever since the attack, observed the men going into the building and understood the situation immediately. He was familiar with the underground's extermination ring and knew that they were wild and uncontrollable.

Gaston yelled at the young man standing over them, "leave them alone this minute! If you knew the whole story, you would kiss their feet!" He pushed the young man away. "It's a good thing I was notified that you were continuing your exterminations of collaborators on this street. I knew you would want to get your hands on them."

Maria and Helena clung to each other. "For a minute, I thought our lives were going to end right here," Helena said.

"I apologize, but the fact that you are a source of information for the underground was kept a secret from everyone— to protect you from getting hurt by the Germans. You played the game and provided the information."

"Everything is already over," Gaston declared. "Paris is liberated! But unfortunately, people have accumulated stores of hatred over this long period, and the desire for revenge, even if unjustified, is being given free reign. I suggest that you don't walk around outside too much. Let the days pass and the rage burn away. Just in case, I will arrange for you to be guarded, particularly because there are very likely still German soldiers or agents in the city."

The whole time Olivier, with his hand over Laurent's mouth, kept quiet inside the closet, hiding and listening to the voices.

Gaston asked the men to leave the apartment, thanked the women, and left himself. He was no longer the same man who had once threatened them into cooperating with him. Apparently, the information they had given and the signals they performed had done their work, and he felt himself to be in their debt.

Suddenly, silence fell; inside the closet, Olivier could not hear anything. He cautiously opened the door and came out of his hiding place to find Maria and Helena in each other's arms. He took Laurent by the hand and they quietly approached the two women.

Helena and Maria saw them coming, silent and terrified.

"That's it, my darlings. It's over. The bad days are over!" Helena told them. The boys breathed deeply, then joined the women in a group embrace, everyone's eyes flooded with tears of joy and sorrow.

PART 3

1

The return to normal life was a strange transition. First of all, the nightclub had closed, and Helena found herself unemployed. She spent many hours with the children, but the question constantly nagged at her: *What has happened to Annette, the children's mother? Could she be tracked down?* At the same time, Helena would wonder how she could ever part with the two boys, for they had become like her own children, flesh of her flesh.

They did not do very much. Helena would go out to run errands, which were mainly attempts to find Annette via the lists of those missing. The lists were posted to help relatives find out the fate of loved ones. On one of these days of searching, she met Gaston at the Paris city hall, which was slowly returning to operation, trying to restore the city to life after the tempestuous years it had gone through. "Gaston!" she called.

Gaston turned and smiled at her. "How are you doing?"

"I'm okay. We're all okay. It's strange, after all the years of being led by fear I finally feel free. Mari is planning to return to Italy, to try and find out what happened to our parents."

"I'm happy to hear that. And the children?"

"They're finally starting to catch their breath, but now questions about their parents are coming up. I'm trying to find them in the lists of people deported by the Germans, but so far with no success. I have no leads to follow. I know almost for certain that the father, Marek, was murdered during the first days of the occupation; the mother, Annette, was taken to the psychiatric hospital, apparently." Gaston smiled.

"Why are you smiling?" she asked.

"Because my brother Gerard directed one of the institutions where they hid more than a few Jews right after the invasion. I can ask him. Come back here in two days. My brother's out of the city at the moment, but he's expected back. If I have information before then, I'll make sure to get it to you."

Helena was excited. She felt that the hand of fate had brought Gaston into her life precisely at the end of the war. He was the one who used her to conquer evil— Helmut and his soldiers— and had also been the one to save her from the vengeance of the underground. Now, he might have the answers that she was seeking to close the circle: to complete her promise to Marek, to find Annette and help her to reunite the little family.

Helena went home and told Maria the news. She hid it from the children, however, not wanting to give them false hopes.

Maria made plans to return to Italy, to her native village. She and Helena feared for their parents' fate and agreed that Maria should get there as soon as possible to try to find them. Two days later, Maria said farewell to Helena and the children and set out for Italy.

Gaston accompanied Maria to the train station for the start of her journey home. Maria's and Helena's lives were still at risk from those who did not know the facts and had access only to rumors. He feared the settling of scores by a drumhead court-martial. Although this phenomenon was becoming less common as the Free French police began arresting collaborators more systematically, there were still cases of revenge killings following summary trials, as well as executions.

Gaston parted from Maria and returned to Helena to tell her the information he had gathered. His brother Gerard had been the one to treat Annette, but to his great sorrow she had been taken when he was away from the institution and he had not been able to trace her. Gaston promised Helena that he would try to find Annette in the tangle of documents that was seized after the Germans abandoned their command posts. Helena felt a glimmer of hope, but she did not have high expectations.

A few days passed, during which their lives began to recover some semblance of normalcy. They started leaving the house occasionally for short walks; once in a while, they would encounter a burned German armored vehicle, and once they even came across the dead bodies of some collaborators who had been executed in a court-martial. And yet, despite everything, there was already an atmosphere of freedom that they had not felt for years.

One day, Helena was with the children as they played on the boulevard, not far from the building where it had all started.

Helena looked up at the building and thought to herself, *Marek, if you could only see them... I kept my promise and we survived. The children are healthy.* Watching the children at play, she breathed a sigh of relief. She rejoiced once more at having been liberated from her imprisonment with Helmut, that the children were saved from the horrors that had awaited so many Jews, and that her sister was saved as well. She hoped that her parents were well and waited eagerly for a message from Maria, but in the meantime no word had come.

Suddenly she heard a voice calling her name.

She turned around and saw Monsieur Dubois. She walked towards him and they embraced warmly.

"You have no idea what a wonderful surprise it is to see you, the children... I was so worried about you. But I followed you from a distance a couple of times, just to make sure that you were getting by. Where is your sister?"

"She went back to Italy to find our parents. And how is your wife doing?"

"Sadly, she was killed in a shootout between the Germans and the underground... It took place just outside our bakery, in the last few days before the liberation of the city. She insisted on opening the bakery and on that day, just before closing, everything fell apart. The bakery was destroyed by an explosion nearby; my wife was unscathed, but instead of fleeing, she stayed there, apparently to assess the damage. Then shooting started between the underground and the Germans who were still alive after the explosion. She was hit and died within a few seconds. I haven't decided what to do yet. The bakery is still in ruins... I think I'll leave Paris and move in with my brother who lives in the south." He glanced at the children and observed, "the children look good. They have smiles on their faces."

"Yes, I went through some tough times, but I managed to protect them. When I was a prisoner, I complied to their demands. In exchange, the the children were not hurt. This is the first time I'm telling anyone."

"I'm very sorry to hear that. We have all been hurt in this terrible war, but we have to pick ourselves up and move on. Have you heard about Annette?"

"No, I'm still searching for information on her."

"I'm sorry to tell you this," Monsieur Dubois began, "but Annette did not survive. She was murdered in the concentration camp in Paris. A few days after the liberation, Annette's cousin from England came to me and told me of her fate. I told her about you and the children, and she was very happy and wanted to find you. She is staying at the Meridien Hotel, in the 16th arrondissement."

Helena did not fully understand the significance of this information, but something bothered her. She said to Monsieur Dubois, "I would be happy for the children to meet their relatives. I don't think they have met anyone, because they were too little." She was trying to digest the bitter news that Annette was no longer among the living. "At the hardest moments, I tried to encourage Olivier and give him hope that perhaps we would still find their mother. How can I tell him something like this now? Those children have been through so much, and now it turns out that the hardest part is still before them. It will leave a scar for the rest of their lives. How will they grow up, orphaned of both their parents?"

"I'm sorry, I have to go home now. My brother is supposed to be coming to me soon. Do you still live in the same building where you brought the children the first time? Maybe I will come visit you before I leave."

"Yes, we're still there."

Just then, Olivier and Laurent approached and greeted Monsieur Dubois politely. He crouched down and hugged them. They both felt uncomfortable; Laurent did not remember who he was, and Olivier did not have particularly fond memories of the man.

Monsieur Dubois released them from his embrace, and they stepped back. He got to his feet.

"I am very happy to see you all. What you did was exceptional; in fact, you have become their mother," he told Helena.

His last sentence left her speechless, but it was the truth. Helena had become the mother of two orphaned boys, for whom she was all they had in the world.

Now, she had to find a way to tell Olivier that his dream of finding his mother would never come true. The child had been waiting so many days for his mother, days that turned into weeks, weeks into months, and months into years, and yet he had kept his imaginary connection with his mother, even though he scarcely remembered what she looked like. How would he handle the news?

One thing Olivier did as soon as the war ended was to take out the pictures of his father and mother, which he had kept hidden up to then at Helena's request, for fear that the pictures would disclose the children's origins and their parents' true identity.

Helena turned to Monsieur Dubois. "I am sorry for your tragedy. I hope that we will all manage to stay strong," and they said goodbye.

One morning after the meeting with Monsieur Dubois, during breakfast, Helena said to Olivier, "I want you to know that you are the best thing that's ever happened to me. From the day I met you as a baby and throughout all those days when the Germans were here, you're the one who gave me strength. I feel that you and Laurent are like my own children."

"But where is our mother?" asked Olivier.

"You know that I've been searching for Maman. You remember the man that we first thought was bad, but in fact he was just watching over us, Gaston?"

"Is he one of the good soldiers that beat the Germans?"

"Yes, that's him. So, he told me that they haven't found Maman, and that apparently the Germans took her just like they took Papa. I'm so sorry, it's impossible to know for sure what happened to her; they haven't found her, and it seems that the same thing that happened to Papa happened to her too." "It's not true!" Olivier shouted.

Helena bent down to him. "My precious boy, I don't know what to say. I want to find your mother very much, so that you could be a family again. I'll do everything I can to find her, but I want you to know that no matter what happens, I'll always be here for you. Like family. Like Maman. I love you more than anything else in this world." She pulled him close, and they sobbed in each other's arms.

2

More days passed, and Olivier gradually began to absorb what Helena had told him. Without noticing, he started to become aggressive towards his brother Laurent and towards Helena. She took care to protect him from himself, as well as protecting his brother, who suffered from Olivier's pent-up frustration and became his target on more than one occasion. Helena would embrace Olivier until his rage gave way to heart-breaking sobs. Slowly, Olivier's aggressive stance softened, but in its place, he became dependent and fearful, terrified that Helena would leave him.

One day, Helena asked him to watch his brother for a short time while she goes out to a meeting connected to her return to work. Olivier had a panic attack and clung to her with all his might, not letting her move. She tried to calm him, explaining to him that she had to go back to work, since their financial situation had become difficult and her savings were starting to run out, but in the end, unable to leave him in that condition, she was forced to miss the meeting.

"Olivier, my love, I will always be here for you, don't be afraid. Laurent and you, you are both my children. No one is going to take you away from me and I will never leave you." She hugged him, and he gradually relaxed in her embrace. She worked hard to rebuild his confidence. It was already the third time that the boy had been faced with mourning and loss. The first time was when Marek disappeared; though he had been very young then, he understood what was going on. The second time was when Annette handed them over to the Dubois family and disappeared from their lives. And now, the third time, when Helena told him the hard truth, dashing his hope that his mother would return.

One morning, a few days after this incident, a soft knock was heard at the door.

Helena went to the door and asked, "who is it?"

From outside the door, a woman's voice answered, "my name is Olga. I am Annette's cousin."

Helena immediately flung open the door and said in great excitement, "welcome! I've been waiting for you to come. Monsieur Dubois told me that you have come to Paris." Noticing a man standing behind Olga, she said, "come in, come in." Olga entered together with the unknown man.

"Let me introduce Mr. Cohen. He's a friend of the family." Helena offered her hand, but his handshake was cold, and she shuddered.

The children, hearing the voices, came out in their pajamas and stood behind Helena.

Olga clapped her hands. "God, he looks so much like Marek!" She tried to bend down to them, but they retreated further behind Helena.

Helena turned around to them, bent down, and said, "this is Olga, your aunt. She has come from England to see you."

"Indeed, I'm your aunt," Olga said, "from your mother's side of the family. I met you, Olivier, when you were just born. I don't know your brother Laurent at all, I only got the news of his birth from your mother's last letters. We tried the whole time to get to you, but it was not possible. I'm so sorry that you were alone all those years." "They were certainly not alone," Helena could not refrain from responding, "they were with me. I brought them up. I watched over them to make sure that nothing would happen to them, and I was here when they had no one else in the world." She spoke quietly but decisively, like a mother defending her children.

"Of course," Olga hurriedly answered, "I meant that their family was not at their side."

Helena persisted. "At the moment, I am their family. They don't know anything else." She was hinting to Olga to refrain from speaking in front of them in order to avoid causing them unnecessary stress. Olga smiled in agreement. She pulled out of her bag two gifts wrapped in paper and said to the children, "I brought you a little gift from England. That's where I'm from. Here," she held out the gifts.

Helena turned to them. "What do you say?"

But both boys were silent, taken aback. This was the first time that strangers had come to their home saying that they were family. Laurent opened his gift, not understanding what all the commotion was about, but Olivier hesitated. He understood that this was his mother's relative who had come to visit, but he knew that his real family was Helena.

Hesitantly, he took the gift and began to unwrap it. The boys sat down side by side and began to examine each other's gifts. They were puzzles, each one suited to the boy's age.

Meanwhile, the adults were free to speak quietly, without distracting the children.

"Helena, I owe you a great debt of gratitude for everything you have done for these little ones. We tried our best to get here, or at least to obtain information. Finally, we managed to get information on the Dubois family, but we did not find out the fate of the children until very recently. It's a tragedy, everything that happened to this family… And in general, everything that's happened in the past four years. All the ruin and destruction. In England, we lived through difficult times during the German bombing of London. Paris did not experience the destruction that we experienced in London. Thank God we survived," Olga said softly.

"I also know that you were a friend to the Germans," she suddenly added sharply, "those who murdered my family." Her words fell like hammer blows on Helena's head.

"Excuse me?!"

"That's what Monsieur Dubois said, that they met you in the stripper's club and that you befriended them."

Helena raged, "I'm very sorry, but this conversation is not to my liking. Who are you to come to me and preach to me about who and what I am? These children are my whole life; all those years, I did everything in my power to save them, and if what you take away from that is that I was a friend of the Germans, then you really don't understand anything, and you have no idea what it's like to live under German occupation. I demand an apology!" She was boiling mad.

"I don't know why you're so angry," Olga responded. "That's the information that I was given about you."

"You have no feelings," Helena shot back, more enraged than ever. "How did the children survive if I'm a friend of the Germans? After all, they deported and murdered the Jews of Paris!"

"Maybe they were here just so you'd feel good about yourself," Olga lashed out.

"I ask you to leave this house immediately." Helena snatched the gifts from the children's hands and held them out to Olga. "Get out of this house." She pointed at the door, standing between the visitors and the children.

Olivier stood behind Helena and held onto Laurent, who had begun to wail because his gift had been taken away.

"I don't understand what you're angry about," Olga tarried. "I just told you what I recently learned." She went on, her voice hardening, "These children are my family, my blood relatives. Annette was murdered by the Germans and I've come to take them."

Helena could not have imagined such a situation. Just when everything was starting to fall into place, when the children had found some stability, love, and family, here was this woman, who did not know them at all, coming to take them away.

"Get out of my house!" Helena shoved them out the door and slammed it behind them.

Olivier had never seen Helena so angry. She leaned against the door, her eyes streaming with tears. He came up and hugged her.

"What does that woman want? I don't want to go! I don't want them to take us! I'm yours!" he said, unaware of what those words meant to her.

Helena sat down on the floor and hugged Olivier, and Laurent came up and clung to her. They were like two baby birds seeking shelter under their mother's wing.

Helena went about for the rest of the day with a sense of nagging unease. Having no choice, she brought the children with her to the nightclub, to the interview that she had missed earlier. On the way there, someone was following her without her noticing, taking note of everything she was doing.

She got to the nightclub and brought the children into the office of the director, Hubert, who was happy to see her. Hubert was the new director who had replaced Jerome, who had left for the United States at the start of the war. She and Hubert spoke briefly about the program, and he told her that in a few more weeks he intended to open the nightclub in honor of the end of the war, and a festive premier was planned with many invited guests. Helena agreed to come back and perform, as long as she could get help with the children. "You know we'll help you. Your story touched all our hearts."

She ended the day with mixed feelings. Although she was returning to her work routine and would have help with the children, the morning's events had left her with heavy fears.

They came home towards evening and went to bed, all three of them together. Lately they had been sleeping in one bed. After the children fell asleep, Helena would move over to the armchair next to them, as though she were watching over them.

Days had passed since that morning when Olga appeared. They did not hear any more from her. Helena would come to rehearsals at the nightclub with the children in tow and bring them into the director's office. One of the cabaret director's daughters would watch them there, as Hubert had promised her.

About three weeks after Olga's visit, Gaston came to the nightclub, bearing surprising news. Annette had been found, in bad shape both physically and emotionally, but alive. After a long period when the hospital staff had been unable to identify her, a relative came and managed to recognize her.

Helena understood that Olga was now with Olivier's and Laurent's mother, apparently taking care of her. For Helena, the news brought joy mingled with sorrow; Olivier and Laurent would be able to go back and be reunited with their mother, but she would be forced to part from the two children who had become her whole world.

She decided not to talk to Olivier yet, until she knew for sure what was happening. Olivier's emotional state was fragile, at best; he could sense his aunt's involvement and feared for his and Laurent's future.

3

Things moved quickly.

The next day Olga arrived with an order from the civil court, instructing Helena to turn the children over to her, since she had been appointed legal guardian for the mother and her children. She came accompanied by a policeman dressed in civilian clothes and by Mr. Cohen, the man whom she had introduced on the previous visit. Mr. Cohen turned out to be the family's attorney, a leading attorney in Olga's home city of London.

They presented the document to Helena, who turned pale and sank into a chair. The children clung to her, Olivier clutching her tightly, as though he knew that in another moment, they were going to take him away from her.

Helena stroked Olivier's hair and kissed him on the forehead. She then pulled herself together and said, "I ask that you come back tomorrow. For the sake of the little ones, this has to be done right, not like this. I know that she has been found," trying to state the fact without Olivier figuring out that she was talking about his mother, "but she is in bad shape."

The detective looked at Olga and Mr. Cohen and said that it was their decision; according to the court order, they were authorized to take the children at that moment.

Olga understood the situation and felt compassion for the children. "She's right," Olga told the detective. "We'll arrange another time to come."

Helena thanked her and added, "I have one more request. I would like to see her, if you can tell me where she is hospitalized," again, without pronouncing Annette's name. "And one last thing: I want to offer my assistance during the first days with them; they are dearer to me than anything."

Olga looked at Helena. On the one hand, she had been a Nazi collaborator; but on the other hand, she had been the one to take care of Annette's children. "We'll be in touch and see how things develop," she said, not wanting to make any promises. The three visitors then left.

Helena hugged the children again and turned to Olivier. "You remember who that is, right?"

"Yes, it's Maman's cousin who was already here before. Why did she come again?"

"I'll explain it to you. I'll try to remind you of everything that happened to us during the war, and then you'll understand why she has come. What do you remember from the beginning of the war?"

"What, when Mari came?"

"Even before that. Do you remember the family that you were living with?"

"I remember Monsieur Dubois. He was nice, but I didn't like his wife. She was always getting angry at us; Laurent cried all the time there, and I had to calm him down. Why are you asking all these questions?" the boy asked fearfully.

"I want you to remember everything that happened. I want you to try and remember Maman and Papa too."

He was silent, staring at her as if he did not understand what he was expected to do.

"I remember that Maman took me and Laurent to Monsieur Dubois one day and left us there. I tried to scream and run away, but she left too quickly." He looked at her as though suddenly struck by lightning. "Why did she leave us?"

Helena stroked his hair. "She didn't leave you, she *saved you*, sweetie. Do you know who came after that? The bad people, the Germans. Do you know what they did?"

"Yes, they killed people."

"Yes, sweetie, they were really evil. Do you know what a church is?"

"Yes, I know. Once, Maman took me there on the holiday where people get presents under a tree. Why are you asking?"

"Because I want to tell you everything that happened, so you'll know and remember. In our world there are people who go to church and they are called 'Christians'. There are also people who believe differently, and they're called 'Jews.' They're like the Christians but they have different beliefs. However, they all believe in God who helps us and protects us."

"Why didn't He protect us, then? Why didn't he help Maman?"

"Maybe he actually did help her… She brought you to us, and that way the bad people didn't hurt you. The Germans wanted to hurt lots of people, and particularly Jews; they did the evilest thing that could be: they killed Jews."

"Why did they only kill Jews?"

"I don't know, but they did not kill only Jews. They also killed French Christians, but they did a lot of bad things to Jews. They also hurt Maman, and that's why she hid you. But I want you to know that your aunt who has come is also a Jew, and she came to look for Maman and for you because you are her family." "So, I am a Jew too?" he asked in wonderment.

"Yes, you're a Jew. But you know you're not different; you and I are alike, right?" Laurent was sitting on her lap the whole time, playing with her hair.

"Olga looked and looked until she found Maman," Helena continued. "Maman is alive."

Olivier's face lit up. "I want Maman! I want to see her! When can we go to her?"

"Tomorrow they're coming to take you to see Maman, and you will go with them to their house."

"And we will all go see Maman?"

"If you want me to, I'll come with you." "But afterwards we'll come back here?"

"Let's wait and see what happens tomorrow. Now we have to get ready and go to work. Help me with Laurent."

"Maybe we could go to Maman today?" suggested Olivier.

"I also want to go; I also miss Maman …" She wanted to finish the sentence, *and Papa*, but stopped herself at the last second. "But we can only visit her together with Aunt Olga. Maman is sick in the hospital and Olga is taking care of her. Let's wait one more day and then we'll go visit her."

Olivier was satisfied, having gotten what he had waited so long for: the news that his mother was alive. But recalling what Helena had tried to explain to him earlier, about his being Jewish, he asked, "what makes Jews different from everyone else?"

Helena tried to minimize the differences, presenting what had happened as a result of evil not connected to Judaism. "Sweetie, there's nothing different about you or any Jew, the difference is all in the heads of other people with evil in them; people who want to hurt whatever they don't agree with, just like that, for no reason. You, Laurent, Mari, and I— we're all the same, and we'll always be for each other. Even when you go back to Maman. It doesn't matter if you're Jewish or I'm Christian. We're one family."

The rest of the day passed quickly, filled with excitement about tomorrow.

4

Morning came. Olivier got out of bed and woke Laurent up. They ran to the armchair where Helena was sleeping— in a rather cramped position, but one she was used to by now. They woke her up with a kiss on the cheek.

"Good morning, my loves. Are you excited?" she asked with a pounding heart. Today they might find what they have been seeking; but she would lose her whole world, for she would lose them.

"Let's go get ready. Your aunt will be here soon and we'll all go together."

She dressed them in their finest clothes. She put on a modest dress, which in fact highlighted her beauty. She had not felt so vital and confident for a long time. Inside, she was agitated; but she gave herself a pep talk: *I'm not their mother. I promised Marek I'd do this, and I've met all my obligations. Now, I have to make sure they return to their family. It will be hard for me, but I'll have to keep moving forward, maybe even have a child of my own...* Feeling strong, she focused on thinking ahead.

Dressed and ready, the three of them waited in the living room. A short while, later they heard a knock at the door.

Helena opened it. Again, their aunt was accompanied by Mr. Cohen, but this time without the detective, which made Helena feel a bit better.

Olga kissed the children and asked, "do you know where we're going?"

Olivier answered confidently, "Yes, we're going to see Maman!"

"Right, sweetie," Olga answered. "Well then, let's go. We're only allowed to visit Maman until noon. She's very tired and sick."

As Helena bent down to pick up her handbag, Olga asked, "are you coming too?"

"Yes, that's what we agreed upon two days ago. Annette was my friend; all through the war, I hoped the day would come when she would be found, and the family could reunite. They suffered a lot, and I'm part of that."

Olga understood that Helena spoke the truth and that there was no point in arguing, for Helena had indeed been the one to save the children.

"So then, let's go," she said with obvious dissatisfaction.

They took the subway to the Hôtel-Dieu hospital, one of Paris' famous hospitals, which had continued to treat the local population even during the war, as well as injured German soldiers and underground fighters.

They reached the hospital and went up to an internal medicine ward on the third floor. The atmosphere in the hospital was difficult. Although several weeks had already passed since Paris and all of France were liberated, the hospital was packed with patients, evidence of the war that had just ended. Wounded men in uniform, with missing limbs, mingled with civilian patients.

The children clutched Helena's hands. As they made their way through the hospital, their grasp tightening until it actually caused her pain. Laurent lifted up his arms, signaling that he wanted to be picked up.

They entered the ward where Annette was lying. Helena immediately noticed that it was a geriatrics ward, or otherwise for people who were not aware of their surroundings.

Olga stood next to the curtain and peeked in. She then turned to them and said, "Maman is very sick, but maybe if she sees you, my darlings, she'll get better. It will give her strength." Olga pulled the curtain back and ushered everyone in.

Olivier, terrified, clutched Helena's leg. Laurent buried his face in Helena's neck.

Helena studied the woman whom she had known, and a tear rolled down her cheek. Annette was nothing but skin and bones, more dead than alive. Her facial features bore only the faintest hint of the woman she had once been. Her expression was frozen, her eyes fixed on the ceiling. Helena knew that she had to act quickly, otherwise, the children's behavior would be the opposite of what everyone expected. These children, after all this time, were meeting their half-dead mother.

She set Laurent down, who refused to let go of her, and bent down to both of them. "Do you remember what we said? That when the bad people left, we would look for Maman and that you'd become a family again. Maman suffered a lot because of the Germans. Let's try to give her the strength to get better: you two are the medicine that can save her." She looked into Olivier's eyes, and as though at the touch of a magic wand, he went from terrified child to responsible adult, charged with a rescue mission.

Olivier let go of Helena's hand and fearfully approached the bed. Olga caressed him and looked with some admiration at Helena, highly impressed by her words. She thought to herself that, despite everything, this was a noble woman.

Olivier stood by the bed, next to Annette's head. He lifted his hand and touched her forehead, then began to stroke her. The touch of his hand seemed to affect Annette, for she blinked. He continued to stroke her cheek. Laurent stood next to his brother, holding onto him.

Olivier whispered, "Maman, it's Olivier. I'm here."

Annette blinked again, twice, as though telling him with her eyes, "I feel you."

"Maman," he repeated, "Laurent is here too." He gently pulled Laurent close to the bed. Then he took Laurent's hand and brought it to Annette's face. "Here, feel him. He's a big boy already."

Annette kept blinking. It seemed to Helena that Annette was trying to smile. Olivier continued caressing her, then said, "Helena came too. She took care of us all the time, until you could come back."

Annette continued blinking. One could sense that she understood and was trying to respond to him.

Suddenly, Annette opened her mouth and whispered with an effort, "O…" Silence. After another moment she uttered another syllable, "li…"

"Yes, Maman, I'm here," Olivier answered her. No one present in the room could remain unaffected; everyone's eyes filled with tears.

The emotional moment was sharply interrupted by a doctor in a white coat who came in and asked them all to leave quietly.

Olga tried to argue with him. "But just a moment ago she made great progress! For the first time in weeks, she managed to say a word. She called her son's name!"

"That's right," said the doctor. "And because of that, she must rest now. Her heart is very weak, she must not get too excited. That's why I asked you to come every day for only a short amount of time; together we'll try to get her stronger. Maman can't handle too much all at once."

Helena looked at Olivier, who was furrowing his brow. He was listening to the doctor with intense seriousness. "Let's leave now. We'll give her strength, but she must rest now. We'll come back tomorrow, like the doctor asked us to."

The doctor looked at the boy admiringly. He had just found his mother and now he was already being asked to leave her.

"I just want to say goodbye to her," Olivier requested, and the doctor nodded.

Olivier approached the bed and lay his head on Annette's shoulder. Annette's hand moved slightly towards her belly, apparently trying to reach Olivier's head, but she did not have the strength. Olivier noticed that and, without moving his head, lifted his hand and touched his mother's palm.

Annette smiled, as though her hopes and prayers for her children had been fulfilled. They were here. She was granted the gift of having them with her again.

They left the hospital. Helena turned to Olga, "I would like it very much if we could all have dinner together at our house. Despite the harsh words between us, we share something in common: we both wish a good life for these children, and for Annette to return to herself."

Olga nodded. She was not insensitive to what had happened in the hospital. They agreed to meet in the evening. Olga asked Helena if they could take a short walk with the children before coming to the apartment.

Helena's heart skipped a beat, but she did not show any outward sign of agitation.

Taking a deep breath, she turned to the boys, "children, would you like to take a walk with your aunt?"

Again, Olivier took charge. "Yes. I'll help with Laurent, and after that we'll go home to Helena!" he made sure to announce. He was skilled at reconciling people.

Olga nodded. "Of course, we'll come later for dinner."

Helena asked the director of the cabaret for the evening off. Being home that evening would be important for creating trust between Olga and the children and her. She kissed the children and shook hands with Olga and Mr. Cohen, then turned to leave. She walked a short distance away and, without their noticing, peeked back at them. She felt as though a part of her body was being cut off. She saw Laurent and then Olivier turning back to look for her, but she hid so they would not see her.

At home, Helena began preparing dinner: appetizers of goose liver from one of Paris's finest delicatessens, roast beef with truffles. These products were still difficult to obtain, but she wanted to make an elegant meal in honor of the momentous occasion.

Just before 6:30 p.m., Olga returned with the children.

"Where is Mr. Cohen?" asked Helena.

"Oh, he's busy. He does a lot of helping Jewish families that suffered in the war. He does everything on a volunteer basis; there are so many cases to handle with the French authorities. Don't worry, you'll have a chance to get to know each other better."

The children looked happy. They had been treated to an afternoon out at the amusement fair by Aunt Olga, and enjoyed ice cream and sweets as well. Suddenly, they had family, something that only a few weeks earlier had not existed.

The dinner was delicious, but Helena and Olga hardly had a bite. Olga did not touch the meat because she kept kosher, and Helena did not eat because she had no appetite.

Olga told Helena about her husband, a wealthy businessman who had contributed to the Allies during the war. His money had gone toward defending civilians during the German blitz on London. She told Helena that her last contact with Marek and Annette was a few days before they were supposed to come stay with her, and that she and her husband had planned to welcome them at the port. She never heard from them since, and had not managed to obtain even a scrap of information about them.

The first bits of information that she had managed to obtain after the war was in the neighborhood where Marek and Annette had lived, from the bakery owner Monsieur Dubois. He told her that the children were alive and that they were living with Helena. The next piece information was the result of strenuous exertion by Mr. Cohen, who managed to locate Annette through his ties with the underground.

Helena, for her part, told Olga what had become of Marek: how she had tried to get them tickets for the train to southern France, on their escape route to England; how on that very same day, when she already had the tickets and travel permit in hand, Marek disappeared; how later, through Monsieur Dubois' stories, she understood that Marek had been murdered. She told Olga of how Helmut, the officer in charge of the Germans in Paris, had taken control of her life and her body, and how she had become his prisoner.

Olga was left speechless. "The stories I heard about you were so different… I-I'm so sorry," she apologized. "Many people think that you collaborated with the Germans."

"I know. It's a good thing everyone thought that; that's what saved the children."

"You know how it is," Helena added. "What's said, or what people imagine, is not always what is really happening. It's possible to believe anything, but it's always better to hear the truth first-hand, and even then, one doesn't always understand what really happened. At the end of the war, just before Paris was liberated, the underground members were in my apartment. They wanted information on Helmut, but also threatened me and the children; they didn't care about anything. I lived in fear from both sides, from both the Germans and the underground. I could have easily lost my life, and then Laurent and Olivier would have been sent with the rest of the Jews to a transit camp or, God forbid, to an extermination camp. According to what I heard, thousands of Jews from Paris were sent to those camps."

Olga looked at her and fell silent.

"The ones who saved me and gave me strength, when my body couldn't stand being near the German officers anymore, were Olivier and Laurent. They were the power source that kept me moving forward," Helena said with sparkling eyes.

Towards the end of the evening, Olga got up and said that she had to go, that she had to be at the hospital the next morning.

Helena said to her, "We'll be there around ten o'clock. I've asked for two days off from work." The nightclub director had given her the time off, even though they were in the midst of energetic preparations to return to the routine that Paris had been anticipating for so long.

Olga came up to Helena and bravely enveloped her in an embrace. They kissed each other goodbye in the manner of family members.

Helena moved the children to her bed after they fell asleep in the living room, then took her place in the armchair and fell asleep herself.

The next morning, like the previous day, Olivier and Laurent got up earlier than usual and ran to Helena, who awoke with a smile. *Life was returning to normal*, she thought to herself. They got ready, ate breakfast, and set out for the hospital.

Annette's recovery happened like a miracle. During the night, she had already managed to pronounce Olivier's name to the head nurse and to move her hands, as though she had received a pill giving her the strength to begin to live again.

In the morning, with the children's arrival and the touch of Olivier's hand, her life force returned to her ever more powerfully. She managed to direct her gaze at him, gave him a real smile, and moved her fingers to touch his hand with her palm.

Those were happy days. Olga and Helena talked a great deal about what they had gone through during the war. Olga, listening attentively to Helena's stories, experienced the horrors of the occupation through her words. Olivier and Laurent drew closer to Annette who, with each passing day, made a little more progress in her movements.

5

A week later, Helena and the children got ready as they did every morning to go visit their mother.

When they arrived at the hospital, Helena saw Mr. Cohen waiting in the main lobby with a grim expression.

"Good morning. Did something happen?" Helena asked him.

He directed his gaze at her, then looked at the children. Helena understood that he did not want the children to hear.

She imagined the worst, that what the children had dreamed of for so long— to return to their mother and be a family once again— would never happen.

Mr. Cohen looked at Helena, nodded his head, and just said quietly, "not with us."

Helena understood that they had lost Annette for good.

She had managed to bear all the humiliation and hurts that she suffered during the war, but this was too much. Unable to stand, she fainted.

The next thing she knew, the children were leaning over her, shouting at her to get up. She opened her eyes slowly to see a nurse crouching beside her, trying to examine her, and the children and Mr. Cohen on her other side.

"I-I'm fine. It was just a moment of weakness," she tried to reassure everyone. The children hugged her, and Mr. Cohen gave her his hand to help her up.

Olga arrived, weeping. She knelt down next to the children and hugged them tightly. Olivier, as always, read the adults' behavior and understood what had happened. "I want to see Maman!" he shouted.

"Olivier, sweetie," said Olga tearfully, "she's already in Heaven with the angels…"

"I want to see her.!"

"It's impossible… She's already been taken out of the ward," Olga told him.

The two women looked at each other and fell into an embrace.

"She will be buried this afternoon, apparently at three o'clock, in the Jewish cemetery, next to the Bois de Boulogne," Olga said.

Olivier tried to run away, but Helena stopped him. "Sweetie, I'm so sorry about Maman. It seems she just did not have any more strength. She saved her last strength to see that you are okay and being taken care of, and when she saw that you are, she couldn't hang on any longer. She's with Papa now. They're together."

"You're just making that up! I don't believe you! There are no angels and there is no heaven!" he burst out with deep frustration and lack of faith in the world around him. As Laurent stood behind him, they collected themselves and left the hospital in silence.

Helena said to Olga, "I'll go home with them. We'll meet at the funeral. I'll get a friend to stay with them, although I don't know how it will go…"

They kissed each other goodbye, and Helena returned home with the children. Olivier resisted the touch of her hand or any closeness. Helena did not give up; the more he resisted, the more she hugged him. Finally, Olivier let go of his anger and dissolved into tears in her arms.

On the way to her apartment, Helena asked her neighbor Veronique to look after the children. Olivier refused to part with her at first, but Helena appealed to his heart. "I want you to think of everything that we've been through together. We're still together, sweetie, forever. I have to go to Aunt Olga now, to an adult meeting." She did not want to tell him that she was going to Annette's funeral.

Olivier listened to her and nodded his head, not wanting to be a burden on Helena. She hugged him and Laurent and asked him to help Veronique with his little brother. He knew his job, especially with people that they were not used to; he was Laurent's anchor.

Helena set out for Annette's funeral, which was a struggle for her. Jews who did not know Annette came to pray according to the ritual and to say the mourner's prayer. Mr. Cohen and Olga accompanied the body, wrapped in shrouds and borne on a stretcher by the surviving members of the Paris Jewish community who now spent their time attending burial ceremonies. It was Mr. Cohen who had arranged the funeral and recruited the community members to help, with the help of the Great Synagogue of Paris. Through the shroud, it was evident that Annette's body was gaunt. *What a tragic end to an unfair life for Annette, Marek, and the children,* Helena thought.

For a moment her thoughts sailed away, and she remembered the magical moments that she and Marek had shared… Now, she just felt pain, pain that she had hurt Annette by betraying her with Marek's. Even if Annette had not known, it was still an unforgivable injury. She tried to comfort herself that part of the connection between her and Marek brought her to protect the children and sacrifice her liberty for them.

The sounds of the prayers brought her back to reality, to Annette's burial.

After the ceremony, which lasted a few more minutes, Helena went up to Olga. "I'm so sorry about everything that has happened to this family… The children were supposed to get their mother back, and just when everything was starting to work out, it's as though she said to herself— *that's it, I can go now…*"

Olga laid her hand on Helena's shoulder. "It's thanks to you that this family was not annihilated. You saved these children. There are no words to describe what you did…"

Helena, who did not cry very often, burst into tears and hugged Olga.

"What now?" she asked.

"I no longer know. I'll go back to the hotel now, but I'd love to come to you this evening, to see the children."

"With pleasure. Tomorrow I have to go back to work." "So, who will watch the children tomorrow?" asked Olga.

"They come with me, they have a room there and a friend who watches them."

"Would you like me to watch them while you're gone?"

Helena was about to say yes, but something stopped her. She was suddenly attacked by a strange fear that she could not explain. *How can I bring her into my house? I don't know what her real intentions are,* she thought to herself. The children were like flesh of her flesh. She was so bound to them that she could not imagine her life without them.

Despite her hesitation, she finally answered: "Yes, with pleasure. It will help me a lot, and it seems to me that the children are already used to you. I'll go home now and get ready, and you are invited to come over." They parted ways and Helena went home.

Together with the children, she made supper. They laughed together; even though it was supposed to be a sad day, she managed to get them to loosen up a little.

Olga came just before six o'clock with Mr. Cohen. The atmosphere became somewhat tense, but she had expected that; they had all had a difficult day. Olivier and Laurent actually managed to alleviate the tension somewhat.

"The children are wonderful," Mr. Cohen said when they sat down to eat. "You've invested a lot in them, and it shows in their behavior, their manners, and in general."

"I have treated them like my own children. You may not know this, but we used to live in the same building before the war, and we were close neighbors. Olivier was such a sweet baby that I fell in love with him at first sight. One of the promises I made to their parents, when we felt that something was about to happen, was to help the children at any cost. We just didn't know how hard that was going to be..." Olivier and Laurent ate and watched the adults speaking among themselves. They did not join the conversation, but they took in everything.

"There's one thing I don't understand," Olga said. "Monsieur Dubois said Annette asked him to take care of the children."

"Indeed," said Helena. "I left the building just before the invasion, so when Annette needed help, I was no longer their neighbor," trying to blur the timeline somewhat. An in-depth investigation would have brought out her affair with Marek, which she did not want to reveal. "They were on good terms with the Dubois family as well. At a later stage, when Monsieur Dubois felt that the situation was becoming dangerous, as Jews were being taken away everywhere and some of the French had turned informers, he asked for my help. And the rest is history."

"At the same time," Helena continued, "my sister Maria came to Paris. She had fled the regime in Italy. Since I was known as a single woman with no children, we created a cover story that she had come with her children."

"Yes, we were Mari's children, and Helena was our aunt," Olivier interjected, with a loving smile at the mention of Maria.

"I understand," said Mr. Cohen. "That's an amazing story, it must be said. I am helping quite a number of Jews who were hurt by the Nazis in Paris. To my good fortune, my family left Paris in the early 1930s, which enabled me to make a life for myself in England. But that's not what I wanted to say. I heard of so many horrors that those people went through... I don't understand how human beings can behave with such cruelty towards other human beings, with no reason, just because they are Jews. Many of them are not even religious; they had no sign to distinguish them as Jews."

Helena sighed, remembering the Germans she had known. "It's hard to call them *human beings*; I can tell you that they behaved like soulless machines. Although they could be polite, the moment they wanted something, they used everything to get it, every method and every means. They didn't see the people around them, only themselves above everything. When you don't value anything around you because you are above everything and you deserve everything, that's what happens."

Olga told her about London, how she suffered during the war from the German bombing, and about the Jewish community in England; she talked about volunteering in the armament factories, as well as her volunteer work with widowed mothers through an Army liaison office.

Towards the end of the evening, the children fell asleep at the table. Helena picked up Olivier, Olga picked up Laurent, and they laid them down together in the bed. They then went back to sit at the table.

"We have to go back to England soon," Olga sighed. "I want the children to come with me, to live with me and my husband." Drums pounded in Helena's head. She had hoped that it would never get to this, but apparently it was only natural; the ties of blood.

Helena sat down. She wanted to scream and banish them from her home on the spot, but she weighed her response carefully.

"You know, Olga," she sighed, "the children don't know anything but me. I'm their supporting pillar in this world. The Germans have finally left, we are beginning to feel freedom and life returning to normal— is it right to tear them away from all this now? I understand that you are their family, but I know what is right for them." She was careful not to insert herself into the equation, lest the fact that she thought the children should be with her might be interpreted as a self-centered interest, something she wanted in order to satisfy her own needs.

"Helena, I don't know what the most correct thing to do is, but I do know that Annette and Marek would want the children to grow up in a Jewish home that would give them what they lost."

"The children lost their mother today for the second time. For several years now, I have been the adult figure in their lives. They call me *Maman*. Does it seem right to you to shake up the foundation of their world that way?"

"Look, Helena, I don't want to shake up anything. But the environment that they are growing up in is not respectable. I am not belittling any action of yours, they're here thanks to you, but I would not want them to grow up in the shadow of the cabaret, if they were my children." Olga was ready to go all the way in her effort to bring the children back with her. For a medical reason, she could not bear her own children. Olivier and Laurent were the closest thing to fulfilling her dream of becoming a mother, especially since they were members of her family.

"I would not want my children to grow up in the shadow of German officers," she added.

Helena was hurt. "Thanks to the fact that there were German officers in the cabaret, those children were saved. I gave my life to the Germans in order to protect those children! How can you say something like that to me again?"

"Helena my dear, I didn't mean it. But I do see these children as part of our family. It's nothing against you."

"All you see in me is an unhealthy environment. All you talk about is the nightclub and the Germans," Helena said angrily. "How can you not see that despite everything they went through, these children are growing up healthy and sane? I don't intend to give up on the possibility of them growing up here with me, in the place where they survived the war. We have to think of everything."

"I don't think there's anything to think about; the only family they have at the moment is in England. They need resources, love, and an opportunity to move away from the place where they lost what was most precious to them," declared Olga.

"Olga, dear, even though you're a relative and thus perhaps have a legal claim to the children, I'm talking here about what's best for *them*, about what *they* want and what *they* need," Helena retorted decisively.

"I respect everything you're saying, Helena," Olga answered coldly, "but I think that after everything they've been through, looking at what is best for their future— they need to live with me in England."

Helena stood up. "I ask that you leave my house this minute. I can't deal with your insensitivity anymore. We were just liberated from years of war, from people who thought they were above everyone and who tortured us. How do you think the children will react when they lose the person closest to them once again?"

"Helena, you're going to have to deal with it. I don't want your connection with them to end, but they're going to live with us. We'll stay here for a few more days to arrange our departure together with them. We can either this the hard way— taking them accompanied by the authorities— or you can be part of the process and also keep connection with them in the future. I understand your feelings, but this is my decision. I am thinking only of the children's good and of their future, and their future is not here."

Helena opened the door for them and waited for them to leave. No one said goodbye.

Helena did not sleep the whole night. The next morning, she woke up the children and they made breakfast together. Towards noontime, they went with Helena to her rehearsals at the nightclub. The day passed without Helena hearing from Olga.

In the evening, when they returned home from the nightclub, they heard a knock on the door. Helena's heart skipped a beat.

"Who is it?" she asked.

"Gaston," came the voice of the former underground fighter. She heaved a sigh of relief and opened the peephole in the door. "Hello." She saw that he was alone and opened the door wide.

"You're still scared, I see," said Gaston with a small smile.

The children peeked out of the other room and then went back about their business.

"Look," Helena burst out, "I don't know why, but I feel open with you, after what we've been through together. On the one hand, you almost killed me, but on the other, you saved my life. What makes me feel comfortable with you is your transparency and truth." "Madame, that's a serious declaration," he smiled at her.

"I have to share with someone what I'm going through, I don't know what to do anymore... Let's just talk quietly, so the children won't hear. Do you know the story of my children?"

"Of course. That was one of the things that made us trust you. Not everyone would do what you did and deal with everything that you went through." Gaston's words brought tears to Helena's eyes.

"What happened?" he asked with a grave expression.

Helena wiped her eyes. "It's the family of Annette, the children's biological mother. Her cousin came from England. As you know, we managed to locate Annette in the hospital, but to everyone's sorrow, especially the children's, she did not make it. She looked like one of the walking dead when we found her. I don't want to think about what she went through all those years... Anyway, after she passed away, the cousin came back and announced that she intends to take the children with her back to England. It is going to happen in the next few days. She's walking around escorted by a lawyer. She also has the backing of the authorities. I don't know what to do or who to turn to! The government offices are still a jungle after the war... Nothing is in order yet."

Gaston cleared his throat before responding. "Look, I just came by to see how you were doing because I was in the neighborhood. I know it's not usually done, but I feel a certain obligation towards you. Tomorrow morning, I'll try to find out some details and see what can be done."

Helena felt a wave of heat pass through her. It was the first time in many long months that she had the feeling of a partner who was trying to help. "I'm really grateful to you. These children are my whole world. They are me and I am them. I just don't understand how we could be separated."

"I know," answered Gaston.

"I'm sorry, I haven't offered you anything since the moment you came in," Helena suddenly apologized. "Would you like a cup of coffee?"

"Oh, no. Thank you. I'll pay you a visit tomorrow afternoon."

"Tomorrow is not such a good day... It's the opening show at the nightclub."

"What about the children?"

"They'll be at the nightclub. I have an arrangement for them there."

"Then, maybe I'll walk you home after the show tomorrow?"

"That would be lovely of you, thank you... I'd like that."

The next day, Gaston sought out the Secret Service man with whom he had been in contact throughout the war and asked him for information on the case. The information was not favorable to Helena. In the wake of the horrors that the Jews had suffered, the authorities were offering overwhelming support for the requests of relatives of those who did not survive the war. In Olivier and Laurent's case, it had been decided to grant custody to Annette's cousin.

There was a slim chance of a ruling in Helena's favor, if it could be proved that being turned over to the cousin's custody would be detrimental to the children. In such a case, the welfare services would oppose the current ruling and make a professional recommendation to overturn the judges' decision. Such a recommendation could forbid complete separation from Helena and would require finding a compromise that would include ongoing contact with her.

The following day was an energetic one for Helena. Her show was impressive: she returned for a moment to what she loved to do, dancing; his was not the stage she had once hoped for, but she was still in the entertainment business.

She earned compliments from the nightclub owner, who said that the show went well, and that the audience was hypnotized.

Late in the evening, Gaston came to pick her and the children up, and drive them to her apartment. At the entrance to the apartment, she found a letter addressed to her from Italy. It was an official envelope. Helena bent down, picked it up, and opened it on her way into the apartment.

The letter was an official notification from the local council of her native village, stating that she had inherited her parents' plot of land in the village. She also learned from the letter that both her parents and Maria, her beloved sister, were no longer among the living, Helena burst out crying and Gaston, who was standing next to her, held her to keep her from falling and seated her on the armchair. "What happened?" he asked in a worried tone.

"Mari, Mari… My parents… Everyone's dead… I don't even know what happened, but everyone's dead…"

Olivier came up to her, understanding from her words that a disaster had befallen them.

"What happened to Mari?"

Helena looked at him through her tears and gave him a hug. "She's joined Maman. Mari is with Maman and Papa now." *How can all this be happening to me now*, she thought to herself.

I'm strong but I can't handle everything… "Is there anything I can do?" Gaston asked.

"I don't know… What can be done now?" Helena sobbed. "Why is this happening to me? Why don't I have a moment's peace…?" She looked at Gaston, and he stroked her hair and said, "Helena, there's lots still ahead of you. You can't fix what's already happened to you, but you have the future. Don't give up. I'm so sorry to hear of this tragedy. If there's anything I can do to help, please tell me."

"What future?!" she sobbed. "And the children, too…" She stopped herself. She did not want to continue in front of the children and drag them into fear of what might happen in a few days if she did not manage to stop Olga.

"Gaston, I want to know what happened to Mari; what happened there, why did she die after everything already ended? She was so young… She went through such a terrible thing here, just because I put her in the role of Laurent and Olivier's mother. She shouldn't have died. I want to know what happened to her."

"Using my connections, I just might be able to get the information," said Gaston. "I'll try to find out everything I can, and I'll get back to you."

Helena could not stop crying, and Gaston asked Olivier to bring her a glass of water. He sat down next to her and took her hand gently between two of his own.

"Helena, I know that this is a difficult moment, but if you want to take advantage of your chance with the two little ones, we'll have to act quickly. You have to file an application to adopt these children. It could delay by a few days the process of taking them away from here."

"I have no strength for anything right now," she answered in despair.

"I know, but you have to. We'll do it together."

Olivier suddenly broke in, "What does *adopt* mean?"

They both looked at him and Helena pulled herself back to the reality in which the children depended on her.

"When Maman and Papa left, you were left without parents. Now I want to be your mother and for you to be my children," she answered him lovingly.

"So, you'll be our mother?" Olivier's eyes lit up.

"Yes, that's what I want to do," she answered with a smile.

Gaston looked at her, thinking to himself what power this woman had. A moment earlier she had received news that her sister and parents were dead, but now she's picked herself up, ready to adopt two little orphans. Life was stronger than anything …

"I know that every minute is precious, but could we do it tomorrow?" Helena asked, looking at Gaston.

"Yes, I already looked into it, and they'll help us file an expedited application for adoption. Anyway, from the moment the process is initiated, the children cannot be removed from Paris." They were starting a process to decide once and for all to whom the children belonged. Helena knew that she would accept only one outcome, and that she would go out in defense of her children, the children that her sister, Maria, had raised.

The following morning, they went to the city hall to file the application for adoption. Gaston was considered a local hero in those days: a member of the underground, a good-looking guy, an idealist. He brought Helena and the children into the registration office, and a clerk shook Helena's hand and gestured her to take a seat.

"Well, let's do this quickly. In principle, you need to bring paperwork and other items, but if the parents died during the war, we accept a declaration under oath," she explained rapidly.

"I don't know what a *declaration under oath* is, but I will do whatever is required." In the forms that were handed to her, Helena filled out the reason for the adoption application and the children's history from their births to the time when they lived in that building. She gave a verbal description of the whole period of the war and life under the occupation. She did not have Annette's death certificate in her possession, but she gave the precise date and the name of the hospital where Annette died.

The children sat next to her the whole time. Olivier, as always, made sure to keep Laurent occupied.

After about an hour and a half, they left with Helena holding a document certifying that she had applied for adoption, a document that should delay the process of transferring the children to Olga's custody. Gaston drove them home. They were growing closer: Laurent, who was very fussy with strangers, held out his arms to Gaston to be picked up. Feeling proud, Gaston scooped up Laurent with pleasure. They went up to the apartment together and prepared a light lunch.

"I will need to travel to Italy, to see what happened," Helena observed.

"I told you, let me look into a few things first," Gaston responded, "then you can decide what to do."

Feeling the family atmosphere that filled her home, Helena imagined for a moment that she and Gaston were a couple, but immediately abolished the thought, saying to herself, *give yourself a little breathing room. It's not the time for a new commitment. Gaston is a good man and he'll help me, but nothing more.*

After lunch, Gaston left. They agreed that he would come in the evening to watch the children when Helena went to work. She saw how the children were gradually becoming attached to him.

6

The following days passed as usual. Gaston and Helena were growing closer and the children enjoyed being around him, from the bedtime stories he told them to the meals they prepared together. This new calm came just when Helena was mourning deep inside for her family that she had left behind in Italy. Sometimes, the thought passed through her mind that if she had returned to Italy, she might have been able to save the situation; that Maria and her parents would still be alive. She sunk into endless thoughts of *what if?* but in the end came to realize that they were not leading anywhere. What was really important was what was happening now, and where she wanted to go from here. At the moment, every minute she spent with the children and everything she was doing for them gave meaning to her life, to her sense of self-respect, to her security, and to her dreams.

A few days later, the final battle began.

At the same time that Helena submitted her application for adoption, Olga had filed a demand for custody of the children as the only surviving family member . She knew that Helena had filed for adoption, and Mr. Cohen was preparing a claim that Olga and her husband be made the children's legal guardians. They collected information and prepared explanations to present Helena as someone who was not suited to bring up the children. They even tried to portray Helena's ties with the Germans as a stain on her past.

Gaston, who obtained information from colleagues in offices where he was admired, learned that there would be a legal hearing to decide between Helena's request to adopt the children, on one side, and Olga's request to bring them up as the only one with blood ties to them, on the other.

Gaston requested that Monsieur Grenier, a learned attorney from an aristocratic Parisian family, known for his resistance to the German regime, take part in the hearing on Helena's behalf. Monsieur Grenier assembled the story of Helena, Maria, and the children in such a way that no one who heard it could help feeling sympathy for the sacrifice that Helena had made.

The hearing was set for the end of November 1944, against the backdrop of the first free Christmas celebrations since the end of the occupation. A week before the hearing, Gaston came, as usual, to Helena's apartment in the afternoon to watch the children. This time, he came with a briefcase of documents.

Before she left for work, Helena sat with him as he pulled out photographs and documents from the briefcase.

"From the information that my friends collected about the case at your family's farm, it seems that in the week when Maria returned, there were still fascists in the area of the village. Some of them hid on your farm. They threatened your parents and Maria. Members of the Italian underground burned down the house and its inhabitants without knowing that your family members were inside. They were sure that your family had left the village a long time ago. You received the document from the municipality several months after their deaths. I am sorry, but that is the truth. The pictures are of the burnt house and the farm, and the page is an article from the local paper about the tragic event. I tried to investigate the incident as thoroughly as possible to get a full picture of what happened."

Helena fell into a chair, breathless. "They suffered all through the war, and in the end, they died at the hands of those who beat the Germans. I don't understand this... All of us survived the war, and in the end the ones who harm us were not the Germans at all, but the Allies, the underground, the ones fighting the Germans... The ones harming us are those who aren't thinking about what they're doing. Olga, too. She's just causing harm... I'm sorry, but that's the reality. If you had not come that day, it's very likely that neither the children nor I would be alive, because of the underground fighters."

"Look," Gaston got to his feet and said, "I'm not justifying anything, but the torture and abuse by the Germans and their allies created in everyone hatred and a desire for revenge. Feelings like that sometimes blind us to the point where we cannot see reality anymore. We only see the target in front of our eyes. The feeling after the victory over the Germans was a desire to destroy everything connected to the Nazis, even if it was a nightclub dancer who saved some children. There's no justice here, only people hurt..." he concluded sadly.

"Well, it doesn't matter to me anymore. I'm focusing on next week. I'm going to go to work; I hope I'll be able to focus on the show and not on the pain my parents and my beloved Mari felt in their last moments... I haven't digested it yet. Mari was here for months, in the presence of Satan himself, and she survived him. When she finally got to hold on to what she wanted, to be home, to be with Mama and Papa, there, in the most protected place, she faced the hardest death..."

"Helena, you have to be strong in the coming week. With your permission, I will ask the lawyer to add this information about your family who were murdered precisely at the end of the war."

"It won't make any difference to them," she said despairingly. "But as far as I'm concerned, do whatever is required so that my little ones stay with me."

Another week passed. Helena's fears grew as the hearing date approached. Gaston was at her side the whole time, supporting her, sometimes even staying all night, sleeping on the couch in the living room. Their relationship did not slip into romance, for they were focused on what was going to happen.

The morning before the hearing, Gaston asked Helena, "suppose you don't get a favorable ruling at the hearing; suppose the judge says that they have to leave for England with Olga; suppose they decide that you're not fit to bring them up. What then, Helena? Have you thought about what you'll do?"

"I'm not thinking about that for the moment. I don't think I'll have the strength to do anything after this. I cannot see myself living without the children. Everyone I had in this world will be gone... After I survived the Nazis, those monsters, what did I do to deserve something like this?"

"Look, the world won't end in any case," Gaston tried to encourage her.

"You're healthy. You're wonderful. You're a woman with values, one who makes sacrifices for others. You're beautiful… I've never told you, but every time I see you, your beauty excites me all over again…"

"Even if things like this land on us," Gaston continued, "we have to keep on and not become slaves to depression and fear. My best friends died at my side; some underwent indescribable torture before they left this world. Some of their families also underwent torture on their account, to the point of murder when nothing else could be gotten out of them. I've seen a thing or two in my short life. I know it's hard, I know that any day we can fall again, and I know that everyday we can choose to start over and live meaningful lives. We just have to decide and get help from the right person. In this regard it doesn't matter what you decide, I'm here for you."

The following morning, the children had to come with Helena to court. This time, the hearing was set to take place outside the courtroom, in a less threatening room, since the children were present.

Mr. Cohen took the stand first, presented Olga's petition and laid out the reasons why he was requesting an unequivocal, immediate answer. He acknowledged that Helena had indeed taken the children in, that this was to her credit since she had saved them a moment before Monsieur and Madame Dubois abandoned them, out of fear of the Germans, but that in fact she was a woman of the devil. He argued that what the children witnessed during the entire period of the war, Helena's occupation as a stripper, a patently immoral profession, left the court no choice but to rule that the children should return to the bosom of their financiallysecure family, who would provide them with the best education and the greatest resources for a good future.

"We will not prevent contact with Helena, and will always be grateful to her," he closed on a pacifying note. "But the children need their family."

"I will begin from the end," Helena's attorney, Monsieur Grenier, rose to his feet and said.

"Do we have any right to object to Helena's request for adoption? Everyone agrees, and it has even been stated by the children's family members, that they admire and esteem the education they received; that they admire her sacrifice. The fact that Helena saved these children not in one momentary act of compassion, but every single day that she was under the occupation and under the murderous control of the commander of forces in Paris. She gave her very soul, and even endangered her sister, all for the sake of the children's survival. And yet, despite everything, the children are not suffering from trauma; they are surrounded by love, they have self-confidence, they are attached to her and love her, and do not see themselves living apart from her. Isn't it enough, what she suffered only a few weeks ago, when she received news that her whole family— including her sister Maria, who served as the children's mother in the cover story for the Germans— were all murdered by crazed people in an act of post-war insanity?"

He then dramatically recounted the story of the Italian immigrant who became the star of the most exclusive strip club in Paris, but functioned in every way as a mother, putting the good of her children before everything else.

After both sides had presented their cases, which took over four hours, the two judges, a woman and a man, asked those present to leave the hall, leaving the judges with the children.

Helena turned to Olivier and said, "don't worry. I'm leaving you now with these two nice people, and I'm waiting right outside the room. They'll ask you a few questions and maybe try to ask Laurent as well. I'm here, don't be scared."

"I'm not scared, I just want to go home," Olivier answered wearily.

"As soon as we're done, we'll go home," she told him tenderly.

Everyone left the room, and the judges came and sat next to the children.

"Olivier," the woman turned to him. "How old are you?"

"I'm seven-and-a-half years old, and my brother is five and a bit."

"Where is your home?"

Olivier told her the name of the street where Helena lived and added: "We live with Helena and Mari, but now Mari is with Maman and Papa. Everyone is dead."

"Did you see Maman in the hospital?" the judge went on.

"Yes. I helped her, but it was hard for her and in the end she died. But now Helena will be our mother, like she was when the Germans were here. She went to ask permission from the woman in the city hall."

The judge could not help smiling at the boy's intelligence.

"And do you know Olga?"

"Yes, I know her, she is Maman's cousin, I think. She was at our house, but she and Helena got into a fight because she wants to take us away."

"And what do you think of that?"

"I don't want to go. I'm Helena's child now, and Laurent too. I want Helena."

"But Olga is a relative of your real mother."

Olivier would not be moved. "Helena is my mother now. I don't have any other one. So, Olga isn't my aunt, she's Maman Annette's cousin," he explained.

"Well, sweetie, you're a smart boy. Do you want to call everyone back in? Help me."

Olivier smiled happily as everyone filed back into the hall.

"Dear friends," the female judge began, "your case is not a simple one. Both sides have valid arguments, strong and true arguments. We've learned the story of your lives, we've met the two wonderful children who also have their own opinion, especially Olivier, even though he is so young. We'll meet again in an hour and present our decision. The decision will be final, not subject to appeal or emendation, since this is only a family court."

"I would just like to clarify," added the male judge, "that the decision does not mean that there is a right side and a wrong side. The decision will be the best possible compromise for the good of all the sides— but first and foremost, for the good of these two darlings." He looked at Olivier, who was all smiles. The boy was thinking to himself that everything will be over today, and that Helena will finally become his real mother.

A short while later they convened again. Gaston took a seat in the hall together with the rest of them, even though he was not part of the hearing.

The female judge rose and spoke. "First of all, we will repeat that we have been focusing on the good of the children. Europe experienced terror for years. One people, the Jews, underwent a process of extermination that brought with it the splitting and loss of whole families. In recent months we have been hearing horror stories. Your story is different; in the midst of the insanity that we have lived through in the past few years, there was a little island of sanity with Helena and the children. She managed to create a warm, loving home for them, which gave them hope. She was in fact their mother and father," the judge looked at Helena.

"Now, when the battles have subsided, we are trying to find solutions for the families who were erased by Satan's horrible deeds," she went on. "We have no doubt that for the sake of the tradition and for family unification, the children must return to the family in which they were raised before the battles broke out. But this will be done only on one condition: that the one who managed to protect them and raise them to be the darling children they are today, will be part of the process. Therefore, we rule that the children will spend two months a year with Helena, on dates to be agreed on ahead of time by both sides, so as not to interfere with holidays and events of either. In addition, Helena can come visit the children three days a month, to be arranged ahead of time. If it happens that she cannot make the visit because of financial difficulties, then, as Olga claimed, since resources are not a problem for them, she will bring Helena to them at her expense. All this is to provide continuity of the children's connection with the people who influenced their lives to the good…"

She was about to go on when Olivier stood up and yelled: "Does that mean we're going with Olga? And Helena is not our mother?"

The judge was taken aback, but knew how to handle the situation, for this was her area of expertise.

"Olivier, dear, Helena will always be whatever you want her to be for you: your mother, or a good friend of the mother who raised you; but you also need to respect what Maman Annette requested, and that is that you return to your family."

"But my family is here! Helena and Laurent!"

The judge went on, ignoring Olivier's words, wanting to bring the long hearing to an end. She went on reading the explanation for a few more minutes. Finally, she said, "the transfer of the children will take place in ten days, so that Helena will have time to say farewell to them. During these days, Olga will spend at least an hour a day with the children. The meetings will take place in a neutral location, and Helena will not be present, though she will be close by."

We know that this is not the decision you hoped for," said the judge, looking at Helena, "but it is the best decision possible given the circumstances."

Helena's eyes were filled with tears, but she kept herself under control. Her noble bearing did not desert her, and she did not show that she was broken. She squeezed Gaston's hand tightly, and he could feel the force of her anger.

"Helena!" Olga called.

Helena stood up, took a deep breath, and slowly turned around to face her.

"I'm sorry. I really didn't want all this," Olga hurriedly said. "I had hoped we could work it out among ourselves without getting to this point. It doesn't matter what you think of me, I really do admire you. I am grateful for everything you did and will always cherish that. We will not cut off contact between you and the children. You will be part of our life and the lives of Olivier and Laurent in whichever way you decide to do it."

Helena did not respond. She turned back around and walked away with the children.

Olga felt relieved. She had gotten what she wanted, even if it had meant hurting Helena. She knew that she would have to work hard now to build the children's trust.

7

Gaston served as a special supervisor in the French Central Bureau of Intelligence and Operations, the BRCA, established during the war. In his role, he had endless access to many information sources and connections throughout the world. After the hearing ended, he contacted colleagues to find out about Olga and her family. He did not find anything incriminating against them, and knew deep inside that it would be impossible to make a claim against them, given that they had lost Annette and Marek and apparently many other relatives of theirs in Europe.

He had nothing new to tell Helena, but he tried to make her time as pleasant as possible in her last days with the children. He was also responsible for arranging Olga's visiting hours.

Helena did not try to turn the children against the decision that had been made; on the contrary, she tried to encourage them. Out of true love for them, she tried to give them the strength they would need for the drastic change that was being forced upon them.

A few days after the hearing, on the first weekend of December 1944, it happened. Olga arrived with a court representative to supervise turning the children over to her custody. Helena was in her house with Olivier and Laurent. She dressed them in their finest clothes and packed two bags. She was reminded of the day she had picked them up from Monsieur Dubois.

"My darlings, I'm not leaving you. You are always in my heart. Olga will take you today to your new home. They will treat you well there, and I promise to write all the time and come visit at least a few times a year. Don't forget me, you're everything to me..."

"I don't want to go, I want us to stay with you!" Olivier said.

"I know, sweetie. But you have family waiting for you. It'll be nice for you with them."

"But I want you!" insisted Olivier.

"I'll visit you, and you'll be with me for two months a year. Everything I promised you, we'll do when you come to me. We'll go hiking in the mountains, we'll go to the seashore… I promise you."

Gaston, standing next to her, signaled that they were waiting downstairs.

"Gaston will take you down to Olga. Come, give me a kiss. You also have a letter from me— read it like we learned to read together. I put it in your bag but open it only when you get to your new home, not before." She hugged them again, then got up and went to her room.

Standing by the door, Olivier wailed, "I don't want to leave her…"

Laurent stood next to him and started crying too, realizing from his brother's sobs that something was about to happen.

Gaston knelt down to the children, picked up both of them in his arms, and hugged them fiercely. Olivier continued to wail but did not resist. He understood everything that was happening: he understood that this was his mother's family, that he was a Jew, and that this was part of what was required to fulfill his mother's wishes.

Gaston brought the children to Olga. "Come, darlings," she called. "We're going to go on an interesting journey, including sailing— have you ever been on a ship?"

Olivier relaxed a little. After all, she was not mean to him, and the thought of sailing on a ship excited him.

"Why can't Helena come with us?" he asked Olga. "I want Helena, she's our mother." Olga tried to explain the situation to the boy. "Helena is not your mother. Helena was your mother's good friend. She saved you, but we are your family. You'll see, if you have a little patience, everything will work out. And Helena will come visit us soon."

Without further ado, they piled into the car. From Paris, they headed for northern France, to the port and the ferry that would take them to London.

After they left, Helena locked the apartment door and holed herself up in her room, ignoring Gaston's knocking. She did not want to speak with anyone just then. The worst of all had come to pass: her family died in the war and now her children had been taken away.

Gaston did not give up. Realizing after some time that she was not going to open the door, he broke in using a technique that he had learned during the war. He walked into her room, causing her to start with fright.

Recovering her composure, she asked in surprise, "how did you get in?"

"Through the door," he laughed. "I know this is hard on you, but I won't let you sink into depression. It doesn't suit you. I understand you don't want to do anything, but life goes on and you're not going to give up. You're going to get ready now and go dancing this evening. I'll come see you."

Gaston worked hard to bring Helena back to life, to believe in her dreams and to flourish. She would occasionally sink into depression, but each time he would help her recover and get back on track. He suggested that they travel together to Italy, to visit her family's village.

Meanwhile, on the other side of the La Manche Channel, the children began the process of settling into their new family in London. Olga and her husband, David, worked hard to help the children acclimatize to their new home. Members of the Jewish community in London also helped get them connected to educational institutions, synagogue, holiday events; everyone knew Oliver and Laurent's unique story.

The children's lives gradually took shape and they developed daily routines, allowing them to focus on their day-to-day life. Nevertheless, from time to time, Olivier was beset by fits of rage, similar to his behavior when Helmut came to Helena, reminding everyone that the children were still in a period of transition.

A few weeks after their separation from Helena, Olga received the first letter from her.

Dear Olga, I am going through a difficult period at the moment. I'm angry at you, but at the same time, I understand you. I would like us to get over what happened and start anew, like a real family. The children and their happiness are important to me. I just want

to be a partner from a distance and see them when conditions are
ripe for that.

Olga went back and read the letter a few more times, thinking carefully
about her response. She decided for the moment to postpone renewing their
tie with Helena, on the excuse that the children were still in the process of
acclimatizing to their new life, and that it would be better not to flood them
with too many emotions at this early stage.

She sent Helena back a letter.

Dear Helena, I was happy and excited to get your letter. I also left
Paris happy, but at the same time— sad and hurting. I know it's
not easy for you. I would like to make the attachment more solid,
but we will need to wait for the appropriate time, when the children
will be stronger. At this point, Olivier has not fully found his place
yet, and is still looking for you. I want him to get a bit stronger,
and then we can arrange meetings and make the relationship more
active. In the meantime, you and I will stay in touch and I'll keep
you updated of everything that happens.

Helena did not like the fact that Olga controlled her connection with the
children, but she could understand Olga's fear— that as soon as Helena
came back into their lives, the process of building their new life would get
derailed. She decided to wait.

In the meantime, she went to Italy with Gaston, to her childhood home, to
find out what had happened there. Gaston took upon himself to organize the
trip and coordinate with Italian colleagues who would accompany them and
handle all bureaucratic matters with local authorities there, including security,
if any would be required. The villagers in the region had not yet forgotten
the war, and there were occasional stories of scores being settled between
neighbors on the background of past collaboration with the fascist regime.

The trip to Italy helped free Helena from her constant thoughts of the
children, flooding her instead with memories of her own childhood.

After a week in Italy, Helena did not want to stay there anymore. She tried to get rid of all remaining traces of the accursed farm where her parents and Maria had met their ends. Gaston, together with his colleagues, arranged what was required, including selling the plot of land that she owned. Helena had no interest in either the sale price or the bureaucratic process, leaving Gaston to handle all the details for her. When they returned to France, her heart was filled with the decision to start anew and leave the pain behind, to pick herself up and go on.

Life settled into a routine. Helena returned to her role as the leading star of the cabaret, but otherwise remained in isolation, keeping to herself in her apartment. She had only a handful of friends. Gaston became her escort, but no more than that. Helena was not ready for a new relationship yet; the experiences of the preceding years had left their mark. She was afraid of intimacy; the abuse she had endured during the occupation had affected her deeply. Gaston, who very much wanted to become her partner, waited patiently for her.

On both sides of La Manche Channel, life went on along parallel tracks.

Several months after the separation from the children, Helena sat down to write Olivier the first letter that she would send to Olga's address in London. She assumed that he was having difficulties in absorbing the new language, among other struggles.

> *My darling,*
>
> *I'm writing you a letter in French, and you can tell me if you remember how to read French like we learned, or whether you speak only English now. I'm writing you a short letter to say that I love you from afar and think of you every day. I will be happy to come visit you the moment you tell me I can.*
>
> *I'll always be here for you.*
>
> *Yours, Helena.*

The letter arrived at Olga's.

Although a bit uneasy at what she was doing, Olga decided not to give the letter to Olivier. Instead, she put the letter back in the envelope, sealed it, and put it in a drawer in her room.

The following morning, when the postman came to their house, she asked him to return the letter to the sender, saying that it had been delivered to her by mistake.

Back in Paris, Helena was very surprised to find that the letter she had written to Olivier had come back to her. Not knowing what it meant, she sent Olga another letter. To her amazement, that letter returned to her just like the previous one.

Helena did not despair. Even though the letters kept coming back, she continued sending a letter on the first of each month. She saved the returned letters in a drawer, arranged in order. She did not know why she was doing that but felt a pull that was stronger than her.

Gaston used his connections to make an inquiry into Olga's family; it turned out that they had moved to a new address. Gaston's men reported that they were a normative Jewish family with two children. The children were observed several times playing in the company of other children their age. Gaston told Helena what he had learned. He gave her the new address and asked her if she wanted to travel there. She did not answer.

Helena continued writing regular letters, but deep inside she decided to move on. She realized that she would never be able to live a normal life if she continued to wait. She tried to get over the crisis with the children by way of a new relationship.

The change Helena had gone through took Gaston by surprise. Helena let him know that she was ready.

They began their romance cautiously. Helena had to learn to trust, for she was scared of intimacy with him. Gaston was gentle and considerate, and, as time passed, she became captivated by his personality. The new relationship that they built between them helped her put some of the painful past behind her. Focusing on living for the moment, they became very close. They would fall asleep like a pair of spoons and wake up snuggled in each other's arms.

Feelings of love for Gaston enveloped Helena, but she never lost her sense that something was missing. She tried not to think about the past, and her memories gradually faded. Every once in a while, however, a memory would surface and take her breath away.

She continued sending a letter to Olivier on the first of each month, receiving it back each time some two weeks later. Her letter-writing became an obsessive repetition of an action that she knew would never get her anywhere; quite the opposite— it only made her sink anew every time. Gaston tried to dissuade her from the practice, but she insisted.

"You'll never understand. They were my whole world. I'm afraid to forget them." Helena was torn between a new life with Gaston and the memories and longings for Olivier and Laurent. Not knowing anything about their life made her crazy. Her head buzzed with questions: what were they doing? How were they getting on? Did they already learn to speak English?

The year 1945 came to an end, before another year had passed, following by another. She clung to her memories of the little children who had been in her care.

A few years later, when she was almost fifty years old, Gaston proposed that they try to bring a child into the world. She was beyond the normal age for earing children.

At first, Helena recoiled, but as the days passed, the idea enchanted her. They began trying to conceive.

A few months later, Helena made an appointment for tests, wanting to make sure that everything was normal and that she was fit to bring a healthy child into the world. She had the tests done in a private clinic with a well-known obstetrician-gynecologist.

The doctor gave her the good news that the tests found everything to be normal. He gave her all sorts of suggestions and recommended that Gaston be tested as well. Gaston's tests also came back normal.

They tried for a while longer, continuing to hope.

"Apparently, it's just my luck," she said to him one day. "I had the children of another woman, who were like my children, but as soon as I want my own children, I can't get pregnant."

"It's true that I would like us to have children. But if not, we'll have to make the best of it," he said.

"What will remain after we're gone, Gaston?" she asked him.

"Not much," he laughed.

"I'm serious. Who will remember us? Who will tell our story?"

"Oh, those are the thoughts of old people, Helena. I'm not thinking so far ahead…"

"Those are real thoughts. I would like Olivier and Laurent to remain after I'm gone, but that won't happen."

"Tell me, if no one remains after we're gone, will you know about it?" Gaston asked Helena.

She laughed. "No, but now I'm thinking about it."

"If you think about it now, then it really won't happen. But if you let your dreams blossom again, you'll be able to live well without drowning yourself in thoughts of a gray, depressing future."

"I'm just expressing the thoughts going through my head. I'm not thinking of such a gray, depressing future."

"I'm thinking a few years ahead," Gaston said, "finding a little village to live in, planting a little garden next to the house, and living in the quiet of nature. I've had enough of urban craziness." "Maybe we'll do that yet," Helena responded.

The years passed and Helena continued to send monthly letters to Olivier, letters that continued to return unopened. Her ritual cupboard in her bedroom was already filled with hundreds of letters.

After years in the cabaret under Hubert's direction, she finally retired from dancing and auditioned as a theater actress. She was accepted to the Bouffes du Nord theater, an ancient and well-known theater that put on modern plays. Like everything Helena did, she threw herself heart and soul into acting and rapidly became the lead actress, starring in dramas they staged.

After one of the premiers of a play about the underground and the war with the Germans, a Parisian cultural journalist asked her about the source of her passionate reenactment of the war period. That journalist received a two-hour-long answer, which laid out the wartime story of her and the children. She was careful not to make any complaint against Marek and

Annette's family, just expressing the sadness and disappointment of losing the two children she had raised.

In the following days, she received several more requests for interviews, but politely refused them all.

Meanwhile, Gaston advanced in his career in the Secret Service. He spent a great deal of time flying around the world, so Helena found herself frequently alone. She read a lot of books and even began writing a play about her own life.

8

Twenty-four years had passed since the two little boys left France.

Laurent, who had become religiously observant, was married off to the daughter of a well-known rabbi in Brooklyn and moved to the United States. He was twenty-nine years old.

Olivier was almost thirty-two years old, living with his girlfriend in one of the peripheral neighborhoods of London. Her name was Jane, she was Jewish like he was, secular and the daughter of a traditional Jewish family. Born in the same London neighborhood where Olivier was raised, had been familiar with his story since childhood, but the two had only met for the first time at university.

Olivier was a mechanical engineer and Jane was a pediatrician. They were already talking about getting married and starting a family, but Olivier felt stuck; something was keeping him from moving forward.

Jane pushed him to take a break from everything and take the time to investigate what was the source of his troubles. She told him wisely, "if you want to live a good life and fulfill yourself— first learn about your past, face your fears. I'm here, I'll wait for you."

Thoughts of the past often overwhelmed Olivier. He knew what was stopping him from moving forward in his life: Helena. *Where is she? why did she leave me like this? Why didn't she ever contact me?*

Why did she hurt me so deeply by cutting me off? Endless questions ran through his head, and he felt a great need to find out about his past. He called Olga, who had essentially been his mother from the age of seven-and-a-half, and arranged to meet with her.

Their relationship was good now, though it had taken him a number of years to be able to communicate well with her. Upon leaving Paris as a child, he had become closed and sometimes lashed out violently towards those around him, with the exception of Laurent. Only at the age of twenty-two, at university, did he begin to relax and open up more.

Olga, already aging, was frightened by talking about Olivier's past. She did not understand what caused him to bring up the issue all of a sudden. The conversation between them that morning turned out to be quite dramatic. Olivier brought up the tough questions about Helena: How could she have left them? How could she just cut them off? How was it that they did not try to maintain contact with her?

Olga broke down. She could no longer stand the pangs of conscience that had pursued her ever since she hid Helena's letters. She opened her heart.

"Olivier, I have to tell you what I should have told you years ago. Helena did not abandon you in her thoughts for even one day."

Olivier was confused. "But she never came here even once, you always said that she didn't answer you..."

"It's my fault," Olga confessed. "I just wanted to protect you and help you build a calm and peaceful life. I wanted to erase your painful past, and I saw Helena as belonging to that past. It was I who cut off contact. You should know that Helena did not leave you even for a moment."

"I don't understand what you're saying."

"Helena tried to make contact with you from the very beginning. She wanted to come and visit you a couple of weeks after you got here, but I stopped her. I told her that the time was not yet right. She kept trying, then started writing letters every month. But I sent them back to her, unopened."

Olivier looked shocked. "I-I don't understand you... Why did you do that? Did you think about us at all? Even today, when I'm already thirty-two years old, I still remember her. I vaguely remember the time when we lived with her, and it comes back to me in dreams; I wake up wondering where she is and what is happening with her. Most people scarcely remember what happened when they were six, but for me, that period is rooted in my thoughts. Fragments of memories keep resurfacing. She's branded in my mind— I carry her around with me every day and I'm going insane from not knowing what became of her!"

"I can deal with the memories," Olivier went on, "but I always thought that it was Helena who broke her promise to stay in touch with us always, never to leave us— and now it turns out that it was you! Why, Olga? Why did you do it?"

"I-I told you... The beginning of your path here in England was not easy. You were angry and confused, you were constantly torn between here and there, between Helena and us. I had to help you settle in. At a certain point, I thought you had erased the past, and

I didn't try to change that."

"I can't make sense of this. Does David know what happened?"

"No. I did it of my own initiative. No one else knows about it."

"When did her last letter come?"

"What does it matter?" Olga tried to avoid answering his question.

"I want to know when she stopped and gave up on us. Answer me— when?"

Olga sighed deeply. "Less than a month ago."

"You want to tell me that she's been writing for more than twenty years, having never received so much as a sign of life from us?"

"I don't know what she understood... But she never stopped writing you. On the first of every month, like clockwork, she sends you a new letter."

"She never stopped hoping that she would get to see us," Olivier shouted in furiously, "she's still writing to us! She must be broken-hearted from everything you did to her! Did you ever think about her either? Do you think that's what she deserved?!"

"Wait a minute..." Olivier paused. "Where are the letters I wrote to her? Did you hide those too?!"

"I never sent them," Olga began to sob. "I still have them."

"Are you telling me the truth, Olga? What kind of person would do something like that to her son... What were you afraid of? That I would get up and leave? You saw that I was progressing. Granted, I was not an easy child, but I was part of your family. Couldn't you have trusted me? You have to let things happen without always trying to control other people." Silence pervaded the room.

"I want to see my letters," he demanded.

Olga got up and went to her bedroom. She opened her closet and pulled out a cardboard box from its depths. The box contained all of the letters that Olivier had written to Helena over the course of five years, up to about age of twelve. At that point, it seems, he had given up and stopped trying to communicate with her.

"I don't believe it. Y-You pretended... You lied to me, all out of a desire to be in control!" He noticed a letter from Helena on top of the pile. It was dated two days earlier, the first of the month.

"You told me that the last letter came a month ago! You lied to me again!" He grabbed the Helena's letter and left, slamming the door behind him.

Olga was left behind in tears. She tried to run after him, but her legs would not carry her.

Olivier stormed out of the house where he had grown up. In the grip of emotion, he broke into a run. Only after a few kilometers, drenched in sweat, did he stop to catch his breath, leaning on a fence. He sat down on a bench, not knowing where he had gotten to. He pulled the letter out of his pants pocket and began to read.

> *My dear Olivier,*
>
> *This year you are celebrating your thirty-second birthday. Twenty-four years have passed since we were separated. I'm still waiting for the two of you, you and Laurent. This year I celebrated my sixty-eighth year, full of hope of seeing you.*
>
> *Your loving Helena"*

Olivier, heart-broken, wanted Jane at his side.

Still feeling a need to move, he set out towards her house on foot, arriving after more than an hour's walk.

Jane was at home, having just arrived after a night shift at the clinic. He came in and embraced her tightly.

"What happened? Did you miss me?" she laughed, then stopped as she saw the traces of tears down his cheeks.

"Olivier, what happened? Talk to me. I've never seen your face like this before. You're white as a sheet."

"It's impossible to forgive such insensitivity, evil, and indifference."

"I don't understand what you're talking about." She came up and hugged him.

Clinging to her, he continued speaking with his face buried in her shoulder. "The woman who saved my life, Helena, I've hurt her more than anything…"

"I still don't understand," Jane said gently.

He let her go and sat down on a chair. Jane pulled up a chair opposite him.

"I was at David and Olga's today. I tried to question Olga about my past, and then, out of the blue, she told me the truth."

In tears, he laid out the story before her. Jane tried to soothe him. She then said in a calm, tranquil voice, just as she always spoke to him when he was feeling weak, "what is your heart telling you to do?"

"I want to find her and ask for forgiveness. If it's not too late."

"Go with your heart, then. I think what has been hurting you all these years has been not having this woman who was so important to you. Go, darling. Go solve the mystery of your life!"

David came home that afternoon and found Olga in bad shape.

"What happened?"

Olga told him everything. David was shocked.

"I don't understand how you could have acted so coldly. What did you think would happen? Didn't you think that one day it would all come out?! I can really understand that boy… We have to help him.

Where did he go when he left here?"

"I assume he went home, to Jane," Olga said sadly.

"I'm going to do now what we should have done from the beginning— support him and give him the feeling that we trust him, and that we will always be here for him. I'll suggest that he make the trip to try and find her."

David went into the bedroom and pulled out a bunch of bills from a hidden shelf in the closet. He then rushed out towards Olivier and Jane's house.

He knocked softly on their door, and Olivier opened. When he saw that it was David, he tried to close the door on him, but David managed to stop him.

"Olivier, just listen to me for a minute. After that, you can do whatever you want."

Olivier left the door open.

"I didn't come to ask you for forgiveness. I don't think it's possible to forgive something like that at the moment. I just heard the whole story from Olga, and I came to advise you what to do. I think you should find Helena, before it's too late."

He took out an envelope and handed it to Olivier.

"There are two-thousand pounds sterling here. You can use it to get to France as quickly as possible and rent a hotel room for the time you're there, until you manage to locate her. If you need anything else, we'll do everything we can to help you find her." David paused.

"I don't know what else to say," he continued, "but I'm sorry. I'm sorry on my own account; I'm sorry for what Olga did. I feel Helena's pain without having ever met her. For me, you are my son and always will be. Go to her quickly. Whenever you want, contact us. We'll be right here, waiting for you. This is the best advice I can give you. I just have one request— please, don't rush to judge Olga for her actions. Today, I can understand why she was afraid. Helena is a special woman; I say that without ever having met her. I say that as a religious and believing man. Very few people would have done what she did, and then tried for over twenty years to make contact with you without ever giving up hope of seeing you."

Olivier, still furious, did not respond. How could one bridge a gap of so many years, endless waiting, an empty space that gaped open and was never filled?

David said goodbye and turned to leave. He understood that Olivier, at this point, would not want to talk to him. Even if David himself did not have a hand in the deception, he was still one of the people who had distanced Olivier from Helena.

9

Early in the morning, Olivier left his house for central London, where he bought a ticket to Paris. The trip included a train ride to the port city of Dover, a ferry to Calais, and another two-hour train ride to Paris.

He could not stop thinking about Helena. How was she? What had she been through? What would he say to her? How had they lost all those years …?

How can someone hurt someone else just to quell her own fears? He was furious with Olga, though he appreciated the push that David had given him. He had thought of the trip himself already, but David gave him the support, the resources, and the reassurance that they were there for him, whatever he decided.

Olivier grew up carrying a feeling that something was missing in his life. He had been impressive as a boy, a youth, a teenager, and an adult, sharp in his opinions and attitudes. His childhood friends, as well as those who met him at university, affectionately teased him that he was a warrior for justice, a sort of superhero.

As a boy, he had gotten embroiled more than once in quarrels with kids who were bigger and stronger than he was, who were bullying weaker children or showing signs of arrogance. They reminded him of past days in which he himself had experienced violence and arrogance.

More than once, Olga and David were called in to his school to try and solve the problems that seemed to spring up around him.

That morning, Olivier purchased a little guidebook of Paris with maps of the city. He then set out on his journey, the same one which he had travelled in the opposite direction all those years ago. He thought to himself, *I'm coming back.*

Olivier thought about his younger brother Laurent, wishing he could tell him everything that he had discovered. But Laurent was far away now, and they had become somewhat distant ever since Laurent had taken on more religious observance.

Laurent had grown into a very closed, withdrawn young man. He was considered a brilliant Torah scholar at the yeshiva where he studied, and his British citizenship made him an excellent match in the eyes of the American ultraorthodox community.

I'll have to send him a message as soon as possible, and make sure that he comes to see Helena, Olivier thought. She was close to seventy years old, an advanced age. He tried to imagine her, but all he could remember was the picture of the woman on the nightclub poster.

Olivier fell asleep on the train to Dover, waking up only when the final stop was announced. He got off the train and walked towards the dock, from which the ferry was scheduled to leave in thirty minutes. He stood on the dock, the sea-scented breeze caressing his face, and sailed away on his thoughts.

The ferry's horn brought him back to the present, and he walked towards the line of passengers waiting to board the ferry. During the ferry ride, he looked at the address on Helena's letter to Olga, then tried to locate the address on his map. He found the street name and circled it, then examined the sites in the vicinity of that street.

Gradually, he began to recall a few place names marked on the map: the flea market, the Sacré Coeur cathedral. Although not exactly sure, he had a feeling that they were not far from where they had lived.

Olivier was so lost in his thoughts that the many miles across the water passed by rapidly without him noticing.

Finally, he reached his last stop, Gare du Nord in Paris. When he got out of the train, it was early afternoon. According to the map, Helena's apartment was quite close to the train station. Wanting to feel his birth city with his feet, he decided to walk. He headed north to Boulevard de la Chapelle, the central avenue, not far from the train station.

He strode along the sidewalk, alert to activity in the street. The aroma of coffee reminded him of the *Boulangerie Café* in their neighborhood; the baguettes in the bakeries suddenly looked so familiar… He came upon a poster for the *Moulin Rouge*, similar to the poster he remembered from his childhood.

After about an hour's walk, which included getting lost several times along the way, he reached the intersection that he had marked on the map. He started walking along Boulevard de la Chapelle, the street whose name appeared on the letter, until the building numbers told him that he was going in the wrong direction.

Olivier turned on his heel and started walking back the other way. Coming towards him was a silver-haired man, dressed in an expensive-looking suit. Olivier did not pay attention to him as he was going by, but as soon as the man passed, something made Olivier turn around.

The silver-haired man did the same thing, turning to look at Olivier.

Olivier tried to figure out who he was but could not do so.

The man came up to him and said, "excuse me, young man, I definitely know you, but I don't know where from. Forgive my boldness, but do you live around here?" Gaston, in his early sixties, still had his wits about him. He was currently working in the Secret Service in a nominal capacity, having officially retired.

"No, I'm not from around here. I understand and speak French, as you see, but I'm actually British."

"Where is your French from? I know that Brits and French don't go together so well," Gaston joked.

"I was born here. I grew up in Paris until the age of seven." Gaston had already figured out why the man's face was so familiar.

"Olivier?"

Olivier was shocked.

"Yes, yes, that's me, but I don't remember who you are…"

"Gaston. Does the name mean anything to you? You knew me for only a short time, just before you left for England at the end of the war."

"I remember something, but I can't make the connection…" Olivier said apologetically.

"I was with you at the end of the war, with you, your brother Laurent, and with Helena…"

"Helena…" Olivier trembled at the sound of her name.

"You disappeared. Why didn't you answer her letters?" asked Gaston.

"I'm sorry, things happened when I was a child that I had no control over. I've come to try and make amends, if it's still possible. I-It' a long story… I only found out two days ago that she has been writing me letters all those years…" Olivier did not want to mention Olga's name, not wanting to blame her for everything that had happened. "I have to find Helena. I know that she lives in this area. Her last letter was sent from here."

"Could I suggest that you have a cup of coffee with me before your meeting with Helena? She'll wait, I promise you."

"Do you know where she is? Can you take me to her?"

"Of course I know," he smiled. "But let's first go into this café on the corner and talk."

In the small café, the smell of cigarettes hung heavily in the air. They sat down in a corner, far from the crowds around the bar.

A waiter approached them. "Good day, sirs. What would you like to order?"

Gaston asked for an espresso, and Olivier, out of politeness, ordered the same thing. Coffee was not his favorite beverage. The waiter called out, "Two espressos."

"Tell me about Helena. Are you in contact with her?" asked Olivier.

"Am I in contact with her? Yes, I was her partner for several years. Eventually we separated, but we remained good friends. I make sure to visit her and help her with whatever she needs. She's almost seventy years old already, and I'm over sixty; we're not young, but in general, we're okay," he smiled. "How old are you now, Olivier?"

"I'm thirty-one. I finished a degree in engineering at University of London."

"And what about Laurent? I remember him as a baby."

"My brother left England and moved to the U.S., to Brooklyn. He got married and already has three children. He became ultraorthodox, which I don't relate to so much... Tell me about Helena— what is she doing now?"

"Oh, not much, unfortunately. After she left the nightclub and the danc-ing, she was a successful theater actress for some time; she even became the leading actress of a theater near here. We were living together at that time. But sometime in her mid-fifties, she began to sink. Her legs were shot from dancing all those years, and sadness overtook her. She stayed home for days at a time and refused to go out; taken together, these things made her age very rapidly. She gave up on the things she loved... Sorrow took her over."

"Sorrow over what?"

"You, Olivier. You and your brother. You were like her children. What she went through with you left its mark. After you left and she didn't hear from you anymore... As time passed, she could no longer handle it. Things were okay at first: we had friends, we were active, Paris was coming back to life. But Helena was mostly busy immortalizing you. Do you know how she did it? With the letters she had written you. That was her memorial corner. She never really parted from you. Memories flooded her every time she sat down to write the monthly letter."

"I don't know how I'll ever be able to atone for all the suffering we caused her. It doesn't matter why or whose fault it is... How can anyone atone for such a thing?" Olivier burst out.

"My son, I don't know what to tell you. The first stage will be to ask for forgiveness. From there, you will have to decide what your heart tells you to do. Helena deserves a happy life. She is a very special woman who has suffered most of her life; she has never had a single period of real pleasure. I don't know what you remember from the war. Do you remember that period?"

"Not really. I just remember that there were people in our house that I didn't like; I remember Helena's sister, I don't remember her name, but I remember there were two apartments, that we were always with her sister."

"Then you remember the main thing. The people you didn't like were the Nazis. They held Helena and her sister Maria prisoner. The two of them agreed to that only because they wanted to protect you, as Jews. But Helena didn't do it because you're Jewish, she did it because she loved you as if you were her own children. She promised your parents that she would look after you. In later years, even though we tried, she never managed to bring a child of her own into the world..."

Olivier cringed in shame and pain over what Helena had endured.

"I'm sorry, darling," said Gaston, "but you must know the truth, because what you are going to see will not be easy for you. You'll have to deal with it and decide what you're going to do. How do Olga and David feel about you coming here?" "Do you know them?" Olivier asked.

"I met Olga at the court hearing where it was decided that you would go live with them. In the days following the hearing, I was the one who accompanied you and your brother in your meetings with Olga, which took place without Helena, to prepare you for leaving her. I never met David, but I followed you from a distance." "Followed me? How?" Olivier exclaimed in surprise.

"I was an underground fighter, and after the victory over the Germans, I joined the Secret Service. To reassure Helena, I arranged to have you followed to see that you were okay. It didn't comfort her, but it calmed her to a certain extent to know that you were growing up and that you had chosen to take the new route and forget the past. Later, without telling her, I continued gathering information on you, to see that you were okay."

"I never expected a meeting like this," said Olivier. "It's bringing back what I was missing all those years. I guess I suppressed it... Maybe I did what was expected of me, not to talk about the past, not to look back. But now I realize that this is exactly what I've been missing all this time. I didn't know who I was, I didn't remember where I came from, I didn't remember who I'd left behind... I want to see Helena. I'm burning up with shame and pain over what was done to her. I will have to do something for her, to give her a little pleasure. I see now that this is my purpose at the moment," concluded Olivier fervently.

"Let me teach you a rule for life, Olivier— don't make big pronouncements. Even though I'm the only one here, and I will not mention your declaration, it's important for you to do the things you truly want to do, and not make pronouncements before you reach your own decision."

"What did you do after you two separated?" Olivier suddenly asked Gaston.

"Me? Oh... My work took me to many interesting places. I advanced to a senior position in the organization, and I also met my life partner, who is younger than me. We have a child, something that made Helena sink even deeper... But that happened a long time after I had left her. In fact, I never really left her. I visit her at least twice a week, and we have long heart-to-heart talks. She has become very weak; the crises she has endured have robbed her of all her strength... Now, come. Let's go see Helena. I'll go with you. This meeting is not going to be easy."

They got up, left the café, and set off down the street. Olivier could feel his heart racing. He was filled with nervous excitement.

A little way down the street, they reached the building. They entered the courtyard through a large wooden gate. It was a typical medieval courtyard, surrounded by four additional buildings. Olivier was stirred by the atmosphere of old Paris.

They entered the building at the corner farthest from the gate, and Gaston summoned the elevator. It was a tiny, compressed cubicle, specially adapted to a building with spiral staircases which had never been planned to accommodate an elevator. They went up to Helena's floor in silence, Olivier oppressed by an almost unbearable tension.

"You should know that one of the reasons Helena doesn't go out is that she doesn't want to climb four flights of stairs. The elevator here is always breaking down, and it's hard for her to walk." "What's wrong with her?" asked Olivier fearfully.

Gaston stopped and turned to face him. "She has a heart problem, called cardiac insufficiency. It's difficult for her to do things. She also has diabetes and on top of all that, she suffers from joint problems— the dancer's disease."

Tears filled Olivier's eyes. They approached apartment number twenty. *Fotticelli* was written on the door. Olivier had no recollection of ever hearing her surname...

Gaston took out a key and opened the door. Olivier realized just how close the two were. It was obvious that Gaston looked after her and took care of her devotedly, beyond the bounds of mere friendship.

"Helena?" Gaston called.

There was no response. Gaston went inside and called again,
"Helena?"

"I'm here, in the work room," her voice rang out.

As he walked into the apartment, Olivier looked around him. The decor was esthetic, but minimalistic; there was almost no furniture, and the room was rather dark. It made him feel sad.

Gaston stood at the entrance to the room, obscuring Olivier almost entirely from Helena's view. Helena sat behind an antique desk, a small lamp illuminating pages spread out before her. Olivier could only see the top of her graying head.

Sensing that someone was behind Gaston, Helena asked, "who is that?"

Gaston looked into Helena's eyes and then moved aside so that she could see Olivier.

From the dark hallway, Olivier took a step into the room, illuminated by the light from the window.

As Olivier was revealed to her, Helena's body began to tremble, and she fainted. Luckily for her, Gaston, with his quick reflexes, darted towards her and caught her before she struck her head on the table. He asked Olivier to bring a damp towel from the bathroom as he laid her down on a small sofa. He took the towel from Olivier and placed it on her forehead.

Helena regained consciousness to find herself with her feet up on the armrest of the sofa, Gaston standing behind her head and Olivier crouching down on the floor next to her.

"Lord…" she sobbed.

She tried to sit up, but Gaston cautioned her, "take your time."

Shaking, she placed her hand on Olivier's face. Wracked with sobs, she touched his face, his ears, his hair. Olivier burst out crying too, his breathing ragged. He laid his head on Helena's lap and she caressed him, like a mother caressing her son to soothe him.

It was silent in the room, except for Olivier's unceasing sobs.

She took his head in her hands. "Olivier, I've waited for this day for so long. Every single day, I prayed it would come. I never lost hope… Oh, my child, you're the most wonderful surprise that happened to me today, this year, in all the years I've lived, in my whole life."

Olivier tried to speak but could not get a single word out through his sobs.

"It's alright," she soothed him. "Everything is alright."

Olivier sensed her labored breathing, presumably a result of the heart problem she had developed with age, compounded by her emotional state.

Slowly, his sobs quieted, and he began to catch his breath. He lifted his head and studied her. She looked elderly, much more than Olga, a fact that surprised and saddened him. Her facial features and her body still attested to the beauty of her youth, but the hard years had left their mark on her. He laid his head back in her lap, seeking her caress.

Gaston broke the silence. "I'll leave you two alone together for a while. You have a lot to catch up on." He turned to Olivier. "How long are you planning to stay?"

"I'll be here for the next couple of days," Olivier answered, his face still soaked with tears.

"Good. Then I'll come by here tomorrow. Helena knows how to reach me if you need me." He kissed Helena on the forehead, stroked Olivier's head, and left the apartment quietly. It was an intimate moment between Helena and Olivier, and he did not want to spoil it for them.

"That moment when you came in the room, I felt like I couldn't breathe. For a moment, I thought I was looking at your father. You look so much like him!" This was the first time Olivier had heard this from anyone. Even Olga, who had known Marek and Annette well, had rarely mentioned them, except when she got into an argument with Olivier. She would then say that whatever she wanted was what his mother would have wished him to do. Olivier's response had always been frustration: "But my mother is not here, so what does it matter what she would have wanted? This is what I want now and that's what decides it!"

"I scarcely remember what my father looked like. I barely remember what happened to him."

The room fell silent. Helena wondered for a moment how he would react if he knew the whole truth about her and Marek. She swore to herself that except for her sister Maria, she would never tell anyone. She would take the secret with her to the grave.

"I will you. I will tell you the whole story of your childhood that you've never heard, from the mouth of the woman who loved you like a mother and who loves you like her son to this day. I'm not angry with you, Olivier, but I would like to ask you the questions that have remained with me, un-answered, all these years."

"I know," responded Olivier. "I'll answer all of them."

"I must ask you first of all— how is your brother Laurent?"

"He's twenty-nine years old. He became ultraorthodox, got married, and started a family in the United States. He already has three children."

She teared up, smiling with a mother's joy.

"And you?"

"I live in London with my girlfriend, Jane. I'm in love with her. She's what keeps me going."

Helena heaved a sigh of relief, but her breathing continued to be labored. Olivier realized that she had chronic breathing problems, unrelated to the emotional experience she was going through.

"Why?" she burst out.

The question he had so feared finally came.

"Why? Why didn't you write to me? Why didn't you come? Why didn't you show any sign of life?" she pleaded. "Although, it doesn't matter to me any more why," she said as though answering herself, "you're here and that's all that matters to me." She embraced him warmly.

He burst into tears again. "I want to tell you that there's no good reason why it happened. I have no logical explanation for it. I just can't bear to think of all the suffering you went through…"

She hugged him again. She smelled nice and her body was warm against his. This was the hug he had been waiting for.

"Oh, Lord, how I've longed for this moment," she sighed. "How I hoped to see you while I was still alive."

Olivier got up off the floor and took a seat next to her on the sofa.

"More than twenty years have passed without ever hearing a word from you, without knowing your fate— if you were happy, if things were going well for you. I didn't know what to think. Perhaps you were angry at me, perhaps you didn't want to write to me… I blamed myself for everything I hoped to get from you and didn't get."

Olivier held her hand. "I'll tell you everything. I remember the day we left. I was so angry! I didn't even remember that it was Gaston who brought me down to the street. He told me that. When we got to London, to our new home, I became exposed to a Jewish home for the first time. David wears a yarmulke. For a long time at the beginning, they tried to connect us to Judaism. People from the community came to visit with their children, so we met other children our age. I'll be honest— it was interesting. All of a sudden, we were in a new place where we felt free, with no more war, even though there were ruins everywhere, even in our neighborhood, much more than there had been in Paris."

"I thought everything was okay," Olivier continued, "but in fact it wasn't. Olga and David tried very hard to connect us to our new home and to Judaism, but in a rather extreme way. They told us that you were a Christian and that the years we spent with you we had been growing up as Christians, but that was not what our mother wanted. They tried to erase our past. In those early years, I tried to please them, thinking that everything they did was for my benefit. I became part of the Jewish community, and I liked my new friends— they were the best thing I had— and I didn't notice that I was forgetting where I came from. From time to time, I would ask Olga when you were coming to visit, and she would always that you had cut off communication and that she did not know how to contact you." Helena snickered bitterly.

"Now I know that that was not true. But I only found out this week…"

"What?!" Helena exclaimed.

"Yes. I wrote you letters for many years in my childhood, but I found out only a few days ago that they were never sent out to you." He went to the corner of the room to get his backpack; he took out a packet of letters and handed it to her. As she took them, she saw her name written as the addressee on the faded envelopes.

"Come with me," she got up and walked to her bedroom. She took a cardboard box out of a closet and placed it on the bed.

Sitting down on the edge of the bed, she lifted the cover of the box. Olivier immediately realized that these were the letters she had sent him, just like the most recent letter he had seen at Olga's.

"I saw the most recent letter you sent. It arrived at the beginning of the week."

She lifted the neatly ordered packets of letters out of the box.

"Do you see all these letters?" she laughed bitterly. "I was actually writing to myself, but I never gave up."

"Helena, I know. I saw your last letter. That's how I found out where you lived, and how I figured out that you were alive and still looking for me. All the letters from you actually arrived, but Olga, in some sick obsession, would return them to you, stamped by the post office that the addressee could not be found. So, I never got a sign from you. I thought you had forgotten me and Laurent. I was very angry until I discovered the truth. I'm not even angry any more at Olga for what she did— she will have to live with that guilt until her dying day. I just regret all the lost years when I wasn't in contact with you, when I didn't see you. I'm angry at myself for what you went through, for your disappointment, for my lack of caring..."

Helena and Olivier spent the rest of the day catching up on the past twenty years. In the evening, Olivier prepared supper for them both; even though he was no great cook, it made Helena very happy. She told him the story of his childhood in Paris, and he asked her about the Nazis and her relationship with Helmut.

"You know that it was not my choice. I did not choose him— he chose me. And since he was the occupier, I was his prisoner. And poor Mari, too... It got even harder when I became responsible for you two, because I knew that if I didn't obey him, I would be putting you in danger. He agreed to ignore the fact that you were Jews, living with me, only because I surrendered to him, and Mari to Fritz. You don't remember this, but Mari was held prisoner for a whole day; she was interrogated under torture and was violently raped by Fritz. She carried that scar with her for the rest of her life, my poor sister."

"And what happened to her?" asked Olivier. "I remember that she left some time before we did."

"Indeed. She returned to Italy, to our parents. She came back home, but almost right away everyone died there... They were murdered by the Italian underground, who burned the farm to the ground because there were people hiding there, fascists who had supported the Nazis during the war. The underground fighters, not knowing that my family was in the house, torched it with everyone in it. It happened just a few weeks before you left."

Olivier got out of his chair, went down on his knees next to her and embraced her in silence. He understood that the death of her family, coming just at the end of the war, was one of the most terrible things she had endured during that period.

"I made peace with the fact a long time ago— all disasters happen to me," she told him. "I tried to pick myself up, and even managed to do so for a couple of years, until my health problems defeated me. It started when I couldn't bear children with Gaston, then the joint problems that forced me to stop the dancing and acting that I loved so, and then finally the diabetes and heart problems..."

In the following days, Olivier and Helena spent many more hours together, filling each other in on everything that had happened in their lives from the moment they had parted ways.

Gaston came back to visit with his girlfriend and their son. Olivier observed how regally Helena welcomed Gaston, even though he was her former lover. She warmly received him along with his son and his girlfriend, who was much younger than him, somewhere in her forties.

Olivier's British accent and the mistakes he made in his broken French lightened the atmosphere and amused everyone. He had not spoken French since he was a child.

A few days later, Olivier said to Helena: "These past few days, I've kept thinking about where to go from here. You've answered a lot of questions that I've been carrying with me my whole life. Now I know exactly what I want to do. First of all, I want to be with you as much as possible. Not because I feel obliged to, but because it's what I want to do; it feels right and good to me. I can really feel the positive energy I get from being around you. I want to make you happy, Helena. I also want to start the family that

Jane is waiting for. So, what I'm going to do now is go back to London and tell Jane the whole story; from now on, I'll divide my time between London and Paris."

Helena smiled. "Darling, I don't want to be a burden to you. I already drove away the one man who would have been happy to help me all the time," she laughed. "I'd love to have you come visit, but I don't want you to split up your life on my account... I remember myself at your age," her eyes suddenly lit up. "I wanted to conquer the world! But unfortunately, the world conquered me," she smiled sadly. "These are your most beautiful years, Olivier— go conquer the world. Do something meaningful. I'll be happy to have you come and tell me what you're doing, how you're fulfilling yourself, what kind of family you've built... But I don't want to burden you. I'm managing fine, despite my limitations. I have help almost all week. I'll welcome you every time you come to visit, but I want to keep everything in proportion."

Without saying a word, Olivier sat down next to her and rested his head on her shoulder.

The next day, Olivier returned to London, to Jane.

Once a month, he would travel to Paris for a few days to visit Helena. A few months after his first visit, Olivier came for a week-long visit, bringing with him Laurent and Jane.

Laurent, for whom religious matters were of the utmost importance, stayed in an adjacent hotel, and attended daily prayers in a nearby synagogue. Olivier arranged to supply him with kosher food from a restaurant run by ultraorthodox Jews in Montmartre. The four of them spent an exciting and significant week together.

Renewing his relationship with Helena helped Olivier to piece together the picture that had been fragmented for so longed, and to move forward in his life. Later, he even renewed his contact with Olga and David. Although his relations with them had become rather cool, his stepparents were unfailingly respectful and pleasant towards him.

Epilogue

In July 1970, exactly twenty-six years after Paris was liberated from the Nazi occupation, Olivier arrived for his monthly visit with Helena. This time, he had wonderful news: he planned to tell her that he and Jane had set the date for their wedding. He carried in his pocket a wedding invitation for her.

Seeing that the elevator had broken down again, Olivier raced up the four flights of stairs. Panting, he knocked on her door, then pulled out the key she had given him to her apartment.

"Helena?" he called as he opened the door.

There was no answer.

He hurried to her bedroom, then to the workroom, finally noticing a light on in the bathroom. "Helena?" Silence.

"Helena!" Olivier raised his voice.

Hearing no response, he opened the door.

Helena was crumpled on the bathroom floor, wrapped in her silk robe.

Olivier rushed towards her in an attempt to save her, but when he touched her, he realized that it was already too late.

He went to the telephone in her apartment and called Gaston, who said he would come right over.

He went back and sat down next to her. "Maman…" he murmured, tears streaming from his eyes.

This time, Helena had left her body for good.

Through his tears, he gazed at her face, which looked tranquil. It seemed to him that a smile played at the corner of her mouth.

He bent over her, picked her up in his arms, and moved her to the bed, covering her emaciated body with a blanket.

On the bedside table he saw a stamped letter, inscribed with his name and his new address in England. He picked up the letter and found that it was sealed and ready to mail. He opened it and began to read.

Olivier my son,

This is the first time I am using this word without making a big deal of it. This is my feeling ever since I had the privilege of seeing you again. I'm writing to you as I did for more than twenty years, month in and month out. I became a mother to children I never bore. One day you were taken from me, and despite the empty hole that was left in me ever since that day in court, I didn't let myself fall. I dreamed of a day when I would get to see you and your brother again. I didn't give up, I stayed alive— just without my children.

And now, when I was already beginning to give up, you appeared, like a dream, out of nowhere. The baby I knew had become a man.

My dream came true— I became a mother for a second time. Despite the years that had passed, you had not neglected me in your thoughts, and eventually you were both brought back to me.

My dear child, I want to thank you, to tell you that today I know that everything I did in my life was worthwhile, every choice I made, every crisis I went through— they were all worth it to know that I enabled my two little boys to live and to become what they are today.

I'm a mother who never gave birth, and you're the family I never had. I'll tell you again— I would relive every day of my life just to see you, to have you exactly the way you are, just as you came back into my life.

My dear son, I ask of you one thing: tell your story, tell my story, tell our story, spread the good news— that despite everything, there is good in the world. When you become a father, teach your son; tell him about us, about what we went through. And give him my love too, even if I don't get to see him.

The important thing, my son, is to know how to give. That is the most beautiful thing that I got to do in my life, and my gift is you two, you and your brother.

Now, after I have sorted through my feelings in your presence, I can tell you that I am more at peace than ever about all that I have done and experienced in my life.

I may not manage to hang on much longer, for I am tired, and my body is betraying me. But I am happy, just like in the days when I used to climb the stairs in Paris and a little boy would smile at me from ear to ear and hold his little arms out to me.

I love you both,

Maman

A single tear splashed on the page.

Olivier smiled. He imagined himself on the stairs, reaching his arms out for Helena, loving, beautiful, stately, and motherly.

He went back to sit down next to her on the bed, touched her cold face said, "I'm sorry, Maman, for all the suffering you went through, for what we all suffered… I would do anything to go back in time, just to give you a little more pleasure, Maman… If there are angels in this world, you're one of them…"

The rattle of a key in the door brought him back to reality.

Gaston came into the room and Olivier rose to greet him. The older man held him tightly as Olivier burst out crying, sobbing like a boy who had just lost his mother.